Blacken

Blacken

Alandra Rankin

PROLOGUE

I travelled here willingly… at least, I think that's the case.

As I ask around, the people that also moved into this small town all share the same story; that they *just had to*. It was almost as if a compulsion; an all mighty force caused them to uproot the monotonous comfort of their everyday life, just to travel out of cities and away from families. They would drive for hours, days, weeks; until inevitably, the pressure lifted, and they arrived inside Blacken's town line.

But my occurrence is a bit different.

I have always been told that I have a Guardian Angel on my shoulder. The night I heard the call of Blacken, I think they tried to stop me on route.

Whatever wanted me here, however, won.

CHAPTER 1

It was barely outside of Blacken city limits where the accident occurred. The front of a small blue car crashed against a tree, causing the timber to split and collapse backwards from the impact. Fumes and smoke billowed out of the ruined engine, illuminated by the orange lights flashing from the ambulance nearby.

"Vitals are stable," the female paramedic stated, glancing at her watch.

"She's a little banged up. Concussed, for sure," the male counterpart added, waving a pin flashlight back and forth across the unconscious female's pupils, "we still can't rule out possible internal trauma, let's get an IV in her and get her in asap."

His colleague nodded, fastening a bandage, before they lifted the patient into the back of the ambulance.

Sirens wailed in the small hours of the morning, cutting a direct path through the woods and into the small city, the female paramedic thumbed through the wallet that previously was in the patient's windbreaker.

"Any ID in there, Rachel?"

"Yes, Avie Conrad. Twenty-six years old. Not a donor." She held up the ID, inspecting it closely, "You're a long way from home, Avie." Rachel replaced the ID in the wallet and placed them aside for her to gather later.

"Do you think she's another one?" The male scratched at his salt and pepper facial hair with the back of his hand, promptly replacing his gloves while hooking up the intravenous.

"I don't know, Dale. Maybe she is. She came up a little shy getting into town all by herself, though," Rachel laughed, her kind brown eyes tracing over the unconscious face. "Welcome to Blacken, Avie."

A dull throbbing caught her attention. Avie couldn't focus on anything else, it continued to rouse her from her slumber. The sensation sharpened, feeling it coming from her eyes and nose, as though she had been hit, the aftereffects causing pain to radiate throughout the sockets and nasal cavity.

The buzz caused her to shift, no longer in the fleetingness of unconsciousness but becoming more aware of the space beyond her eyelids. Avie felt *odd*, an ache spread throughout her body, a beeping noise caught her attention, she felt out of place. She didn't feel *correct*.

Her consciousness finally came in, causing her eyes to flutter open. The brightness of the room stung, making her wince and need to rapidly blink away the excess tears. In her swimming vision, she noticed her arms splotched with a few bruises, laying neatly outside the tautly tucked blankets. The material was an ugly pale green, the kind she saw in infirmaries, and her forearms were attached to a few wires and tubes. She followed their trail to find the source of the beeping: a heart rate monitor.

The hospital? Why was she here?

Her bed was already on a slight incline, yet she felt so weak and sore in her movements, it produced a struggle to even sit up. The beeping rose in pace, and by the end of it, she was a little out of breath.

"Hello?" she had called out, her voice dry and croaky, and only leading her to cough. She tried again, louder, "Hello?!"

A nurse came in seconds later.

"Oh! You're awake, Miss…" Her finger leads over her clipboard, searching, "Ah, Miss. Conrad, how are you feeling? You've been unconscious for a while, must be hungry at this point."

She walked over and examined the monitors as she spoke with idle conversation pleasantries. Her dark complexion caught Avie's eye against the washed-out navy blue of her uniform, a mocha bob bouncing as she walked.

"I'm in a bit of pain, but I don't understand what happened, why am I here?"

The nurse stopped what she was doing, turning to face the bruised woman with a concerned look on her face. Avie was able to see her badge, seeing her name was Caroline Ericson.

"You were in a car accident, what's the last thing you *do* remember?" Caroline checked the contractions of her pupils, the light hurting and causing her to squint.

"That I was driving, and it was nighttime. I guess that doesn't help… Was anybody else hurt?" Her eyes trailed after the nurse's finger, back and forth, up and down.

"No, the paramedics said you had hit a tree. Do you know where you are?"

"Of course, Pace Medical."

Caroline's thin eyebrows raised, her motions stopping to gaze seriously down at her, "Miss. Conrad, you're at Berridge General. In Blacken, British Columbia."

"*What?*"

The woman was flabbergasted. How the hell did she end up all the way out here, of all places? Her mind raced; she was just driving around running errands at home. How could she have gotten somewhere that took possibly *days* to drive to?

"Is there anyone you can call? Family or friends that might help jog your memory?"

She shook her head, "No, I don't know. I don't know… I've been by myself for a while."

"It's alright, these things happen. At least you got to walk away with just a few bumps and scratches! We're going to get neurology to look at you just in case it is anything more serious, but short-term memory loss can happen after a bump on the head. Your wallet and notebook were turned in as well, how about I grab them for you, Avie?" Caroline smiled gently at her, her purple lips splitting to reveal a perfect smile, Avie couldn't help but reciprocate one back.

"Yes, thank you, Nurse Ericson. I'd appreciate that."

"Call me Caroline if you'd like, I'll be back in a little while."

After the nurse left, an exasperated sigh escaped. Both hands came up to comb through her ginger locks, finding a few spots tender and covered with a bandage. She grimaced. Just how bad was the damage?

Spotting the bathroom, the redhead took her time to shimmy to the side of the bed, adjusting her legs inch by inch before finally resting the shaking appendages on the cold flooring. She was in a hospital gown, the top of her knees poked out and revealed a dark bruise on the left, wrapping from the top and down the side of her knee cap.

Avie almost couldn't help herself from touching the green and purple discolouration, wincing before laughing at her terrible decision.

It took her a few times to try and stay up on quivering muscles, feeling a rush of dizziness. Yet she managed and was stable enough to limp to the small enclosed bathroom. The young woman leaned onto the IV that wheeled with her, happy to have some stability from the cool metal as the door swung open for her with a push.

Flicking on the light, the dim wattage allowed her to see the damage. In the mirror across her, the woman saw the aquiline bridge of her nose covered with gauze and a strip of tape. It was split skin, she figured, not broken to her relief. Her eyes were swollen and dark, both able to open and close without pain at least, only when she strained it would cause discomfort. A bandage was wrapped around her crown, a couple thicker dressings rested on her forehead and a small cut traced vertically on her bottom lip.

"Jesus," she told her reflection, "you look like you've had better days," she laughed once, turning in the door frame to lean up against it. Avie huffed, letting her eyes fall closed.

What the hell was she doing out here? She thought back to the last thing she remembered.

An opened drawer. Out of tape. Picking up tape from the drug store and developed photos across the street. Drive thru. Driving home. Road was closed. Detour. And then...

Her eyes opened.

"The vibration."

It came on suddenly, no onset warning to prepare for such an unusual experience.

Taking the recommended detour leading into an unknown part of the city, she promptly got lost.

"Damn it. Everything looks so different at night, where am I even going?" The woman turned onto a street that she was positive led back to the main road. That was when it hit her.

It was the most surreal experience; an almost vibrating commotion emanated from her body, causing her to exhale from shock, winded, and unable to inhale again.

Avie pulled over, needing to park, taking gasps of precious air while panic rose in her chest. This was not normal. The sensation that washed over her felt almost on par to the bass at a music concert—the music pumped up so loudly that deep tones hit right through to the core.

It was an itch that made her squirm, should she go to the hospital? The feeling had her wanting to do **something**, *a compulsion to just move.*

With a few shaky breaths, she calmed herself down enough to start driving again, becoming entranced; driving in various directions, finding that it caused the feeling to lessen. It felt better, if only a fraction. But the compulsion kept on.

The young woman continued to drive, the feeling a compass of sorts to her. If she turned one way, it came back to its initial intensity, if she continued down the 'correct' path, it reduced. All of it very peculiar. Still, Avie pressed on with driving for what felt like hours.

The further she travelled, the better it felt.

The redhead had no idea what she was being led to, but she didn't want to stop, the curiosity burning through her veins.

Even though the vibrating sensation decreased as she advanced, her apprehension grew. She was only stopping to rest at motels or inside her own car, the need for an answer taking over. What exactly was she being led to? Or rather, would it even have an end?

She was too far to stop now. Avie pressed on with her body reverberating akin to a tuning fork.

The forest surrounding her made the woman uneasy. The mountainous area she drove into made her feel small and watched in the darkness, paranoia growing as it seemed to stretch on forever into the unknown. Mentally, she kicked herself for not stopping at the last town about an hour or so back to rest up for the night. She yawned.

Just how much further was it until the next town?

It may have been that she ran over something. It may have been that her tires were overdue for an inspection. It could have been anything really, even what some may call a form of Divine Intervention. However, in that moment, the front tire on her small punch bug blew out, causing her to lose control, swerve, and overcorrect, all before colliding head on with a tree.

Forcefully, the airbags deployed, knocking the wind out of her while the car came to a sudden halt, her small stature receiving more damage from its power.

And then darkness…

Avie thought over the memory a few times, staggering back to the comfort of her bed. How could she have forgotten such an experience? A million questions rang through her mind, but the one that was prevalent was the issue on how she was found in the first place.

The woman was all alone in the middle of the woods.

Was it possible that someone just so happened to also be travelling at that time? Was there a concerned passerby that called into the nearest town for her? If so, she hoped they left their identity so she could personally thank them.

A knock at the door took her out of her thoughts, a tall man in his late forties or fifties came in swiftly after. His hair was swept back and away from his face, she regarded him quite handsome, he fit the term of 'silver fox' especially in the way that he smiled, revealing twin dimples below high cheekbones.

"Hello there, Miss. Conrad! I'm Dr. Marshall and I'm just gonna take a look over you. I understand you have a bit of memory loss and confusion?" He walked over to where she sat, starting the same regiment that Nurse Caroline did.

"Well yes, initially, but I remember the accident now and pretty much everything up until then. I think I was still in a bit of shock."

"So, a pretty short short-term memory loss, huh?" he drawled, laughing at his own joke, "Well I'd say that's a good sign! We can set you up a lil' later today to run a few tests, just to rule everything out, but it sounds like nothin's taking a toll."

"Good, I'm so glad. I feel like I've been pretty lucky."

The doctor chuckled again, "You must've had someone lookin' out for you, Miss. Conrad."

She may very well have.

As the doctor left, Avie kept herself occupied with the small tube television mounted on the wall across her, waiting the few hours for him to return for her testing. After only two hours filled with a mix of news stations and cartoons, Nurse Caroline came back to escort her to another section of the hospital.

She sat in the small room with the oblong machine, seeing the doctor enter shortly after, a glint in his smile and another friendly greeting.

"Dr. Marshall, I was hoping to know who I could ask about how I was found in the middle of the woods?" The redhead sat on the MRI machine, fiddling with a ring on her pinky before having to take it off and place it in a bin.

"Tell you what, Dale's a good friend of mine and your first responder. An' he told me that you crashed into a spruce a little outside of ol' Blacken here. You almost made it into town, assuming you meant to arrive here?"

She thought back, not remembering seeing a sign for the town, but if she really was as close as he said, a few concerned citizens must have heard her crash or had seen any smoke.

"I think so, I wasn't looking for a particular destination. I feel a lot better since I've been here, more or less," she laughed, pointing to her face and outlining the predicaments.

The comment caught the neurologist's attention, looking back up at his patient, "How do you mean by that?"

The woman in question looked down, embarrassed, smiling and laughing quietly from nerves. She didn't know how to bring it up without sounding *strange*, not even sure if there was a term for it or if she could do the explanation justice. Was it worth even talking about, especially since it stopped?

"I had the strangest sensation start up a few days ago," she began, nervously trying to go back to fiddle with the pinky ring that was no longer there, "like I was quivering or having some sort of high intensity vibrating from inside of my whole body. I know it sounds weird and I don't really know how to describe it properly, but it seems completely gone at this point!" she spoke fast, trying to get her thought process out before she was judged by the doctor too harshly.

He only chuckled, giving her a light pat on the shoulder, "S'alright, nothin' I haven't heard before. Now why don't 'cha lie down and remember to stay as still as you can while you're in there."

Avie cocked her head, confused to what he had meant, "Wait, do you know other people that felt like that? Or what it even was?"

Dr. Marshall started to walk away, "I'm sure you're gonna find a lotta interestin' people in this town, Miss. Conrad. Now, let's start the test."

A matter of hours later, results were in from the MRI and CT scans.

The woman asked for more information on the town, if they could provide her with a map or anything she could research. Her interest peaking full blown after Dr. Marshall's comment, Avie couldn't get more information out of him, him simply explaining that he couldn't, and that other residents could more than likely help answer some of her burning questions much better than he could.

The young woman was studying a map of the small town, finding some points of interests, intending to explore and ask around after getting out of the hospital. She also circled two motels to look at while she stayed. Finishing a circle around the library's icon, Caroline knocked and came in with her results.

"I've got good news! Nothing concerning was found, and even with your memory back, it looks like we can discharge you today, Miss. Conrad."

She sighed with relief, "That's wonderful news! I've been itching to get to know your town, is the Gala Motel any better than the Rare Bird one?" The red pen tapped a few times on the glossy paper, her fingers expressing eager energy.

"Better to stick with Rare Bird, it's newer. The doctor also gave you a prescription for your pain and the chills you've been having, you can pick them up at the Pharmacy," Caroline pointed its location on Avie's map, "nice and close to the motel too."

She returned Caroline's smile, "Thank you, I'll make them my first stop. I'm also really, *really* hoping to find a good restaurant. I'm really sorry but the cafeteria here is…"

"Pretty *blasé*, right? It unfortunately has to be that way, no matter how much we rally," Caroline let out an airy laugh, before pointing to a few personal choices, "you can't go wrong with these few here, and this one across town as long as you stay away from the fish."

Avie snickered, "All right, that's been noted! Thanks for the heads up!" She wrote the memo down beside the legend on the map. The woman let out a steadying breath, glancing over the placements on the map, still unsure of one thing. "Caroline, do you know anyone else that had a vibrating body experience? Someone that I could maybe start talking to?"

The nurse's demeanour changed, the middle-aged woman looking sterner at her question, "You can try Jim at the hardware store, I don't know too much about anyone else. I prefer not to get mixed up in that hysteria."

Avie felt the tone grow heavy, "Sorry, I didn't mean anything by it. I appreciate all your help."

"Mmhmm," she hummed in acknowledgment, before leaving her to her own devices.

Well, that was weird.

It was odd to see such a shift over a simple question, Avie wasn't sure what to make of it. More questions came up, the whole phenomenon struck at her innate curiosity, she needed to find out more, needed to find out why there was a calling to this town that she followed. It affected its citizens in some way, but she was still very much in the dark about everything. There was a starting point at least.

Jim who worked at *Home·Aware* was her first stop.

It was time to get some answers.

CHAPTER 2

The sky loomed heavy with darkling clouds, a sure sign of an intense rainstorm coming at any time. The wind picked up enough for Avie to pull her windbreaker closer, attempting to block out the chills, to no avail. August rain waited beyond the trees, bringing in a bite to the atmosphere. Frost ran its threatening fingers over the evening, a promise it could come within days by the dropping temperature in the surrounding mountains.

Traversing through the streets by the map in her hands, she felt good to get up and walk around for the first time since leaving the hospital. Even though her muscles protested in their sore state, she needed to stretch them out, knowing it was beneficial to build up her strength. Besides, she had been resting plenty, Avie could rest once she got a little more information.

Her eyes searched the street ahead of her, locating the hardware shop on Blacken's main street. Promptly after entering the store, a wash of warmth caressed her, finally out of the wind.

"Hello, anything I can help you with?" A man appeared at the cash register to her left, flashing her a smile which crinkled his eyes, wiping his hands with a dark hand towel. He couldn't have been any older than his late forties, but his face was worn. Avie thought absentmindedly that he smelled of tobacco, the scent wafting through the building.

"Yes, I was hoping I could speak to Jim?" She stepped further inside, walking up to the desk to converse with the gentleman.

He motioned to his name tag, "Well you're in luck, Jim is in!" He chuckled, "You have a special project you're working on?"

The redhead fidgeted, not really rehearsing what she was going to say.

"I, umm, well actually I was hoping to talk to you about something else. A nurse at Berridge General said you may be able to help, and I'm sorry if it sounds weird, but do you know anything about having your body... vibrate?"

Jim's smile dropped while his bushy eyebrows rose in being caught off guard, "It's been a very long time since anyone's asked. I had it take me here thirty years ago now, so I can't rightly remember what it felt like, just that it took over my whole body. There's not many people out due to the weather, would you like to come and sit, maybe have some coffee?"

Avie agreed, knowing it may be a lengthy discussion, excited in the fact that he knew the sensation. She was led to the back; a break room of sorts, an old coffee machine brewing caused the space to smell like rich java. The large pot sat next to a few other appliances and next to a half-eaten sandwich on the counter, bright lights slightly flickering overhead.

"I had just started a fresh pot; you take cream or sugar?"

"Both, please."

Jim motioned her to sit at the small table while he fixed the cups of coffee, "So, miss, what's your name?"

"Avie, Avie Conrad."

"Well Avie, you look like you were in quite a scuffle, you mind if I ask what happened?" Jim sat across her, handing her coffee over.

"I crashed into a tree, just outside of the town. But since I came here, that feeling I had stopped. Do you... I mean, is there any answer for that?"

Jim sighed, taking a sip of his black coffee, reverie dancing behind his eyes, "Geeze... How many years has it been since anyone asked about this...?"

She tilted her head, feeling some lingering tenderness, "You don't have a lot of people experience it?"

"Well... No, not really. And there's not *really* an answer. The locals of Blacken don't like to hear or talk about it. They almost brush it off as some sort of witchcraft or conspiracy. I, like many others, can't ask too many questions without being ostracized. It leaves people not wanting to pursue that curiosity."

She sipped at the coffee, mirroring Jim's action at the natural pause. He looked down, breaking eye contact while staring down into the black abyss of caffeine held in his hands, speaking with a low longing. It almost felt like he was someone who gave up his search, one of the ones he was talking about—on the verge of being an outcast for asking of the strange sensation they had no control over.

"But why is that? Why do they care so much about others trying to find an answer?"

"Most people around here are religious, it's the crutch they lean on whenever someone tries to go out of their way to explore what's been going on and drawing people like us in. It's been a long time since someone new came in. I honestly thought I wouldn't talk about this phenomenon again. I thought it must have stopped."

She looked away, "I know it must be difficult, it's just... This all sounds very strange. Nothing in the town is doing this? There has been absolutely no one able to figure this out? Doctors? Scientists?"

"Anyone who has tried, I have no idea about. We are only a small group in this already small town, in the end, the majority rules over silencing our voices. I suppose we have a few theories to go off of, but it's really nonconsequential. Once I got here, I tried to find out a few things, but I came up short in any conclusions. It's still a mystery with more questions than answers. Though, the only discovery we have is that when we try to leave, the feeling comes back. It's a spectacle that no one has been able to figure out, but it hasn't hurt anyone."

"No wonder they think it's a weird conspiracy, to keep people in town like that... Do you think it affects the same people? Like, did we all come from the same place, just to be led here?"

"Not sure. I came from too big of a city, the same is said for a few others, probably even the same as you, I'd imagine. Us older folk seem to not have to worry about the how or why. I live for Blacken's community, it's all I've ever dreamt about, it is a great little town for finding yourself and I think a lot of folks see it that way. I can't speak for everyone, of course, but I'd rather have the vibration that led me here on the back burner while I got to enjoy the convenience of simple living."

"Jim, this thing that brought us here, with no one in town able to ask what's causing it… Do you think they're keeping it a secret?"

"I have no idea. I still have as much information on this as you do, Miss. Conrad," he chuckled, downing the rest of his beverage.

Her mind was reeling, why wouldn't people want to know more? Things couldn't have led her here just to live in a small town. The populace seemed older, less driven so it would make sense that they just left well enough alone. But what about the kids? Were they stopped just by the others who preached religion or even tradition? Were the two parties fighting out in a conspiracy against each other?

"You said that it's been a while since people who experienced this came in. How many usually come to live in Blacken?"

"People came in every month or so, left the same way too."

"They can leave? How can they when—I mean, I thought you had said…" she trailed off, not understanding even further.

Jim chortled, in the same flippant nature a parent would give to a child asking a silly question, "Like I said, it's a mystery with more questions than answers. But some of the others *can* leave without it, I figure they return home because they had the same drumming buzz to do so or leave to another town. Who knows? In either case, they don't stay long."

"So, there are people that come and go with this. Has anyone asked them what they did so that it *doesn't* come back?"

"Well, some people have tried. Some of 'em built bridges here, and those close to them have tried to get into contact… but they can't. It's as though they started a whole new life, I never knew anyone who has left, really, but I would like to know what goes through their head when they do. Have you contacted your family since coming here?"

She stopped, feeling embarrassed. Avie hadn't even thought about it, even though they may not even bat an eye as they had when she moved to the city. They didn't need to know, however what Jim said was making sense, maybe the affected population that came in and out didn't have very many people connected to them, as she did. Maybe that was the connecting factor?

"No, I don't really have anyone."

"Then you're like most of us. We don't have a lot that we left, though some do, could be all coincidental though. People build lives here, the community is great, you'll be making friends in no time. There are, however, plenty of people who don't know what this situation was like, and they don't like hearing about it. It's been a long time since another came in, you may be the talk of the town, Avie."

She looked away, a small flush tickled at the back of her neck from the thought of people talking about her *en masse*, "Did you ever notice how long people like us usually stay then?"

"Don't get me wrong, I've noticed people can be here for the rest of their lives, but they also come in a lot older than you. They stay for a number of weeks at least if they do leave. If the sensation comes to people at random, it probably lets them go the same way. In any case, I don't question it, it's not like it's a big deal if it leads people here to *Blacken* of all places."

More questions burned in her mind, the more information she was given by Jim, the more she wanted to figure out what exactly was going on in town, why the phenomenon was happening, why it wasn't seen as a bigger deal by the townsfolk, why it led people in just to let them go?

"I've seen that look, just be careful asking around, it can be awful if you push too hard. I can try to answer any questions you may have. For now, I hope you stay a while. Blacken is very hospitable."

She nodded; not sure what else she could ask. The young woman was not getting any direct answers, only speculations, it was frustrating.

Avie stood to thank Jim, shaking his hand, "Thank you so much for your time, it really is incredible, this town. I want to stay for as long as I can and get to know Blacken better."

"You'll get along great here, I can feel it, Miss. Conrad. I've got to run back to the shop, but you can take your time. I hope you'll feel better soon!"

She smiled in the middle of tracing a medicated salve over her lip, "Thank you, Jim. I'm doing my best," she laughed.

Her time with Jim gave her a little more insight to the town, but it still didn't explain very much. Avie sought an answer on what was causing the sensations to begin with, it had to have been something more interesting than just a 'God's Will' explanation coupled with the inability of the people wanting to know more.

She thought about if anything was reported on the town, or what was going on, then its history may have a few jumping off points or clues on where to start digging up answers.

Pulling the map out of her back pocket, she found the library just a few blocks over. Her attention was grabbed by the abrupt wind howling against the building.

Looking down at her windbreaker, she grimaced at the lighter clothing. Braving the weather in her walk, Avie shivered heavily upon entering the library.

She held her arms across her body, a feeble attempt to keep the extremities warm while rubbing up and down to create friction. Her teeth chattered while walking into the dim lobby. The young woman observed her surroundings, unable to find anyone else in the building, not even anyone at the reception.

Her footsteps echoed in the quiet building, it was so silent, even for a library. The lack of persons, coupled with the storm brewing outside— darkening the lobby through the grand windows, made her uneasy. The space wasn't over all anything lavish, small town, small buildings, she assumed. However, the woman was hoping to find another friendly face like she did with Jim at *Home·Aware*, but even glancing around the open area, she couldn't see any staff wandering around.

Maybe they were busy elsewhere?

Reaching the reception desk, Avie placed her palms down on the cool marble, "… Hello?" she tentatively called out.

A man with dirty blond scraggly hair and beard to match popped out from the desk, seemingly to have been interested in something on the floor or low shelving. Small glasses framed his face as he pushed them up with a large hand, cradling a stack of folders with the other.

"Yes, hi, I was just… Um, hello! I'm here, yes, hello," he struggled to speak while attempting to catch the falling papers, his tweed suit moving in a flash with his erratic juggling movements.

"Goodness, you scared me!"

He placed the paperwork down between them while strewing his words, "Sorry! I didn't mean to; I was having problems with the sorting and—holy hell... Are you alright?" The man finally looked at her, taking in her features.

Avie rubbed at her arm, "It's just a couple of bruises, I was in an accident a few days ago."

"You're also shivering! Have you been outside with only *that*?" He looped around the marble desk, showing off his tall and lanky form, "Do you need some hot chocolate? I also have a large sweater that might help warm you up from the rain."

She shook her head, holding up a hand, "Oh no, it's not a worry, you don't have to go through the trouble."

The scraggly man looked around the library in an exaggerated manner, "There's nothing going on here, hasn't been for a while. C'mon, you're gonna catch a cold. I'm happy to help if you wanted to keep company and warm up for a bit?"

It was a very tempting offer, Avie felt as though she could not warm up; a mix of the weather and the chills that lurked in her body since the hospital.

She sighed, giving in, "If you're sure, I would absolutely love some."

His smile lit up his face, radiating the cerulean eyes. "Done deal. I'm Owen," he held out his hand for her to shake.

"Avie. Nice to meet you, Owen. You're the first person I've met that looks about my age," she laughed, finally meeting people in her age group.

He joined in her laughter, "That's Blacken for you! How old are you anyway, if you don't mind?"

"Turning twenty-seven in October."

"Almost time to celebrate for you then! I just turned twenty-five a few months ago, still trying to get used to that milestone," he laughed.

They walked over to one of the tables and sat, Owen bringing a sweater and hot cocoa. She held the Styrofoam cup in her hands, having the heat flow through her with the help of the coat hugging her shoulders.

"So, did you forget to check the weather before going out?"

Her eyes raised to meet his, this Owen was pretty straight forward, it seemed.

"Um, I actually, uh… I don't have anything else. I didn't really pack anything with me."

"And so, you came to the library instead of a winter shop?"

The woman in question took a sip of the drink, careful to avoid burning herself before setting it back down. Thinking over her words, she took Jim's advice in heed, "I was hoping to get some more information on the town. I didn't get too much from some of the locals."

She traced the lip of her cup, eyes trailing her thumb as it danced in a semicircle. Realizing Owen hadn't responded, Avie grew worried she still said too much. She glanced up, seeing his features gleaming instead.

"You're one of them, aren't you—that came into town because of the body tremor? God… It's been forever since we've had anybody new."

"You know about it? Are you one too?" She became visibly restless, enthusiastic to get more information on the subject. She didn't really know what qualified as 'one of them', assuming it was just having the vibrating that led someone into Blacken, but she couldn't be sure if there was more to the mystery.

"I'm not but, I've been extremely interested in what's been going on, unlike most people. It's like they don't even want an answer to something that could be the biggest mystery since the vortex of the Mirny diamond mine."

Avie shifted even further, growing more excited with everything the blond was saying.

"I know! What's up with that? There is this mystery that's just begging to be solved at this point, and no one's asking questions. All I can think about is what the bigger picture is. I was hoping there was more information about it here, if anything's been reported. Do you happen to know?"

"Avie… I've been waiting a long time for someone like you to show up. Someone just as interested. Can I show you what I have been working on?"

Nodding enthusiastically, she followed the young man into a side room down a staircase, locked off and only accessible with the key ring attached to his belt. Inside were a few papers, newspaper clippings, maps and scribbled notes along most of the photocopied pages. Avie looked over the newspapers, old dates standing out amongst the scientific hypotheses as to what the town was experiencing, especially with the people who had come and gone.

She looked at census reports next to them on the table, reading over the fact that, more or less, people seemed to be coming in and leaving at a level pace—keeping Blacken at a steady population.

"I've been looking for any information," Owen started, "something that might distribute a pattern, something to give an idea on what's been going on, why only some people are affected. I know it's not a lot, but I've only been working here a few weeks, so, it's a start at least. There is a ton of information on the town archived and I have hardly managed to scratch the surface."

"It's incredible! You've found a good number of data to go off of. People affected like me, they come in and just leave. I want to find out the reason."

He scoffed in a laughing manner, "I wish it were as simple as that… Nobody hears from those people ever again. They don't leave, they go *missing*."

Avie's hands gripped the papers tighter, flinching, "What do you mean they go missing? They go missing and no one bothers to find out what happens to them? How many people?"

"Oh, I mean they are *technically* missing; they all have missing persons reports filled out, but it's just *normal* in Blacken. Everyone seems to believe if they had come in so suddenly, who is to say they didn't have the same feeling to go somewhere else? Or even back home? I'd bet a good couple of weeks or even a month spans over until someone disappears, only going by these charts at least."

"That's terrible! Nobody wants to know what happened to them…? What kind of town is this?" The papers slammed into the table, disrupting a few at rest there with the gust of wind.

"Hey now, missing could mean anything, but not once have they been found dead. People don't die here because of this, if they did, then everyone coming in would fight the urge to stay and get the hell outta dodge. We don't know what happens, that's what I'm trying to figure out here."

Avie calmed her breathing, her rapid heartbeat falling to a slow murmur after processing Owen's words. He was right, it was a mystery, and nothing was concrete. But she was also one of the ones affected, she didn't care to find out the hard way what happens to people involved.

"Can I help in any way?"

His eyes widened, "Really? You mean it? You don't find it... too much?"

She smiled, "No, I mean it. It feels like there could be some actual answers in here, somewhere. I want to help find them; it could be really exciting! And, well, I need all the help I can get. Could you imagine actually solving the phenomenon? What Blacken—what the *world* might do with the info?"

He sighed content, readjusting his glasses, "It's my dream. Avie, would you be willing to hang out later and go through some archives?"

"I would love to, but is that even allowed?"

He laughed, "Nobody has touched them in decades. As long as they don't go missing permanently, we should be fine. Besides, I work here, it's not like we are stealing them. Just... *borrowing* for the greater good."

The woman echoed his laugh, she found the librarian to be blunt, but a fun character, and someone she would be happy to spend days with trying to solve the unknown. His enthusiastic energy and passion matched her curious wonder and infatuation.

A match made in heaven.

"For the greater good then," she held out her pinky, him almost immediately locking his own together with it.

"Our secret, for the greater good... Avie, I think this is the beginning of a beautiful friendship."

They shared a smile, "I couldn't agree more."

CHAPTER 3

It has been a very long time since Avie felt a connection with anyone. Being completely alone for the better part of five years, she moved away from her immediate family and into the city with high hopes of finding an escape. Throughout the years, however, the young woman struggled exceptionally to make friends or even break out of being seen as anything except 'the new girl' by her co-workers—constantly being brushed off despite her best efforts.

She and Owen just clicked, an out of the blue connection bringing them together over a common interest, the compatibility further strengthening the relationship the longer they spent time together. After years of trying, Avie finally was able to call someone her friend. Her first friend.

Owen was honoured with the title, not really having friends of his own either. The blond jokingly calling them two peas in a pod, separated from the town with their interests and even age. He happily called her his friend in return.

"I'm falling asleep; we need to take a break," the librarian complained while leaning back in the office chair.

They worked in the basement, combing through file cabinets filled with information for what could have possibly been hours. Since there were no windows, the passage of time was iffy; the only way of knowing would be to head back upstairs where the grand clock hung in the reception area. Both young adults too wrapped up in searching to think about moving from the collections.

Avie rubbed at her eyes, "I'm pretty sure I've gone cross-eyed... A break sounds amazing."

She turned to watch him stretch awkwardly in his seat, before grunting in satisfaction from the relieved muscles. "Hungry?" He smiled, locking her eyes from across the room.

"Oh my god, yes." The redhead started walking over to him, stomach rumbling from the thought of food, too enveloped in the task of searching; the sensation of hunger did not register until now.

"We'll have to go upstairs, so save your place!" He gestured to the disarray Avie collected, emphasizing his point.

She looked at the muddled piles searched through and future piles to further scrutinize, cringing at her mess. Avie turned back to see Owen starting up the stairs, jogging to catch up with him.

At the top of the staircase, she saw the blond in the foyer dialing on the house phone at his desk. Owen caught sight of her and waved her over, his ear to the receiver.

"*What kind of pizza?*" he mouthed to her once she was close enough, starting an order for delivery.

"*Veggie!*" whispering back, she leaned across him on the desk, watching him frown. He stuck his tongue out while miming puking with a soft gag.

"Yes, I need a large Can·a·di·an pizza for delivery please," Owen spoke, enouncing each syllable while playfully staring at Avie.

Rolling her green eyes, Avie retaliated, playing dirty. She gave a soft, dramatic gasp before pulling out her best pouty face, bottom lip jutting out and quivering, the split healing over the week to a soft scratch while her eyes shimmered with false sadness.

He chuckled, trying to block the look with his hand, "And a medium veggie as well."

Avie dropped the look and grasped at the hand in her face, mouthing a "*Thank you*" back as Owen finished on the phone with the local pizza joint.

"That's not fair, and you know it," he returned the receiver to its cradle, "you have to get us something to drink to make up for it."

She laughed, "Oh I do, do I? Anything your majesty requests?"

Owen scrunched his nose, "I wasn't actually serious, you don't have to!"

"It's too late, I'm already on my way out the door!" Avie turned and began walking out, "If you don't say what you want, you're going to get nothing."

"Get me a fruit punch," he shouted.

The woman only chuckled in response, a bounce in her step as she walked over to the corner store.

A violet jacket wrapped comfortably around her, keeping her much warmer than the last time she navigated out in a nippy wind, thankful for the ability to stretch her legs after being in the library's basement all day.

In the short walk, Avie thought about the money she had left over, counting out some spare change she still held onto. She applied to several different jobs in town, trying to get something, anything that could provide a steady income. The Rare Bird Inn she stayed at was draining her savings, she couldn't stay there forever either, the redhead wanted to rent out an apartment too if she could at least get a call back.

It was late, the evening hours setting in with the sunset while she walked, the town coming to a close with people going home to family and friends. It was her favourite time of day, the bustling busy hours finally swelling to a close and allowing the streets of Blacken to breathe.

The small bell fixated atop the shop door rang gently, signalling her arrival. The old woman at the register lowered her newspaper to greet her new customer.

"Ahh, Miss. Conrad," she greeted happily, "you look better and better each day I see you!"

Avie indeed noticed a dramatic change in her eyes and lip during the past ten days, the cut at the top of her nose being the only stubborn thing to heal.

"Good evening, Mrs. Harris, how's business been today?" Avie chatted back, continuing to the beverage section in the small store.

"Same as usual, dear. The handful of school kids seem to be my only patrons."

"That's a shame, have you thought about bringing in something more than snacks?"

She reached the register, the short and plump woman on the other side started to ring up the few bottles Avie placed down.

"Oh, I could, I just don't know where I would put anything. Hardly room in the store as it is."

"You'll figure something, if you can come across the country by hopping train cars, you can figure anything out."

Mrs. Harris laughed loudly, "That was a long time ago, dear. I have been meaning to ask, have you found a job yet?"

Avie shook her head, "No, still looking."

"A young lady like you should get lots of offers, you're great with old folks like me. Gerald at the flower shop was looking for someone's help, how about I put in a good word?"

She blinked at the offer, stunned at the suggestion, "Would you really? That would mean the world! Thank you!"

"Just make sure he doesn't push you around! He's used to doing everything his way and can get a little unbearable."

"You would know best."

They laughed together, having fun with the exchange of goods and currency.

Mrs. Harris patted her hand, "But you let me know if my son crosses a line, we need more people like you helping us out in town."

"I will. Thank you again, I hope you have a good night."

"You too, dear. Take care."

The young woman collected her items and headed back into the brisk night.

As soon as she could, Avie would go and bring her resume into *Flora Adora*, jumping at the chance for work, even though it would be working under Gerald Harris.

She experienced firsthand the extent of how strict and demanding he could be. Watching him press further demands upon a woman running ragged to keep up with customers, upset that his worker did not do a certain task within his time constraints as he only gave out criticisms. He was a perfectionist, and while that probably helped keep his store in business for so long, it also hurt his employee rate.

Many only stayed so long before moving on, but Avie was desperate, wanting so bad to secure a job and an income, anything to get her on her feet. She didn't get a call back for any position applied to as of yet, and she hoped that this may be her break.

"Thank god you're back, I was about to run out to try and find you!" Owen was in her face as soon as she walked through the threshold, grabbing at her arm in an attempt to lead her.

"Whoa, what's going on?" She set the bag down on a table as she passed it, allowing the librarian to pull her back towards the archives deeper into the building.

"I couldn't help it, I wanted to look and see if I could find anything while we waited on food, I think I've got something."

"You did?! Why didn't you say so?" The initial confusion was replaced by determination, her legs working extra hard to keep up with Owen's long strides.

She was led to a newspaper article from the town on the microfilm viewer. Sitting her down, he enhanced the image, "I was just messing around with these, figured I'd jump back a ways. It isn't much, but I thought it must be one of the first cases reported."

Avie stared intent at the screen, watching the letters become readable.

"Strange occurrences point to magnetic fields in small town," she glanced at the date, "February 1919. Oh my gosh you weren't kidding."

"Keep reading…"

She read over the article, and as old as it may have been, they raised valid questions about the logic of the town's phenomenon. But the more she read, the more she didn't understand. The science was outdated, saying the cause was due to the iron in people's blood that caused them to travel to a magnetic field inside the town of Blacken. That couldn't be possible with the makeups of blood or Earth's magnetism.

"Owen, this is incredibly dated. None of what they printed scientifically holds up."

"But what if the answer was as simple as a scientific reaction? Truth is sometimes stranger than fiction and do you think anyone here had thought to try?"

"Do you think it's magnets?"

She had been serious, but Owen cackled as though she was having a laugh, "It's gotta be something, it would rule out any easy answers. Besides, there's a million things we could test, magnets could hold a small part in the overall phenomenon."

Avie looked at him, the passion sparkled in his blue eyes, she could see a possible answer somewhere in the future, having it backed up by science could get them on the map.

"Let's fucking do it then."

Owen broke into joyous laughter, picking up Avie and spinning her around, "I couldn't have asked for a better mystery partner! We have to have a name for our team, make it official."

"Isn't that what kids do?" she laughed from his actions, eventually being set back down onto her feet.

"You don't think it's fun?" Avie plainly looked at him, reading his expression as sincere. He wanted to have fun for fun's sake, not to be judgmental...

Giving in, she smirked with a terrible suggestion, "What about... The Dewey Decimals?"

He scoffed, "I'm mad I didn't think of that. It's perfect for us!" They laughed together at the cliché team name, walking back up to the main sitting area as their laughter died down. "Alright, just in time!" Owen spotted the pizza delivery man walking into the foyer and approaching the desk, meeting them adjacent instead once they were in his sightlines.

They toasted their pizza slices once they had settled, tapping the triangles in the air, "Here's to the start of, well, *something*!"

For the next two days, Avie and Owen investigated magnetic poles and fields, as well as solar energy and if it had any effect or correlations. So far nothing had been conclusive, much to their dismay, but they only started to dip their toes into a plethora of trials and questions.

Avie strolled over to the library once again, a spring in her step. It was now her usual spot, frequenting the place to meet up with Owen and work on finding a possible solution to the town's unknown. What initially started off seemingly paranormal, started to be peeled back as explainable with simple science. It was just a matter of finding the direct cause.

Owen's dishevelled locks caught her eye as soon as she entered, her mentally noting how he needed a haircut before she greeted him, "Guess who got the job?" She triumphantly raised her arms into the air, catching cerulean attention.

Maybe Vivian Harris already got her good word in. When Avie walked into *Flora Adora*, resume in hand and anxiety gripping her bones, she was almost sure Gerald would turn her away at the inquiry.

To her pleasant surprise, he stated he needed someone right away, reluctantly. Albeit, she had to work odd hours to make up for some lost profit in the past few months. Avie was over the moon to be getting hours to begin with. She was sure if she dedicated herself to helping, that the hours of work would steady out to a normal schedule soon enough.

"You did? Hell yeah you did!" He rose to meet her, Avie's raised arms wrapped around the back of Owen's neck, while his slid around her, embracing tight in a celebration. The taller of them rocked their bodies from side to side, squeezing tighter once before letting go, "So when is the first day?"

"I start early tomorrow, I'm so ready to get out of that motel!" Avie uttered, relieved.

"I don't doubt it, we should celebrate when you can. I know Gerald might keep you busy as much as possible. God, he's such a hard ass..."

"Absolutely, I wouldn't mind the extra hours though, it would help a lot. He couldn't be that bad overall," she sat down, stretching out her left leg, massaging the flesh.

Owen took notice, "I hope you won't push it, or he won't push you, I'll kick his ass if he does. Is your knee still giving you trouble?"

Avie heard the worry in his voice, "It's really not that bad, I think the weather is affecting it, if I'm honest."

He chuckled quietly, voice hardly over a whisper despite the empty building, "Oh no, now you're sounding like one of *them*."

She snorted, imitating an older voice as she leaned forward and cupped her ear, "What's that, dearie? You'll have to speak up!"

"I knew it, you are older than me, after all. It was only a matter of time before the change took over." Owen gently slammed a fist on the table in an inflated manner, smirking at his friend across the painted wood with false horror in his voice.

"Oh, as if! I'm gonna be young forever," she broke out in giggles, enjoying the playful back and forth her and Owen often did.

Eventually, the pair made their way into the geology section, picking up where they had left off. They didn't have much luck with the topics picked to start with. What began with magnetic fields led to research about wind and light pollution, along with starlight and the sun. The information just didn't line up consistently or couldn't get past speculation and theory to begin experiments on.

"I don't know if this will be much luck either. Anything else on your list?" The woman exhaled forcefully as she leaned into a book, her nose nearly touching the fold.

He pushed away his own book, sighing in much the same way, "I did have a theory. Something darker if you're interested," he waggled his eyebrows, "maybe the town is on top of an ancient burial ground, its victims targeting the ancestors of those who wronged them!"

She shook her head in disbelief, "Hmm, wow, *incredible*. And any other theories, Einstein?"

"Just the usual things; electricity, radiation… Extraterrestrial lifeforms."

The redhead deadpanned, "I meant things that could actually have an effect!"

"We've looked at a few of the other variables, I'm just throwing outside-the-box options into the mix." Owen shrugged, light heartedly entertaining the idea.

Avie laughed once, "Yeah. *Aliens.* Totally plausible. Little green men wandering around, that's why there hasn't been anything in the news about any sightings or—" She stopped herself mid-sentence.

It just clicked in her train of thought. Missing persons, no bodies found. *Abductions.*

"Holy shit. That actually makes sense…"

"You're messing with me, right?" The blond cocked an eyebrow, his arms crossed as he leaned back in his seat.

Avie waved him off, "No, it's actually plausible, you said that there were missing person cases in Blacken, but never a body count to go with them. What if it really were aliens doing this?"

"Drawing people in, and then taking them away?" He was intently staring at her, enamoured with the woman running with the idea of his.

She could see her reflection in his oval glasses, expressing the same look of intrigue.

"Should we abandon this part of the project and see if we can find anything more *not of this world?*" Avie whispered, leaning forward across the table, meeting Owen halfway.

"I don't think we have a choice, nothing else gave us enough evidence," also whispering back, he was mere inches away from her face.

Perhaps they were both worried about someone overhearing them, despite the dark and empty library. Skin breaking out in goose flesh across the two of them, they conversed about the paranormal, voices never cresting over a whisper. It was a far-fetched idea, but then again, the whole town's situation was just as such.

Excitement rose as they continued to speculate, the only thing that took a hold of them enough to connect the dots was the unbelievable. Could there really be aliens visiting Blacken? And if so, why? For what purpose?

As much as they wanted to find a scientifically plausible answer, this was more captivating, breathing new life into the Dewey Decimal team and their search for answers. It was time to switch gears from searching the abnormal into researching the supernatural.

CHAPTER 4

"You were right. Gerald is being a hard ass."

Avie slouched on the striped couch, wine being poured into her out-stretched glass as she huffed.

"Wow. Not even a week in and he's broken you," Owen laughed before he twisted the bottle in an elegant fashion to stop the flow of liquid.

They were celebrating Avie's new job, finally. The blond invited her over for dinner and wine, having a night off from spending time in the library to be able to enjoy the other's company in a more comfortable setting.

"Hardly," she scoffed, "it's a flower shop. I don't understand why he needs to create so much mess and hassle."

Owen swirled the pale drink it its glass, "But all that mess and hassle got you an apartment. You're officially a member of Blacken, welcome to the club, Avie."

He lifted his glass to toast, Avie meeting his glass halfway with a soft clink.

"Even more reason to celebrate, good thing we're getting them all together in one night," she laughed before taking a sip, pulling a face, "it's so dry, is this what you usually drink?"

"Usually, yes," he took another swig, "I don't like sweet things, it makes my teeth hurt. I can get you something else?"

"Oh, no, it's good wine! I'll still drink it. Guess I've been too spoiled with the sweeter stuff." She gulped another mouthful, smiling into the wineglass as if to prove her words.

"Aww c'mon, we're supposed to be celebrating you! I want to make sure you're having something you like."

Owen set his glass down on the coffee table in front of them, standing and making his way to find something in the kitchen. Avie followed him, still taking sips of the dry wine in an attempt to not seem rude.

"It's fine though, see?"

Opening the fridge, he ignored her words, crouching in the doorway and searching its contents. "Hrm, what if we threw some fruit in it? That's fancy, right? Might help the taste," he wondered aloud.

Avie couldn't respond.

The blond waited a few seconds. Realizing he wasn't getting a reply, he stood upright and turned to face her with an eyebrow cocked, watching in that moment as her shaking hand fell numb and glass slipped through her fingers.

"Avie?"

The glass dropped and shattered on the linoleum, Owen hastily moving around the door of the fridge to get to her, mindful of the broken pieces. Her distant expression caused immense worry to wash over him as it showcased to her, blurred in all his motions.

She went numb, her mind reeling into overdrive and causing everything around her to suddenly halt, caught up in the slew that was her psyche.

Owen grasped at her shoulders, "Avie! Avie, c'mon, talk to me, what's happened? What's wrong?" He tilted her chin up with a gentle thumb and finger, causing her eyes to meet his.

"It's back. The vibration. *It's fucking back*," she eventually stammered out, eyes wide in an internal panic.

"What do you mean? It's impossible! How the hell do you mean it's back?"

"I don't know, I just feel it! The same as it was when I had to be here. What does it mean, Owen? What does it mean?!"

Avie was terrified. All the conspiracy theories conversed in the past few days littered there in her mind. They mingled with the foreign feeling, the itching underneath her skin that she knew all too well. It didn't make any sense; everyone had it stop when they came into town…. She was still in Blacken!

Were there actually little green men responsible? Were they coming to take her away?

Were they going to kill her?

"Whoa, whoa, breathe now, Avie. I've got you. I'm here. There are never any witnesses to the disappearances, remember? No one's going to take you away, you're going to stay right here. We will figure this out," Owen spoke as if reading her fears. The thoughts inside her racing as fast as the frequency drummed through her circulatory system.

He breathed with her, trying to get her to calm.

Deep breath in, let it go, repeat.

He held her face in his hands and kept direct eye contact.

Avie's breathing started to slow by mimicking the man in front of her, just his presence being a huge help with calming down the intruding thoughts. God. She wouldn't know what she would have done if she was alone.

Owen's hands moved, readjusting the woman's arms to rest around his shoulders before picking her up. She made a noise, not expecting the action, and before she could ask what was going on, she was set down on the couch.

"Stay and relax, I'm going to get you some water, I'll be right back."

She tried to focus on a spot across her, the buttercup walls and mac-ramé plants strung up swirled around each other unless she absolutely focused her vision. Grabbing the afghan from the back of the couch, she wrapped it around her shoulders just as Owen returned. Avie sipped on the cold liquid as he sat beside her, rubbing small circles on her back.

"Was it something to do with the alcohol?"

"I don't think so, I've had a few drinks before, and nothing happened then. Damn it, I can still feel it. Could it really be something beyond our comprehension? Why is my experience with this different from everyone else's?"

"Whatever is happening, the rabbit hole goes deeper than expected. This opens up way more questions. I've got a heating pad; do you think it might help?"

Avie nodded, wanting to try anything to relieve the pressure.

The blond returned with medication and a warm bag, giving her a massage to try and ease the stress and lift some of the vibrating that wracked her body. It took a few hours of distractions and trials, but eventually, the feeling tapered off, much to their relief.

"I'm sorry," she spoke from his shoulder.

"Hm? What for?"

"I feel like I ruined the night, we were supposed to be celebrating."

Owen turned, she readjusted to see his face, "You don't have to be sorry, Avie. You didn't do anything wrong. This is an awful thing that makes you uncomfortable. It took over. All I want is for you to feel better. The night isn't ruined, just interrupted."

She smiled, relieved at his words. The guilt hit her hard over the fact she couldn't do what they originally planned for the evening, all she wanted to do was have a break and a fun night, but it turned into an ordeal.

"Can we watch a movie? And maybe I can have some of that wine with fruit?"

Owen chuckled, "Absolutely."

They watched an old movie, the hours dwindling into the early morning as they finally enjoyed each other's company, the sensation finally long passed.

—⁃∞∞⁃—

Owen mulled around the small space, looking for an appropriate place to set the box he cradled in his arms.

"Would just anywhere for these be alright?"

Avie watched from where she made up her bed in the next room, seeing him struggle with the heavy box, "Yes, that can go anywhere! Thank you!"

She smoothed out creases from the satin sheets, glancing out the window, finding that the line of the forest met on the other side of the street. The redhead grabbed an empty box before standing to meet Owen in the living space, looking in tentative apprehension at the mess she would have to sort on the wooden floor.

A multitude of boxes littered the small space, they piled up on furniture and counter space, leaving the floor a maze to weave in and around. Avie had been able to pick up a few items for her new apartment, as well as have other materials expedited to her new town. The librarian helped out tremendously with a few of the necessities she needed to get by before she could start spending again.

Owen huffed, setting the container of books and papers he brought from the library down on the ashen kitchen counter; the only thing that separated it from the open living room.

"I gotta say, at least the kitchen and your bedroom look nice. Your sitting area looks like a hoarder's den."

"Half of the stuff here is the junk you bring from the library! I've got nowhere to keep all of it," she laughed, starting to organize the boxes of various knick-knacks onto a bookshelf in the corner, "are you sure you don't mind helping unpack this much?"

"Of course not! I wouldn't leave you to do everything on your own, besides you were able to get everything in before any snow hit. If it was the middle of winter, you may have been on your own," he sucked in a breathy laugh, joking around with his friend.

"Thank you for being *such* a gentleman," her tone dripped with sarcasm as she wiped at a smudge on the floral wallpaper, "have you found any other leads for the Dewey Decimal team?"

Owen thumbed through a few containers of movies, reading each title before packing them in the T.V stand, "Just a few more natural occurrences we can look at. Extraterrestrial and U.F.O information is in short supply."

"Damn, it figures. I wonder what happened the other night then? Do you think it will ever come back?"

"I guess it's a wait and see. But if it does, call me. I can be over in minutes."

Avie nodded, finishing placing items from the box and standing up to stretch out. A whine escaped, drawing his attention to her.

"We've been moving and unpacking for hours," she glanced at her wristwatch, "it's almost time for lunch, want to brave the rain and go over to *J&K's*?"

He agreed with excitement.

Soft music played in the diner as they entered and were seated. The small mom and pop shop had an older 1950's aesthetic, with black and white tiles, jukebox, neon signs and thunderbird car themed seats. *J&K's* was easily the most fun diner in town and had amazing food, of course meaning it was always busy.

"Heya, Avie!" A woman with dark brown hair highlighted with silver came up with pen and paper.

"Hey, Sandra! It's been a bit, how've you been?"

Sandra flashed her eyebrows, pulling a brief exasperated face, "Busy as usual, though it's good to see ya again. And this must be your friend… Owen, was it? Can I get you two somethin' to drink?"

"Just water for me, please."

"Same."

Sandra nodded, "I'll come back for your order in a bit, sugar." The older woman started off to other patrons in the restaurant on quick feet, leaving Avie and Owen to their own devices.

"She's never remembered my name before. What have you been up to?" He leaned forward, voice a bit lower as if he were worried the waitress could hear him over the noise of the restaurant.

"I'm usually in when she works, she's been on constant overtime because of scheduling mix ups and call-ins, and we just get talking every time. Sometimes I've talked about you with her; all good things, don't worry."

"Sandra always acts like she's got a bug up her ass. Maybe she can take a lesson from you, you're always too nice to everyone, I don't get it."

The waitress in discussion walked up and set down their beverages, "Do y'all need a little more time?"

Owen looked down and away, readjusting uncomfortably and fiddling with the glossy menu; outwardly worried if she heard his comment.

"I'm good, Owen?" He nodded in response. "The usual for me, please," Avie sang, handing the pamphlet back.

"Gimme the Big Breakfast."

Sandra scribbled down the order on her small notepad and collected their menus, "Sounds good, we'll bring that out as soon as we can."

"I've never seen her on the right side of the bed. She's really taken a shining to you!" Owen commented, bewildered at her change of character as she strolled away.

"Sandra's got a lot of work to cover, and a lot of people who treat her like an expense. Everyone deserves kindness. A little of it can go a long way," she smiled, sipping on the ice water.

"Yeah, I guess I haven't really thought about it. You were the first person to be nice to me, too. But you can't help everyone, some people are beyond that."

The pair began to chat over what happened with Avie the other night, gathering any info they could about what may well have caused her to feel the vibrating pressure again. It was unheard of. If people *did* feel the sensation again, it was because they left Blacken. The Dewey Decimals had a whole new can of worms added to the mystery, one that caused another detour with the investigation.

"They examined me at the hospital when I first got here. An MRI and CT scan was done, and they didn't find anything abnormal, they released me after they got the results. I'm absolutely certain it wasn't anything else. You couldn't forget it."

"I've got to say, I am feeling a little left out. If I just knew what it was like, maybe I could help more, maybe we could narrow some choices down."

"You've talked to a lot of people about it, right?"

The waitress returned to their table with food, Owen in the middle confirming Avie's question.

"So sorry for the wait! Anythin' else I can get 'cha?" Sandra was slightly panting from running around the lunch rush.

"It looks amazing, we should be all good, Thank you!"

"I second that, it's perfect timing, thank you."

Pleasant surprise wrote over Sandra's features, "Enjoy, sugars!"

Avie turned her attention back to Owen once she left, "See? She's already starting to treat you the same way. All because you were giving her a break and treating her like a person."

The blond nodded again, mulling over the change in Sandra, "I was starting to think you had a superpower. Or maybe it is."

Avie giggled, digging into the chicken parmesan, "I think the world just needs a little bit more love, that's all."

They ate, resuming conversations about the additional wave of vibrating and how they could figure what was causing it to come back. Or even if it would come back again. The woman briefly brought up that she could talk with Jim, even if he didn't seem to have very many answers to begin with. It may be worth a try. *J&K's* atmosphere was bubbling with other conversations, masking their own.

The redhead picked up on a conversation that came from the couple on her right, *"Did you hear? They think Dale went missing…"*

She didn't mean to eavesdrop, but the conversation was along the lines of what they both were looking into… probably. Keeping concentrated, Avie waved at Owen to be quiet and listen too.

"What, why? When did he leave? He had such a good job here."

"Who knows, maybe he went back to the States, I hear they pay better. It was just a few days ago now."

Jade eyes widened, locking them with Owen's pale face. Her attack was only a few days ago.

Shit, this wasn't good. Was it just coincidence? Owen grasped her hand.

"Owen, we need to do something, I don't like this. I don't like knowing people are going missing with no follow up," coarse whispers fluttered over the table.

"I know Avie, we're working on it. We'll find something soon, there are clues, we just have to follow them."

Squeezing his hand, the woman nodded, worried about the fates of those in Blacken, and herself. Who really knew if they would find any answers any time soon? Would it be too late by the time they discovered something?

The knowledge that someone actually went missing recently since she came into town kicked the investigation into a new gear. Avie wanted to find something, *anything*, that could make sense of why people disappeared. It took a few weeks, the Dewey Decimals going through both natural and supernatural elements, trying to cover all bases.

They were running in circles; all the information blended together and didn't go anywhere. Any time they discovered something that looked as though it could lead to an answer of some sort, came up as a red herring, leading them back to square one.

The pair were no closer to any answers than they were at the beginning.

"I know these things take time, but shouldn't there be more? Should we have found something after a *month* of searching?" Her head rested on the table after pushing a manila folder to its other side, "Maybe it's why so many people accepted religion as an answer. This shit is frustratingly confusing."

The librarian came to sit down beside her, "I know it's tough and I know it feels impossible, but we've got all the wrong answers out of the way, the right one has to come soon. Once it does, we can figure out a way to stop what's been going on."

She leaned her head on his shoulder, "You always know what to say. I hope we can find out more, I just have to be patient. I guess, overall, I'm worried that it will happen to me too."

"That's why there's more priority now, you've felt the hum again and we don't know what that means. We won't rush anything, you look exhausted. You should really go home and get some sleep," the blond was idly rubbing circles into her back as he spoke, causing Avie to feel the wash of sleep kick in with all its power.

"I suppose you're right. It would help to rest up for work tomorrow too."

She got up to leave, throwing on her coat for protection against the chilly air. The temperatures once again dropped near freezing in the mountainous September atmosphere, gracing her every time she stepped outside.

"If your boss isn't in, I might be able to run you some food!" he called out after her.

Avie waved back at him, "Here's hoping! Have a good night, Owen!" With that, she walked out of the library and into the night, seeing puffs of her breath as she shuddered, drawing the coat closer to her body.

The walk home was going to be a long one.

—————

It was back.

The same call she felt to draw her into town, the same pull that hummed in her blood and whined in her bone marrow picked up its frequency in the small hours of the night. Familiar vibrations woke Avie from a dead sleep, causing her to shoot upright from her bed in a panicked state. She clutched at her heart, the bass baritone of the buzzing affecting the center of her circulatory system harshly.

She gasped for air, sweating, desperately trying to crawl out of the mulberry satin sheets and onto the cool wooden floor—all the while focusing only on the vibrating in a feeble act to calm it down herself. It was worse, it was *way* worse this time around.

Avie couldn't take this. There was something else, something she was supposed to do or find; nobody else had the forceful hum continue after they moved into Blacken, but here she was, continually suffering.

Finally, after resting on the cooling wood beneath her, her body accumulated to the shock, allowing her to breathe without it catching in her diaphragm. The woman wasn't taking any chances of another harsh attack like this to happen again. Promptly, she staggered up on shaking knees and all but threw on her violet coat before rushing out of the door, shoes hardly hanging on.

The unexplainable phenomenon of Blacken, an all-encompassing drive to move; to *seek*. Most seemed to think the town itself was the driving force, even Avie in the first few weeks. It was naive to think that it would stop as it did for others.

No, she knew better after having her body under the powerful vibrating strength long after moving to the town.

It wasn't a phenomenon of the town.

Something else was calling, and she had to find out what.

CHAPTER 5

The bitter night caressed her exposed skin, her body shivering upon walking out of her small apartment and into the streets.

Instinctively, Avie wrapped her arms around her frame to keep her core warmer if only a fraction. The young woman was disoriented, the drumming in her veins occupying her thoughts. She had to steady herself before starting to move forward.

Picking a direction at random, she started walking, turning down different streets to see what course her body may lead. It was just like when she was coming into Blacken; her body was her compass to where she needed to be led.

A fleeting voice of reason attempted to break through the overwhelming obsession to pursue, telling her to go to Owen first.

Of course, the thought was pushed away as soon as the pressure lifted a tinge when Avie turned down a set of streets, leading out of the town and towards the line of trees. It relieved her, the affliction lessening becoming her only interest.

Into the forest… Was she being led to where she had her accident?

She could very well get lost if she went through the tree line, unknowing where she could end up while being turned around and around by this thing in her body. However, she also didn't want to continue to feel like this; to have the vibrating wrack her body, to have people she knew disappear never to be heard from, to be unsure of her fate and if she was destined to be missing as well…

Avie took her chances, and she dipped into the line of trees to enter the woodland.

It was so dark, the only light she had was the moonlight above her, helping only slightly in its half phase as she tripped over roots and fallen branches. The cacophony in her simmered down the further she went, common sense instead taking its place to course through her.

"What the hell am I doing? I should go back. What if I run into a bear? What if I run into *worse*?" A mountain of 'what if' scenarios rushed into her mind, all the while her legs carried her further into the woods, contradicting her want for safety.

Up in her own mind between the vibrations and her paranoia of the forest, she almost didn't register until a few steps in that she waltzed into a clearing. Her face scrunched in confusion, taking in the new surroundings with her adjusted eyesight.

There was, what looked to be, a small abandoned manor in front of her. It stood tall, narrow, and foreboding—absorbing the night around it. Only a few speckles of moonlight trickled through the trees and patched its worn wood, the dwelling easily camouflaged in the nature surrounding. It was an odd sight to see, but not unheard of. Yet Avie never heard anyone mention anything about it, not even Owen. She absentmindedly wondered if he even knew about it as she cautiously took steps towards the looming building.

It had seemed the perfect area for whatever supernatural activity happening in the little town to take place at. Either that, or a serial killer's hideout.

Avie twirled the ring on her finger, eyes darting for any possible movement. She had to figure something out while she was here, she came all this way and if the sensation did keep coming back at this intensity, it would drive her mad. Or what if she was chosen next?

For some semblance of safety, the woman grabbed a small bough at her feet for protection; figuring it was a decent sized bat if anything got too close.

Her teeth chattered. Still, she approached the front door, a shaking hand reaching out for the handle. *Please be locked. Please be locked. Please be locked!* Avie was terrified to enter, the unknown inside outlined all kinds of danger, yet she couldn't stop. Her rational mind and determined mind fighting out in an exhausting war.

The handle turned under her touch and the door opened for her.

The wood squeaked on rusting hinges, opening inside to reveal the dark space. Avie cursed for not having the foresight to have brought a flashlight with her, the moonlight having to make do once again as it streamed through the windows.

Jade eyes accommodated after a few long minutes of standing in the doorway. She took notice of a few graffiti tags and dusty open cans of food strewn about in the entrance, it looked like a few squatters had taken refuge in the past. A broken banister held the small staircase beside her, she was almost certain she may fall right through the steps if she tried them. Hesitant step after hesitant step was taken, the branch clutched tightly against her body.

The place definitely *seemed* abandoned, Avie couldn't see any signs of inhabitants in the darkness as she moved through the level of the manor. She certainly didn't want to announce herself, choosing only to blend into the creaks and moans of the wood, the lack of light perhaps a blessing in disguise. Moving through the living space, old furniture had been covered with sheets, books stacked all over and overflowed in the bookshelves. A grand fireplace stood to her right, reaching up high and mighty, drawing her sight to where almost every inch of the roof beams above her were covered with dust and cobwebs. She could feel as though she was close to a discovery for the source of drumming inside her, so close yet just out of her grasp.

It had to be here! It just had to...

Reaching the other side of the living room, a straight shot through the manor, she entered the kitchen, leading to a back door. There was a dining room adjacent that she eyed cautiously, unsure of the darkness emanating from it. Avie really didn't have the ability to explore the other levels of the house; her heart in her throat with apprehension at just exploring the main level. Her rational mind won over her.

She opened that exit with no hesitation, ready to leave the creepy atmosphere the place gave off. Back outside, Avie rested on the door after she closed it, heaving a sigh of relief as the adrenaline had a chance to calm down.

At the back entrance of the abode, what would have been a garden in warmer weather lay there in its abandoned ruins. Wire branches of the hedges enclosed the yard, their skeletons serving as a decent barrier of privacy even in the season. A large broken bird bath sat in the center, groups of dianthuses surrounding the faded stone—a short walk away from the small shack amidst them. Curious, she took the chance that her answer resided there instead.

Avie took a few steps toward the fountain and froze.

There was something in the periphery of her vision. *Movement.* A hunched figure there on the outside of her sight lines. Dare she turn to see it?

Her head peeked slowly, eyes following the path, hesitant to look. Her feet firmly plotted to the soil, frozen in place while crippling fear occupied like ice in her veins.

Eyes locked onto a flurry of wings, stretching up taller than any man she had seen. They blocked out the moon in the distance. Avie noticed a heavy-set man laying at the figure's feet, his look more than likely mirroring her own; pure shock at seeing such a thing, soaked in awe. The ginger man must have been taking up all the creature's attention, away from her nervous footsteps attempting to lurk away from its massive form.

Avie couldn't take her stare off of it. Fingers went numb, unable to support the heavy wood in her hands, they trembled and let it fall to the peat beneath her.

The noise caused the mass to sharply turn towards her, giving the woman a glimpse into large deep red eyes, glowing in the low light. The moment their eyes connected, the breath knocked out of her, a gasp following with raised shoulders as she struggled to comprehend what exactly she was seeing.

Fight or flight kicked in and she was able to get her legs kick started with adrenaline to get the fuck away from that *thing*.

Would she be so lucky that it wouldn't abandon the man already entranced at its feet? Or was Avie as doomed as the day she first heard the town's—no, this *creature's call?* It was an entity, a form beyond this world, she was sure it was the being that called her blood and bones to the town of Blacken. To it.

She looked back and cursed her bad luck. The thing with its massive feathered wings had indeed chosen to run after her. Its witness.

Her body ran for the tree lines, she couldn't outrun it, the only way she could possibly think of escaping was to hide, move under guise of the darkness and the canopy the trees could produce. Confuse the *thing*, get it off her trail enough for her to get home, get to *safety*, get to Owen to tell him what the hell was going on.

Storming into the forest, she zig-zagged through the trunks and roots, hoping to stand a chance of making it out alive. Flying faster than she'd ever imagined her feet could take her, she ducked and weaved in her limited vision, getting to keep some distance between her proverbial cat and mouse chase.

Her knee gave, causing Avie to fall, bowing behind a particularly large tree trunk.

She stopped herself from crying out with great strain, hissing silently while crawling out of sight, she took in the area around her. Quaking hands covered her mouth, a breath was held in morbid anticipation, listening, waiting.

It was close, attempting to locate where she had disappeared on her trail, or were hiding. She couldn't hide, it would find her. She was sure it could *smell* her.

Without making a sound, she deftly took off the warm jacket, exposing her skin to the harsh mid-September. She could feel hot tears stream down her cheekbones as she silently prayed to be allowed to escape alive.

The woman steeled herself, rubbing the damp earth over her arms and through her hair, hands balled tightly clutching her jacket after her rushed mud bath. It was closing in, there was no time left.

With all her might, Avie threw the jacket to her left, hearing the giant move towards the noise, giving her the opportunity to run right; thankful that the dark cover was seemingly enough that her trick worked. She ran on light feet, mind hyper fixated on running fast and quiet; it would have been almost impossible with the dry leaves licking her sneakers, but because of the rain fall earlier, she was thankful for the stroke of luck with the tri-coloured foliage too damp to crinkle under her step.

She had to be close to being back into town by now, it felt like running a marathon, hours ticking by instead of minutes as she gasped for breath with burning lungs, refusing to stop. Avie stumbled and fell forward, somersaulting down a small hill and into the hard glow of orange lights illuminating a road, a street, housing...

Out of the fucking forest.

She laughed, shaking and crying, hands clutching at the roots of her scalp.

She made it.

But she wasn't completely safe, still having to get out of the immediate area.

Her legs started to fiercely shake, using all their strength to sprint at such a pace for so long. The adrenaline wore off, leaving her steps in agony while Avie needed to keep going, to get to Owen. Owen would know what to do, how to keep her safe, how to make her feel better.

Owen, Owen, Owen.

She needed Owen.

Trembling, Avie huddled her arms over her torso as she wobbled on screaming muscles, just trying to move, placing one foot in front of the other took all of her will power. The little blue house came into her vision, she started to count the steps.

25... 26... 27... 28...

The thing in the woods staying in the back of her mind as her vigilance mingled with pain and cautious optimism. Owen's familiar house was right there, right in front of her...

147... 148... 149...

She spammed the doorbell, fingers frosty red and nails scorching blue. After waiting for the feeling of eternity, warmth opened the door. Owen in his scraggly bedhead with an accompanying beaten down robe opened enough to reveal tacky sailor pajamas. It was the most comforting sight even as he berated her in the lateness of the hour and her choice of wardrobe in the weather.

She could only smile, finally safe.

The last of her strength left her, leaving Avie to collapse on the front door stoop, him barely managing to catch her before the impact could. Owen picked her up in his arms, taking in the frigid temperature of her body, skin covered with scrapes and caked with dirt.

"Holy shit, Avie... what happened to you?"

"I need. To use. Your shower..."

At the very least, she thought if she could wash off her scent, there would be no more trail, no horrendously tall cryptid smashing through walls to capture the human that cost them their privacy and possibly a meal. However, once she moved into the bathroom, the idea of having a shower didn't work, Avie couldn't stand for that long, so instead decided to take a long soak with scented products much different than her own.

The hot water soothed her muscles, the whine still reverberating throughout her. The young woman rinsed out her hair, the masculine scent masking the honey one she previously applied. Avie thought about what she had seen. The eyes of the dark figure terrified her. She felt as though she interrupted something she *really* was not supposed to see, let alone escape from. The dark red burned into her retinas, creating a snapshot memory every time she closed her eyes. Once again filling the tub with clean water, the woman soaking in its comfort as she sat and processed.

The redhead couldn't describe it, but she felt the overwhelming block in the back of her throat to not share the information she bore witness to.

But why though?

She should be telling Owen what happened out there in the woods. Avie should be telling any person who would listen so they could stop what was out in the forest. But she couldn't bring herself to think about attempting to do that. It sounded crazy to her, and she was the one to bear witness to the thing with feathered wings. How could she possibly convey it properly? This was way beyond the scope of her ability of understanding. Her energy was zapped, leaving her beyond the point of exhaustion, her body hardly able to control the motions of cleaning up, let alone converse over the situation she experienced.

Avie went out there for answers, and, well, she may have got a fraction of one. She was lucky this time, how could she keep that luck to find out more? Would Owen run in with gusto at the mention of something *not human* in the woods? He very well might without a second thought to his safety.

Twisting her hair to dispel extra water, she figured she was too tired to think clearly about what happened, and that she could ponder and explain more in the morning. She came out with borrowed PJ's, toweling her damp hair. Owen started a warming fire, still crouched adding firewood before he took notice of her entrance.

"Hey, are you feeling okay? I made you some tea."

Sitting on the couch, Avie slumped into its comfort, "I'm exhausted, the vibrating is back, it's draining me, but I'm alright. Thank you, that's exactly what I need."

"I put your clothes just on the recliner here, did you want me to wash them?" He adjusted to come and sit next to her, bringing the steaming cups to sit on the table in front of the pair.

"Burn them. I just need to rest for a moment." She leaned the damp curls on his shoulder, feeling as though she may pass out at any second.

"Avie, why would I do that?"

"You've got the fire going anyway. Please? It's important."

He nodded, the scruff of his beard scratching on the top of her head. Hesitantly, Owen spoke quietly, "Did you find something with your vibrating?"

Her eyes opened up, looking down into her lap, "… Yes and no. It came back in the middle of the night, but it's much worse. It felt like I couldn't even breathe, and I knew that it was trying to guide me to find something else. So, I followed the call—kind of like how I first came into town, you know? I ended up in the forest where this old abandoned manor was."

He bristled at hearing that, but still waited for her to continue as she sat up, "And… Someone else was there, I think. Two men were, actually. One of them chased me out and I was terrified they were following me, so I tried to lose them in the woods. I couldn't see what they looked like or anything. It was so dark there, and I was unbelievably frazzled."

"I understand. I've seen that place a few times; it has an intimidating atmosphere. I'm not very impressed you went out there alone in the middle of the night, that's idiotic. I would have preferred you call me at least so I could have gone with you. I mean, look at you, you're shaken up. Frozen to the bone and collapsing on my doorstep!"

Avie sighed, "I know, I wasn't really thinking straight. I just wanted answers to make the pain stop."

"It's painful now?"

"Like someone turned the intensity way up, I had a hard time moving at first. I'm sure it is trying to get me to find something else in town." She reached out, picking up the tea, slurping at the seeping liquid as it cooled down enough for her to drink comfortably.

"There may be something in that area, we should do some investigative exploring once you're feeling better." Owen drank from his mug as well, eyes sparkling with a possible lead behind his concerned features.

Avie spun the ring with the side of her finger, "Perhaps, but it didn't feel better once I was there. It may be further in the forest."

Damn. She just lied again, why did she continue to lie to *Owen* of all people?

Deep down, she knew she was scared. Avie feared what could happen to her or Owen if they went there. Even talking about the creature made her worry of repercussions. She didn't want to end up dying in the pursuit of knowledge. But then people would keep dying if she didn't intervene…

She sighed heavily, questioning her cowardice.

His arm wrapped around the back of her body, having her embrace further into him, Owen nodded slightly, making a small noise in confirmation, "Let's get you upstairs, you're exhausted. You should sleep in the bed instead and we can talk more tomorrow."

A dreamless sleep was gifted to her, sleeping heavily in a few hours grace. That was until warbling from a bird outside roused her from her slumber.

Avie awoke to gentle sunlight streaming in from the parted drapes, seeing a little brown bird perched on a branch outside the window. She stretched out, feeling the muscles in her legs giving protest due to how much strain they were in earlier.

Oh... Something very out of the ordinary happened last night, yet the woman questioned if any of it had been a dream. It couldn't all have been real, right? The experience feeling all too surreal the more her memories came through.

Still, the feeling she had last night stayed in the forefront of her mind, Avie didn't want to tell anyone about *it*. Not yet at least, the thought of Owen rushing headstrong to the manor giving her hesitation. However, if that man escaped from the manor as well, the blond would find out eventually. He would also want to know why she didn't tell the truth...

Of course, they speculated about aliens, but could she really confirm that entity was as such? Avie had no idea about how to approach the subject with Owen. She owed him the proper explanation, at least, even through her worry... Dragging her hands over her face, she got up to just get her confession out of the way.

Walking down the staircase, she found him already awake, sipping on a mug of coffee and watching the news. He turned upon hearing her, "You're awake! Did you end up sleeping alright?"

She nodded and smiled, "Yeah, it was decent. You?" Avie sat next to him on the love seat, taking in it was still early in the day from the television in front of them.

"The same. Here, I've made you coffee," he stood to retrieve the drink from the kitchen, bringing it back to her. She sipped, careful not to burn her lips on the steaming liquid, humming at the comfort of having a warm drink made just the way she liked.

"I wanted to apologize for scaring you last night. I really am okay."

"Hell of a night for you, you shouldn't be worried about me. If you remember any more about the mystery men though, I'll take that as an apology!"

Avie smiled, shaking her head, her words coming out before she even thought of them... "I've got nothing..." Damn it, she was supposed to have told Owen the truth! She was only digging herself further down, now frustrated by her own inaction...

"Well, feel free to stay as long as you'd like. I've got today off, and so do you."

She looked at him puzzled, "What do you mean? I'm scheduled in a few hours."

"I called in for you, you shouldn't be under that stress and then have to deal with work stress. It's just one day, I figured you might need the rest."

His heart was in the right place, and she did appreciate the time to rest and figure some things out, but it shouldn't have been his call.

"That does sound nice, but next time, I'll be the one to call in."

"Yeah, yeah of course. I'm sorry, I didn't mean..."

She waved a dismissive hand, "No, don't worry about it, I know you just wanted to help. I think I'd like to stay and inconvenience you to make up for it."

"It's only fair," he laughed, "want any breakfast?"

She nodded vehemently; her stomach not satisfied with only coffee.

After spending the day with Owen, Avie started on her walk back home, the sun beginning to set with the shorter autumn months as she walked; sky illuminating in a soft pink tone for her.

The thoughts of what she was going to do still plagued her. The red-head didn't know how to continue forward with the information she accidentally stumbled upon. She certainly didn't want anyone else to die, but she didn't want to either. It was incredibly risky to even enter the woods now that she knew what lurked within them. That creature was more than likely on the defensive.

There was also the fact she still had questions that needed answers— Owen's safety lurking in her mind with how to proceed. She had to steer him away from wanting to explore the space until she could figure something out. First things first, she had to find what became of the man called there too.

With her key in the lock, Avie opened the door to her place, the small space seeming darker after being surrounded by Owen's larger and brighter house. She threw her keys on the counter beside the door and made her way into her bedroom, intent on finding a start in her own investigation.

Flicking on the light to her room, she quickly realized she was not alone.

The creature from the woods the night before came out of the shadows once she had entered and flooded the room with light. It dropped down behind her, talons unceremoniously clattering on the hardwood, effectively blocking her exit. Avie jumped, spinning around to the source of the noise and inhaled a scream at what she saw. She had a feeling that this thing might track her down, despite her best efforts to avoid it.

Her brain almost couldn't process the situation, she didn't know what to do in the circumstances that she was trapped in. Reacting without thinking, she started to smile nervously in her odd tick and breathlessly let out a laugh, speaking to the creature.

"You must be quite upset with me…"

She spoke while backing up, trying to put more distance between them as it matched her step, bridging the gap, snarl wearing on its face. Avie got to take in the creature's appearance for the first time: it looked male, towering over her with chestnut feathers covering up and down his body, those wings that blacked out the sky last night were instead curled around him as he was confined in a small space. Longer feathers even caressed around his head, coiffed around his cranium and nape, practically giving the appearance of hair swooped back. Small quills drew around, surrounding and outlining his long and angular face and even covering down the bridge of a nose—skin pale over the rest of his face. The eyes that she saw burning red, cooled into an amber with dark vertical slits for pupils.

One of the massive wings unraveled itself and crashed into the light overhead, causing sparks to fly, and bathed the room once again in darkness; keeping secret from any prying eyes while he blocked any escape.

Avie hit a wall, still gazing into those amber eyes, pulse drumming in her head and hands shaking. He leaned down and she clenched her eyes, certain he would attack at any moment.

"*Understatement.*"

CHAPTER 6

To her surprise, he talked. And hell, he even understood her. His voice was low and seeped with irritation but held a softness in the lilt of his pronunciation.

Avie's eyelids snapped open in astonishment, looking up to meet his gaze once more at hearing him speak. Why would he bother coming to communicate if he was just going to kill her? She couldn't take her eyes off of him now that she was locked in his vision, danger emanating from her every nerve.

Finally, the words stumbled out, matching her shaking body.

"Are you here to silence me?"

"It is not in my best interest to kill for the sake of killing, nor be discovered. You had the opportunity to speak of my existence yet have not. Why?"

He stood upright, using his full height to loom over her in an intimidating fashion. His eyelids lowered, the light casting small shadows onto his face as he leaned away, studying her and awaiting a response.

The creature had followed her out of the woods. He saw her at Owen's and overheard their conversation. Avie's blood turned cold. This being now knew whom she was closest with. She mentally kicked herself for even going out to that manor in the first place.

The woman was sure that he was the cause of the vibrations. He was the thing that led people into town... To do what exactly? Use them as a food source? If he wasn't here to kill her, then he must have already fed on that man before her at the manor...

"I d-don't know. I was s-s-scared." She never stuttered in her life, but this being brought out true terror.

A smirk lit up on his face, the action frightening in the darkness, "Scared? Are you scared now?"

He was having fun at her expense.

Avie's breath was drawing heavy through her nose, every part of her screaming to leave the situation. The wall pressed cold on her back, and the dark figure stood before her, she was akin to a mouse before a lion.

"ARE YOU?" his voice boomed, wings cast off of his body and opening to expand his size. She startled, seeing claws curling at his sides before squeezing her eyes shut.

"Y-yes!" she squeaked out.

The creature laughed in an undertone, amused.

"What even brought a lowly human like you to snoop around my domain? I have never had two show up at the same time before." She watched as he regained his posture, the enormous wings wrapping around his body once more. It reminded her of a cloak, draping over his torso and the majority of his legs.

Avie's eyes flicked back up to his, quiet with her answer, "I-I thought you were the one that called me there."

An eye ridge lifted at her comment. She didn't sound as afraid as she had been, clearly upsetting the cryptid.

"And how was I to do that?" he drew out the words, unimpressed.

"The... The blood, the bodies. You're the one that causes them to vibrate, right?"

He chuckled again, "I do not control blood, *I just drain it*. Bodies come to me. You are lucky I have already fed; I am not liking your tone."

That comment made Avie wince, head spinning with mental visuals of how this supernatural being fed on its victims, the ginger man seen at the manor center of said scenario.

Her eyes fell from his, darting as she thought the obvious; what was he here for? If he already ate and he wasn't going to kill her, then what was his angle?

"What do you want?" she could only whisper, unable to raise her head.

A hand reached out through the mass of feathers, the appendage dark and featherless, only having three attached fingers and thumb with equally dark talons protruding. Avie watched as it connected with the bottom of her chin, drawing her face up. "I am just ensuring my safety. You have not outed my being and I expect you to continue to do so. You made it so easy to find you when you left something trying to escape, remember I can easily find you again, and I know those close to you."

She flinched and then cringed… Her jacket… She left it in the woods. That's how he found her. That's how he had followed her to Owen's.

Fuck… Owen, he's wrapped into this now. She had to switch the conversation, keep him safe.

"For what it's worth… I'm sorry."

He looked irked; her words unexpected, the hand on her jaw retracted as though it burned.

"*What did you say?*"

"I'm sorry. I didn't intend on telling anyone, but I made you come all the way out here."

His eyebrows knit together in confusion. He was definitely caught off guard. Perhaps he was only used to others fearing him, begging for their life once they met him. Those people were drawn to him, just as Avie was. She was sure of it. This creature was attached to the mystery of Blacken in some way. If she wanted to find some answers, then she needed to be on his good side. She needed to be alive and she needed his help.

He took a faltering step back, before catching himself in the action. His demeanour quickly changing back to his previous haughty manner with a frustrated huff and a quick bite of bottom lip—exposing too sharp of teeth even in the darkness. The being stared down at her with scorn, the silence heavy between them. It looked like he wanted to say a plethora of things, yet nothing was uttered, trapped in the back of his throat.

Instead, he shook his head with a scoff, leaving in a flurry of feathers through her window.

All Avie could do was blink. Confused at his actions, and at her own. Just as fast as he was in her vision, he left. She let out a breath holding in her lungs for some time, the adrenaline tapering off, causing her legs to shake and give out, hitting the floor with a *thump*. This bird-man hybrid was intriguing to say the least. And it didn't kill her, which was further interesting.

The woman couldn't imagine he had much conversation with people beforehand; there would have been something in reports and newspapers if so, or even tall tales and urban legends spreading through the town.

She didn't sleep very well that night. Too many questions raced through her mind at what just happened.

"I figured you may need a coffee."

Owen waltzed into *Flora Adora*, a blue and white Styrofoam cup in his grasp. Avie lit up at the mention of caffeine, needing the energy boost from her uneasy slumber.

"Thank you, yes, it's been a long shift." She took the cup, eagerly gulping down its contents.

"So, is the boss in?" He looked around nervously.

"No, he went out for banking purposes, I take it you're not here for official flower business?" Her green eyes amused as she smirked.

He leaned on the counter, "Well, here I was thinking, I've been to that building you were at a few times. I didn't find anything out of the ordinary when I was there, but that was before I met you. I think you could have some sort of superpower with your vibrations to bring out the supernatural there. I was hoping you and I could scope it out?"

She scribbled down a finishing sentence in the company workbook, "I think it was just a vagabond that was there in the middle of the night. I don't think it's safe to be lurking around there just yet."

"True, hardly anybody knows about it since it's kinda way out there. But in the weather here, they're probably taking up the place until it's warm again," he sighed and hung his head, "maybe when it warms up, they would move on?"

"Who knows, but we want to solve a mystery, not wind up as one of the missing statistics."

"We can figure a way around it for a later time then, for now we'll focus on the data!"

The welcome bell chimed, signalling Gerald returning to the store.

"Any messages, Avie?" the boss called out, distracted in an envelope.

She stood upright and professional, "No, Sir."

"Good, continue on then."

Owen coughed awkwardly, "Yes, just the salmon rose bouquet. That is everything," his voice lowered an octave. She wondered if he was disguising his voice as to not be recognized as the person who called her in. He even handed her a few bills, committing to the part, Avie ringing the purchase and bouquet up for him.

After the workday, all she wanted to do was slump into the green cushion of her couch and not move for the rest of the night. Working in the mornings *and* evenings reminded her of the old routine of her teenage years, however she did not retain the same stamina.

The shrill cry of her landline interrupted a particularly entrancing paragraph in the book she held. Silently cursing, she shoved a bookmark into the pages before rushing off to pick up the receiver and cradle it on her shoulder.

"Hello?"

"Hey Avie, it's Owen, I'm sorry to bug you again."

"It's okay, what's up?"

"Nothing really, but uhh, there's something that's been bugging me… The other night when you were at the manor, did you see anything else?"

Her smile dropped, she couldn't let him know anything about the events, too worried that he could get hurt if he tried to do his own investigative exploring.

"Owen, If I did see something interesting, you would be the first to hear all about it. All I can remember is the two men."

"Right, right, yes. Sorry. I just wanted to make sure all the bases were covered, still hoping for some sort of lead in this. I know you'd let me know. Talk to you later?"

"Talk to you later, have a good night." Avie hung up, a shaky breath escaping her.

It felt horrible to lie to Owen, but she was only doing it to keep him safe. He would do the same for her, and in the end, if anything did come from the mystery, he would understand. She knew he would. Leaning on open palms on the side table, she sighed at the predicament as her head hung down.

The thing evidently made his way into her apartment once again. In a burst, looking quite exasperated in appearance, he confronted her in the living room.

"Why do you not tell him the truth? Why do you not tell him of my existence?!"

She jumped at the intrusion, her hands coming up to rest at her heart. A mental note was made to buy better window locks; this couldn't keep happening. Just how long was he lying in wait? She was right beside the door, Avie could leave easily if she wished. Instead, she stared at him, reaching over, it took the entire length of her arm to grasp at the light switch, flicking it off and drenching the living room in darkness, much like their last encounter.

The woman thought that he may be planning on killing and feeding on her if she did go and tattle. But she wouldn't be playing his game. It frustrated him to be discovered by a human who was doing nothing about it, she could see that now by his reaction.

"I may not agree with it, but you're only eating to survive. It's not my place to tell the world about you. I understand it, I don't *like* it, but it isn't right of me."

He huffed, "More innocent humans will die. You know this, correct? So, tell away. Why not try to stop me?"

"Why not stop *me* then before I can?" her voice was filled with confidence, a complete turn around from how she was merely hours ago. "If you're so worried, then why are *you* hesitating?"

The being was caught aback, blinking the illuminated eyes in a thought process. Hands at his side balled up and released several rapid times, the motion drawing her attention.

Then, he rushed.

He pinned her up against the wall, eyes drilling into her own as a twisted sneer painted his face, "I am above you, tiny *thing*, beyond your comprehension. And yet you do not fear me, you do not care to even have decent manners before me? Oh, I could kill you in an instant, before you drew your next breath. But I do not kill unless I need to feed. And you had better count the blessings of the stars that I have already. Now answer: What. Is. Your. Plan?"

Each word was enunciated as the look he gave became incredibly powerful, his eyes changing from that cool amber, bleeding into crimson around the corners. The tone was as red as when they first met unofficially, perfectly showcasing his anger. Her mind swam. Of course, terrified, but also so very intrigued. There were so many inquiries she had that only he could answer. He hasn't killed her by now, there were further motives with him; she also wanted to know his plan.

Avie blurted out the first thing she could muster.

"I'd like us to be friends! We could help each other."

Stepping back, he let her go, handling her words in a curious manner before laughing hysterically.

"Friends? With you, a *human*? Did you not hear what I had just said?" His wings flew back in a dramatic fashion, catching view of him holding onto his stomach as he laughed through his speech.

She raised her voice, an attempt to be heard over the noise, "Of course, I did! Are you out there all by yourself? Don't you get lonely?"

He stopped the raucous laughter in an instant, face dropping to a stern look. Returning his amber eyes to her jade gaze.

Awkward silence fell upon them, she fidgeted, wanting to break the apprehension. "Do you have a name?"

He visibly bristled, after her last question, she may have made him uneasy.

"I would not dare you to have the privilege of knowing my name."

And then in a sweeping moment, he turned to leave, escaping through her bedroom window once again.

This time, however, the woman ran after him.

"No-nonono, wait! Please wait!"

She reached out, the streetlight a few yards away barely painting her hand in its glow. But he was gone, disappeared into the night. Avie sighed, disappointed. She was just getting *something* from him.

It was odd. He was an asshole, absolutely, but he wasn't necessarily an evil entity. Truly, she meant her words, understanding he was just feeding to survive by his own accidental admission. She did want to know more about him and if something else could be used instead… Building a friend-ship could help in the pursuit of that knowledge and it didn't seem like it was an impossible feature; incredibly difficult, sure, but not impossible.

Only time would tell if he would show himself to her again. Avie hoped he would, having the feeling that he was going to in the future soon. He had his own intrigue and inquiries, she could help. She *wanted* to help.

The proverbial plot had thickened with the addition of the creature.

God, Owen would shoot her if he knew what she was keeping from him.

CHAPTER 7

It was an event that rocked Blacken's residents. The body of Garret Kipper had been found September 17th, nearby a ravine in the wooded area surrounding the town.

Waking early to go for a jog, the morning washed out any colour as she stepped outside, making the sight of a couple in yellow pajamas moving into the line of trees easy to spot—exclaiming that police found something. Curious, she followed, making her way through the small crowd gathered within, unsure as to what was going on or what could have been found to warrant so many townsfolk in this terrain. Many onlookers circled around, demanding answers from the small town's police department.

"We cannot give out any further details at this time, please disperse and give us room to work!" The female officer was mitigating the crowd, her voice commanding attention.

Finally, Avie laid eyes on what the mass had gathered there for; seeing the face of the man before he was covered with a white sheet.

Her heart palpitated in her chest as her stomach dropped, surroundings starting to blur in motion. She recognized that face, it was the same one she saw while at the manor. The same man with his light strawberry blond hair and matching stubble, taking up the feathered creature's attention; having the unfortunate luck of arriving there first.

"*But I do not kill unless I need to feed. And you had better count the blessings of the stars that I have already,*" the creature's voice rang in her head. It was one thing to hear about it, but to actually see the aftermath of the event made her squeamish, worried about the fate of her fellow persons.

"—The body has been found under unusual circumstances; we will be going over the evidence. If you have questions or tips, please call the department. As it stands, everyone needs to leave the scene," the officer's voice cut back in sharply, drawing Avie back into the moment.

The crowd dispersed, moving away from the yellow tape, her following suit in a daze while thinking over the Chief of Police's statement.

"Who are they trying to fool?" a woman still wrapped in pajamas spoke from her left, catching Avie's attention, "Everyone knows Garret, it's no use keeping his identity anonymous."

It was the first time she heard his name in reference.

"Yeah, and did you see his arms? Poor guy actually did it," the other piped out.

Did what? Was it the unusual circumstance? What did the officer mean?

Avie thought at first that the Chief meant something along the lines of what that being could have done to Garret. If there was evidence involved, it could have been anything. It could have even been...

She stopped dead in her tracks, having to support herself on a tree trunk as a wave of dizziness hit. She left her jacket in the woods, which was damn committable evidence tying her to the body.

Maybe they meant something else. Maybe she could... No, if she were found trying to locate and remove the coat while an investigation was in the area, it would look even worse. The woman started sweating despite the cold weather.

Avie decided to go to Owen, let him know what was going on with her tie in with Garret.

The redhead rang his doorbell, knocking frantically at the wood.

"Avie! Holy shit I was just trying to call you, did you hear?" Owen stepped aside, letting the young woman in, a hint of excitement behind his words. He was excited over more answers coming in to be sure, but it was just unfortunate timing given the circumstances. Word indeed got around fast...

"Yeah, that's why I'm here..." She paced, anxiously playing with her golden band.

"Can you believe they found a body? Do you think there is more out there? Just hiding in the woods?"

"Owen, he was one of the men I had seen out at the manor."

He stopped, registering her words, "Shit, you may have been the last person to see him alive."

Avie's fingers steepled in front of her mouth in a nervous fashion, "I left my jacket out there, nearby."

His expression turned thoughtful, remembering the night she had come to him freezing. Damn it, she also asked him to burn her clothing after she soaked in his tub. She could see the proverbial gears turning in his mind as he thought it over.

"I don't have an alibi to go against being in the woods at the same time. I know it looks bad; I'm terrified that they're going to think I was involved in this somehow." He raised his eyebrows at her in a questioningly way. "I wasn't, Owen!"

He took his glasses off to wipe them, "Right, but… Yeah, you're right, it looks really bad, Avie."

She collapsed onto the couch, hands encompassing her face with a frustrated groan.

"Couldn't you tell them there was someone else there?"

"I didn't even see what they looked like. It would be no help."

The blond hummed, "Your best bet may be to wait it out. Tell the truth if they ask, they may have a few leads already. They may even release more information sometime soon. I mean, where's that drifter going to go anyway? To another abandoned house and hide?"

Avie let the hands fall from her face, staring at the ceiling. Briefly, she thought about asking the feathered creature if he would be able to find the coat and bring it to her, but that was quickly dismissed—he wouldn't want to be doing her any favours.

She thought back to what she saw at the crime scene, Garret was pale, much more than a normal body would be. Figuring he had some blood loss at least with what was visible to her at the time, it was possibly caused by the creature in the woods—meaning it would be the first time he was sloppy, leaving evidence of his presence behind. It didn't really make sense that he would allow that to happen, after being so intent on making sure he would be kept a secret.

The woman would see if he could answer that question.

"I would hope so, it would help to get tips from the public... I just wish I was there longer, maybe I could have seen something more or done something that could have helped."

"Hey, don't beat yourself up about this. You could have ended up the same if you were there any longer. We're damn sure not going near that manor now."

She turned to see him, "I haven't even thought about that. I was so concerned about trying to remember more details, I didn't even..."

He stood to sit beside her instead, "You're safe, that's all that matters."

Avie leaned on his shoulder, "They're going to be reopening a lot of missing person's cases because of this. Do you think that there will be more people found?"

"I hope so, it would bring more closure to the town."

Humming in agreeance, her mind still occupied on what the future may bring.

It was common knowledge that missing persons were the ones that left everything to move into Blacken, accepted as fact that they moved back after not being constrained to the town. But now, there was a body, proof that missing may indeed also mean dead.

The town went into an emotional frenzy, worried that their loved ones too were deceased somewhere in the woods, maybe even in other cities that they came from. Others were not as convinced, since it was only one person found dead in the town's extensive history. This one case may have been a fluke, a change from the otherwise norm of Blacken.

"Hello, are you Avie Conrad?"

A knock at her apartment door interrupted her dinner late into the evening, opening the wood to two constables standing with pen and paper in hand, badges outstretched.

"Yes, that's me. How can I help you?"

They flipped closed the leather containing the metallic ID, the one to her left clicking his pen, ready to take notes, "Just had some questions regarding the body of Garret Kipper being found early this morning. We're going around and seeing if anyone had any information that would help the case."

Heaving a sigh of relief at hearing nothing was brought up about her jacket, she described going to Owen's late that night, unable to sleep. Even walking down the streets in the late hour, but unfortunately not seeing a struggle or anything suspicious.

"Thank you for your time, Miss. Conrad, if you remember anything else, give us a call," with their words, they handed over a business card, and promptly left.

They really didn't find her coat in the woods. Avie wondered if someone found it and decided to use it as their own, seriously starting to question if bird-man moved it when he used it to find her that night. Yet another question she could ask, if she was going to receive an answer was up for debate.

In the next few days, dozens of missing person's cases were indeed escalated and reopened. Police were forced to go over old evidence, eyewitness reports, out of city departments and follow-ups, including dredging the lake and combing the woods. People were now aware that individuals who had gone missing in the past simply didn't go back to an old life; they disappeared, not heard from whatsoever. It caused a few residents to move, despite their knowledge of the call inevitably returning once they traversed away from the town, a few speculating they would be back in no time.

However, despite the police department's best efforts over the course of weeks, anyone else that disappeared were not found. It was still early, but if there were so many cases of missing people over the decades, something would have been discovered by now. They ended up pulling back from the extensive search within their borders.

Owen and Avie tried everything in their power to get insider information, hoping anything the detectives could give them would help their own case about what was really going on behind the scenes.

The blond was like a kid on Christmas with the new revelations, getting slivers of information only added to his passion for the project they started. The woman believed their first flaw as a team was too many jumping off parts, but he disregarded that, stating they needed as much information as possible to be accurate.

Avie finished stacking the case files collected in her bedroom away, assembling the laundry she gathered from the community dryer and got to work on folding as she sat comfortably on the bed, a program idly chatting on in the background. She huffed, unimpressed at the pile done, still needing to fold another basket, and possibly start on a new load, her procrastination getting the better of her and leaving her more work to do all at once.

In the middle of moving a pile of shirts from her couch to the bedroom, the cryptid's voice startled her with his unexpected intrusion, "There were people poking around my home. I cannot imagine what they wanted to find there."

Hands dropped the clothes she carried, "I'm so sorry, I didn't send them to find you, I haven't told anyone! They've been looking over the whole town for missing people."

His laid-back attitude put her on edge, not exactly sure what he was expecting from her. He sat down in her armchair, picking up a t-shirt from a folded pile, examining the garment. Avie gathered up the scattered mess on the floor, she thought about turning off the television, it was her only source of light in the space. She really did not want him to smash it as he did to her light bulb.

"I figured as much, that is why I am not here to interrogate on the matter. Have they found any?"

She simply shook her head once his eyes were taken off the cloth and met hers, putting the pile she held back down into the basket. He unceremoniously dropped the shirt back on top of the neat stack beside him, tsking.

"Such a shame, they drove me out of my home all for nothing. You could have told them there was no use, after all."

"I said I wouldn't tell anyone." Sitting down on the bed, she faced him, "They did find a body, but I don't know if it was your handiwork."

His eyebrows lifted expressing his intrigue, "Do tell."

"That man that was at your home the same time I was, he was found. But you wouldn't want to leave evidence behind that could lead anyone to you, right?"

"I remember him. Yes, he ran as soon as you did, I found him later, already dead."

She wasn't expecting an answer, to have been given one was a shock, Avie pleasantly surprised by it. It however raised the question on what happened to Garret that night.

Still, a smile peeked through, "I knew it. I knew you wouldn't make a mistake."

He gripped the sides of the chair, talons slightly ripping the material, "So casual once again, do you honestly believe a friendship will blossom if you are just nice?"

She swung her legs to sit cross style to face him better, breaking eye contact to nervously tuck a lock of hair behind her ear. Damn it. That *was* kind of the plan here…

"What really brought you here? It wasn't just to give me a hard time was it?"

He chuckled darkly, "You say as if you were expecting my praise instead?"

"Don't get me wrong, I am happy you came back. I wanted to see you again."

Those talons finally punctured fabric, the feathered creature standing in agitation.

"Are you ignorant or just plain *stupid*, human? What is it that you do not understand about I kill your fellow beings for a food source? You could be next; your friends could be next. Why do you not try to stop me? Why do you even try to be nice and civil and kind and—and—"

"Because I think that you deserve some," she interrupted, causing him to pause on an intake of breath and simply look at her.

"You could've taken me out at any point. You could have tortured me to get the information you wanted; you could have hurt those who were close to me just for fun, but you didn't. How else can I respond but with some kindness?" She stood to meet him, standing before him, the closest she had been voluntarily, "I meant what I said; that I would like to be friends. I would like to know more about you… I think about you constantly, you're unlike anything I have ever seen. But I understand that I am just a nobody to you. You're not the bad guy here, at least, I don't think you are."

A hand came up between them, signaling for her to pause as the feathered being stepped back, looking away and amidst his thoughts.

He continued to step back, "I do not get it. I just. Do not. Understand." Suddenly, his head perked up to meet her eyes. He flew back up to her, grasping her arms, "Humans fear me, they hate me, no one makes it out alive when they meet me. You know your fate. So, fear me! Hate me!"

He slightly shook her, as if that would make her think like all the other humans he met.

"I can't! I can't, I'm sorry… Sometimes I think I'm nothing but afraid, but then my curiosity takes over and I want to know why you're here, what I should call you, where did you come from? I want to try to know, at least try to understand who you are." Avie placed her hands over top of his forearms in their hold, a bold move.

She continued, "Why did you come back, then? If you don't want anything to do with me, why come back and bother talking with me? Why even entertain that? Why? Please, tell me why!"

Her words were getting somewhere with him. She saw him take them in, think them over, question his own motives. Maybe he really was lonely to try to continue any communications with a human.

The being spoke through gritted teeth, "… Because you make me curious too."

It was a breakthrough; an incredible moment Avie didn't think she would get to see—an admission to something. This odd back and forth that they had which made no sense to her, finally broke through the fog, just the smallest amount, in order to understand the existence before her.

A knock on the door startled them both, turning towards the sound. He let her go, holding his own fists tightly. She looked back at his form, eyeing him intensely, a mix of desperate zeal and disappointment in the interruption reflecting back at her. The redhead couldn't imagine how he interpreted the look.

"I don't want to answer it, I don't want you to leave yet."

The pounding continued.

"Avie! Open the door!" Owen's muffled voice came through the wood.

"... I cannot stay."

She spoke in a rushed whisper, "Will you come back? Will you come back again?"

He looked at her, his gaze narrowed. Avie wondered how she sounded to him, asking him to come back, practically pleading to see him another time.

"I have a lot to think about first." In the brush of his wings, the giant was gone into the night again.

The harsh wracks against the door continued, causing her to curse, stomping over to throw open the wood on its hinges.

"Thank god, I was about to start kicking. I think I found something—a photo from a while back, it's hard to make out but hear me out on this one."

Owen made his way into the flat, pulling out the picture to show off with pride.

CHAPTER 8

He could see her residence from the tree line.

Perched in a tree, snow fell from a higher up branch, landing on his shoulders as he surveyed into the town. He groaned, disturbed at the sudden cold before shaking off the offending flakes with a roll of his wing. Her lights were off, but a soft glow still came from the abode, much the same as the last time he had been there.

Under the guise of night, he moved, swooping down and travelling the short distance to the window by her fire escape. His talons curled under the pane, surprised when yet again it slid easily up and open for him. This human *must* be daft.

A few days passed since their last contact, he stood the same as he did before, however, she was not there. He almost felt... disappointed?

No that couldn't be, perhaps it was more akin to him wasting his time when she couldn't even be in to greet him. He paced back and forth, pondering if he should even bother to come back at a later time, the aftermath of their last meeting floating to the surface.

He entered his home, the scent of damp wood and pine once again welcoming him back as he walked through the threshold. Talons at his side clasped and released while pacing the living room over the interaction with the human.

This person wanted to see him again. She thought he was good despite what he did to her race. Gave kindness when he hadn't even tried to reciprocate. But the few times he's met with her, he did want to go back.

There was something strange in what she said, about vibrations in her body.
He wouldn't mind learning a little about that, it may help him with his meals in
the future, right? He guessed that could be worth seeing the female again.

He looked over at the coat she had left in the woods, now resting on a covered
armchair. Walking over to hold it, he thumbed over the fabric, inspecting it in the
darkness. He remembered the internal struggle of picking the thing up to begin
with, intending to toy with that human once again; never imagining the conver-
sation to steer in such a way.

"Friends. What a thing to want with someone like me."

An odd jingling and clicking noise caught his attention, drawing him to
watch the door. The young woman entered, flicking on the lights and shutting the wood behind her.

Her face lit up with excitement upon spotting him in the small space,
rather than in the past where dread and apprehension expressed on her features. She turned off the bright lighting once again, leaving them bathed in
a soft washed out blue glow. "You came back!"

He didn't respond, focusing too heavily on rationalizing the human's
behavior. Amber eyes watched as she moved, drawing the curtains closed
before turning on lights strung along the wall, giving the room more lighting, yet still dim.

"I made sure to set up a few things if I got to see you again. The curtains are black out, no one can see in. I didn't know if you didn't like harsh
lighting, so I got dim wattages for these."

He hummed in retort, seeing her place in more detail. A small space
compared to his, with yellow flowers separated by blue borders vertically
lining the walls and a few paintings detailing abstract humans interacting
with various items and each other. Far less furniture occupied here compared to the ones littering his abode. For the better part of a few minutes,
he wandered around the enclosed room, touching items, running his hands
over the spines of books on their case, picking them up, scrutinising. His
back was turned when he finally broke the silence.

"Tell me more about your body vibrations."

Turning, his eyes were drawn to the movement of her toying with a ring on her finger, "Well, it was what brought me into town in the first place. It stops when people get here, mine did too for a while. Then the feeling came back, and it's getting worse every time. It feels powerful, like it clenches around my bones and I have no idea what's causing it. I seem to be the only one that still has it."

"Other people experienced this too?"

"Yes, apparently a good number of people travelled into the town because of that odd feeling in their body. It was a guiding map and stopped when they were led here. Most thought it was a form of intervention or an anomaly of the town, so they stayed here. No one else I know of ever had it come back, except maybe if they left Blacken. Which is why I'm so confused as to why it keeps happening to me."

Nodding, taking the information in, his feathered self placed the book down and situated on her couch. She sat across him in a dining chair, gauging his reaction.

"And you think I have something to do with it."

"I'm not sure how," she laughed nervously, "but I think, in some way, yes."

"Is that why you are trying to get close to me? For answers?"

The female shook her head slowly, "I would like to know about you, but not just in that way. Like, like… What's your favourite colour?"

He felt his face scrunch at the absurd question, "Favourite colour?"

"Oh my gosh, I'm so sorry, do you only see in black and white?" The expression blanched.

He chuckled, "Typical human! So ignorant!" His laughter continued as he waved a dismissive hand, "No, I see an array of colours and shades, possibly more than you humans do, but I have no basis for that."

"Then which one do you like seeing the most?" Perking up, the human looked excited for the answer. Her energy was full of expectation and childish glee—a different experience for sure.

"Why would I need to answer this?"

"It's so we can learn more about each other, it's fun!"

"This is for children; we were just discussing matters more serious."

The female bit at her bottom lip, a question on her face, yet a debate expressed over saying it or not.

"You don't like having fun? It's okay if you don't have a favourite."

He stumbled, "I, um…" *The nerve of this human…* He had to prove that he did now. "The deep licks of ocherous fire, the faded gamboge spark of the sun setting on the horizon and burning crescendo in early mornings. That is my favourite"

Her face changed. Instead of the eager smile, eyes softened while her mouth parted slightly, she looked surprised—entranced.

"That's beautiful. You really do see more than we could." He smirked, feeling his ego swell. "Could I ask… something more personal?"

The smile dropped, instead he leaned forward with his hands clasped together, eyes bearing into hers. He knew these heavier ones would eventually come up, though there were never any conversations lasting longer that the usual questions:

"Who are you? What's going on? Why is this happening?"

It never went very far with those humans.

"It depends, you can ask, but I may not answer."

She nodded, the apprehension practically dripped off her in the low lighting, "Are you from another planet?"

Tension held in the air after the words left her red lips. She waited patiently as he studied her, running her question around in his mind, debating whether to lie or simply tell the truth. He leaned back, breaking away eye contact for a moment before returning. Settling on the latter, he breathed a low whisper,

"I am."

The female let out her breath, inhaling and exhaling in the thrilling moment. Goosebumps pricked her skin, evident even in their distance. The air became electric between them as they sat, awash in the revelation.

"I knew it. Oh, Owen would be so jealous if he only knew I was talking to an alien."

His face twisted, "That man has been a thorn in my side for years. I do not know how you can stand such an annoyance."

"But he's really very sweet. He's a lot of fun to be around and always has some interesting knowledge—"

"That is enough," his voice cut through her so low and quietly.

She stuttered to a close, vision resting back to him, "Right, we're not talking about him, this is about us." He nodded in agreeance. "And there was really nothing you knew about the vibrating?"

"It is just as much a mystery to me; I have not heard of this situation until you."

It was the truth, after all. How was he to become interested in a human if they were to become a meal shortly after?

This human asked a fair bit of questions, his response to only about half. Yet she answered every single one he asked—about the strange sensation she had, to when she felt it and what it was like. They conversed about why he didn't go out to kill unless absolutely necessary, remarking how some humans tasted wrong and he would be hungry again shortly after if that was the case.

"Can you have livestock instead of humans?"

"No, I cannot. If I am unable to feed properly on certain humans, I certainly can not survive on less intelligent heaps of meat." She nodded thoughtfully, taking all the information in. "And this does not disgust you in any way?"

The female laughed lightly, "In some weird way, it's all actually very interesting learning about you. Maybe because it's a secret. Maybe because you're something more than a human being. I'm not quite sure."

"You find me interesting?"

It was a sentiment he never would have thought to hear. All he ever came to know was fear from these humans. The sudden change from one in particular had struck a chord with him, made him feel different. At first it made him angry, his ego getting in the way and refusing to acknowledge a change in perspective. Humans were food sources, not something to connect to. Then the anger dissolved into confusion—attempting to process a human's innermost workings and hidden plans, what they meant after every little remark.

She leaned forward, an intense look read on her face that made his mouth part open for a heavy breath to escape, "I am deeply fascinated with you."

The resolve broke, the look in her eyes showcasing no hidden motives, a look that reminded him of someone from his past, yet he couldn't place. This human truly did find him fascinating instead of one to fear now. She truly did want to know about him.

He stood abruptly, walking over to where she sat, he may regret this in the long run, yet he extended his hand anyway, "Come with me. I would like to show you something."

Tilting her head in uncertainty, the hand was taken regardless. He noticed a tint in her cheeks at what was his kindest gesture to her, leading her to the window where the fire escape sat outside.

"Follow me, I will wait for you at the tree line."

Disengaging their hands, he leapt, moving with swiftness to keep out of sights. Landing on a branch in mere seconds, he turned back, locating the small human. She had been much further away than he anticipated, not as fast as he was, still he waited for her.

Finally, she reached the line of spruce trees, looking around for his figure. He watched her below him, searching around in circles. With a leap, he landed behind her, startling her enough to jump and spin around.

"This way."

He led the way through the maze of branches and roots, hearing her pant from attempting to keep up with his stride, wandering the forest until they came across the manor once more.

She took in the clearing, "This is?"

"My home, so to speak. This is where I have been living, I figure you may want a proper look at it. If there were anything here for you to discover, I can allow you free reign. It actually has a lot of charm."

An astonished look met him, "You're going to show me your home? This house?" She gestured to the building.

"What, did you think I slept in a tree? You do not have to if you want," he chuckled, opening up more with the human. Or Avie, as she was regarded? It was what that annoyance called her…

"No! No, I do, I would love to. Thank you." She eagerly jogged the short distance to catch up.

As they arrived at the entrance, he opened the door for her, allowing her entry first. Avie walked in, taking in the same space he presided, taking in the sight of the first floor.

"I've been in here before, that night. I thought I was being led to this building." Her hand traced over the graffiti on the wall beside, "Do you get very many unwelcome visitors?"

"Not for a while, have you seen upstairs at all?"

She eyed the staircase warily, "Are the stairs safe?"

"Strong as bricks." He stepped to the side, gesturing for her to try them out.

Upstairs, he showed her his sleeping arrangements; various soft materials gathered in a makeshift bed. Many stacks of books littered the room, a large window allowed the moonlight in and draped across a small elegant loveseat—a wood burning furnace sat cold in the corner.

Picking up a title, jade attention skimmed over a few pages, "Can you read in this lighting?"

"I often use the fireplace in the living room, it makes it much easier."

Avie smiled, closing the book, "You've done a lot of reading."

"It is the only thing I can do to pass the time."

The human looked back to him, realizing his lack of hobbies. Searching the room again with her eyes low, she seemingly counted the hardcovers occupying this space alone. She huffed, a visible debate happening across her face as her expressions changed.

"These are probably how you know so much about us."

Handing the hard cover back to him, he took it from her fingers, his talons brushing against their softness, "And why I am so confused as to why your actions differ so much from these humans. No alien nor monster usually fare very well in the end."

"I don't think any of them had the chance to meet one."

Her eyes were shining again, he could see even in the moonlight. That expression had always made him feel... self-conscious. He cleared his throat, shaking off the thought, turning to place the book in one of the many piles.

"It's not fair, really. Most of us even have a tendency to treat others who don't look or act a certain way the same."

He turned back to her, "How do you mean? Everyone looks different."

She expressed her sympathies about certain human beings treated as though they weren't just that; human beings. People who were perceived as unworthy by society all from something they couldn't help but be born with in some cases, drastically altering the way they live their lives.

While he had heard of such things, it still didn't make sense how people looking different could be mistreated by their peers. That's not how things worked way back home...

"Well, I have a few books that may help put it into perspective, if you were interested?"

He raised an eyebrow, "I suppose I do not have anything better to do."

She looked around the space awkwardly, "Well, I, um... I really like your place. It's beautiful in here, but it could use a clean-up if I'm honest."

As if for emphasis, a few of her slender fingers brushed against the white fabric haphazardly covering the chaise longue sofa in the room, drawing lines in the dust there.

"Would it not be suspicious if anyone came across a clean discarded manor?"

Avie wiped the dust on her pants as she grinned, "I thought you said it's been awhile since you've had any 'guests'?"

Damn. She was right.

"*Touché*. I should keep it proper, at least."

"I could help with that," she said, laughing.

The pair returned to the apartment shortly after the tour, unable to find anything of interest for her odd sensation much to her evident disappointment. Arriving back at her home, she searched around the flat for two books she had mentioned previously. Finding one was easy, finding the second proving to be a game of hide and seek.

"I hope you like these, they're classic literature."

"It is new material; I am sure I will enjoy the change."

She appeared sad at his statement, "There can be more that you can do now, if you're bored of just reading?"

"I enjoy it, but it is tiresome. What did you have in mind?"

"Have you ever painted? I have supplies you could use. Maybe I can bring them when we spruce up the place?"

The idea mulled over in his mind, "I could give it a try. After all, I see in other shades, maybe they will translate well to canvas."

A laugh was hidden behind her hand, "You're probably a regular Da Vinci."

He gripped the books tighter, "Right, the painter. He was merely a human; cake walk in comparison to my spectrum," he chortled, joining in on her laughter.

"Let me know what you think when you've finished, or if I can help clarify anything." His feathers shimmered as he nodded, turning to exit through the bedroom window, "Wait! Wait, before you go... I just wanted to say thanks, you know, for making the effort."

He turned his crown to observe the sudden statement. While it was true, he wasn't expecting to have such fluidity with chatter. This human made it *easy*. While finding him interesting, the more she brought up, the more he found her similar in return. It wasn't just about the mysterious drumming, there was something more that made him seek her out.

"You are welcome."

The mass of feathers cocooning wings pushed him into the night's sky, kissing the stars as he set out to his home in the woods.

That night, he took up one of the books Avie gifted him. Engrossed in a new story, he followed a character trapped and raised inside a grand church, kept secret for the way he looked. Even other humans were treated poorly due to living as an 'incorrect' race in the eyes of the antagonist. The main character arc propelled the lead to save the woman he unrequitedly loved and die because of the silly sentiment. His feathered self liked it in terms of believability, and it felt like he did understand the point Avie made earlier... sort of.

It at least outlined the differences someone could face, fiction or not.

He sighed, seeing the sun peeking from the horizon as he sat the paperback on a nearby pile. Laying back and stretching out, he considered getting some sleep, the lingering fingers of fatigue tracing over his eyelids.

Turning to face away from the window, the other title filled his vision. *Then again...*

He picked it up, holding it over his face as he read the introductory.

───⁕───

She was cooking, seeing through the same infamous window of her bedroom to the other side of the apartment where she stood.

Lifting the glass, he helped himself inside, gripping the book he brought with him.

"I do not understand this one. I mean I do; I understand it in the literal sense. What I do not understand is the reasoning? I spent dawn reading through it, all day even, and then once I finished... I had to read it again. It is powerful, it is energetic, it is mysterious. Why would the female not return his feelings? How dare it end in this way!"

He paced back and forth in the combined kitchen and living room, rambling off the thoughts, seeing that he startled the human with his sudden appearance and monologue.

"Because she did not love him, she pitied him," the small female said, quieting the flame on the burner.

He stopped, softly outraged, "Love? But she loved that one not seen since childhood? *And* she chose him? He hardly acted better!"

"It's how her heart worked... She never let go of that love she had. I think she really did care for Erik, and was grateful for him! But she was still scared of him because he wanted to control her."

"But he... Erik had nothing before her," he said, lifting the book.

"I know, I find his life unfair too... No matter his actions, I think he still deserved love." Her eyes lit up with a thought, "There's a movie too, they add on more to the story if you were interested."

"I want to watch it. But not here, I am… *uncomfortable* being in the human area for very long."

Avie smiled gently, "I think I have something that will work."

The movie captured the same feeling he had when reading the same title—his feathered self really getting into the flick, into the characters, into the 'villain' portrayed. He feels a sense of relation to the main character; they were both just trying to live, albeit in seclusion, finding solace away from humans and perfecting their passions, turned away for being different.

Avie set up a small box attached to a screen and a movie player, allowing them to watch in the comfort of the manor. It was a very kind gesture, a lot of work coming from the human granting him the ability to watch a *movie*; something he never thought possible.

"It… It is not fair, it is even more unfair," he spoke as the credits rolled over.

"I think they should have been together too."

He turned to look at her, seeing her vision still holding the screen, "I know it sounds weird of me to say; but I think she did love him, their connection was more real, and I think it made sense for them to be together in the end. The Comte loved her after he saw that she was beautiful and talented, he didn't even remember her. Erik fell in love through getting to know her." She turned on her last sentence, shrugging and making eye contact—the impact of words heavier as he processed the new viewpoint.

They paused, a contemplative silence filling the air between them. He thought over his words, wanting to know more about her thoughts and perspectives, but still struggling with the new experience.

He sighed through his nose, "What would be your favourite colour?"

The change of subject had her questioning before gleaming, a small smile tickled her lips and a quiet laugh poked through, "I haven't thought too much about it, I think it's pink, just like the dianthus nearby."

He turned further towards her, "Any your favourite novel?"

"The Princess in Unknown. A story outside the realms of this world, she escapes her life as a princess and starts a life of adventure with dangerous time trials on high seas and a vizier who would stop at nothing to track her down."

"That does sound exciting. I would like to read that as well."

She nodded, "Anytime. Which one is your favorite?"

Looking away and grabbing something on the end table where they sat, he returned the possession to her line of vision. It was the copy that she had given him. Avie smiled with glee.

"If you like it that much, then please keep it!"

Taken a bit aback by that, he faltered, "But I- I mean I could not... I do not have anything to give to you."

"I don't want anything back, I'm happy that you like it. I want you to be able to read it whenever you'd like."

"... Thank you."

They discussed more about the movie they had watched, he was quite enamored with how they changed details and plot, but it very well was among the same story in the book.

"And the uh—" He mimed a stiff imitation of a movement from the film.

"Ballroom dancing?"

"Yes, dancing, of course. The dancing you humans do as man and woman, what does that do in terms of enjoyment?"

"It's like an expression of art, just like a song, as well as a connection or an experience any two people can enjoy. Do you have that where you're from?"

He scratched the back of his head, embarrassed, "It looks a little different, but indeed we do, and it means relatively the same."

"Would you like to learn something new?"

"*Human dancing*? What would I even need to do with that knowledge?"

"It's something fun to do, and I think you would be very good at it."

That stroked his ego, his expression cool as he thought it over, "... We would need music."

She practically jumped at the agreement, shouting a quick "*I'll be right back!*" before leaving the manor, returning a matter of minutes later with a boombox. Avie set up the portable machine, getting a few songs ready to play.

"It's not ballroom music, but it's the closest I have."

Soothing music began to play as she grabbed both of his hands, the instruments picking up a light tempo while beautiful strings coerced with woodwinds, emotion behind every note. She showed the steps, explaining that the gentlemen lead, and the ladies follow, both stepping in tempo a certain way.

"One-two-three-four, see? You're a natural!"

He picked it up fast, no longer watching their feet and confident enough to look at his dancing partner without the feeling of uncertainty in his steps. Yet it didn't seem the same way it had when watching it on screen.

"If you are to teach me, at least do it correctly, we are supposed to be like this," with the drop of one arm, it swung back to hold onto her lower waist, bringing her in much closer to him. He twisted his other to hold her arm up more, copying the look portrayed in the movie.

"Yes… I suppose you're right."

She looked at him in that way again, with large eyes he couldn't read, seeing them in all their might in the moment—in a way it felt like they never really left, just dimmed in every other instance.

With a raise of her hand, it was placed upon the top of his arm, him being much too tall to keep it hiked up upon his shoulder, the soft plumage caused her fingers to sink in slightly at the touch. He didn't dare break eye contact, nor did she as they swung around the wooden floors, becoming bolder in actions, spinning her around, mimicking things he had seen.

Avie laughed, a string of giggles leaving the redhead as she was having fun with his feathered self. It was something he never dared dream would happen from their first meeting, even their second! Her laughter becoming infectious, he let out his own chuckle as the songs played on, allowing them to have this moment of bonding. In a way, he felt like he needed it. He's been alone for far too long….

The music swelled to a close, and he dipped her gently for the finale. She was smiling, those large green jades darting between both of his. His own gaze was strong as it fixed on hers, thinking over his next action. He brought her back up, only the crackling in the stove adjacent them could be heard. They hadn't broken away.

"Rhulle."

Her eyebrows crinkled together upon hearing the unfamiliar word, "I'm sorry... what was that?"

"My name. It is Rhulle. You may have it."

Even in the dim glow, Rhulle noticed a discolouration happen on her face while her features softened, that expression returning with the same glittering wonder.

She decided to test it out, "Rhulle..." The female smiled, "Thank you for a wonderful gift."

CHAPTER 9

The chips crunched loudly, causing Avie to turn up the volume on her television just to hear what the narrative was explaining as she lounged in bed. A particularly large chip splintered while biting into it, causing crumbs and fragments to fall onto the sheets below her.

She sighed in exaggerated annoyance. It was her own fault for eating in bed; a bad habit she could never break out of. It was probably for the best if she put the bag of potato crisps away and out of her sight.

On her way back into the bedroom, her eyes caught on the corner of a glossy photo recklessly tucked between the mattress and box spring. Momentarily having the conversation slip her mind, she pulled the square loose from its bindings—studying the blurred, grainy, black and white photo of a dark figure with extended wings.

"Thank god, I was about to start kicking. I think I found something—a photo from a while back, it's hard to make out but hear me out on this one." Owen made his way into the flat, pulling out the picture to show off with pride.

Avie took the image from him, seeing it depicted a view of the forest but also something much more prominent in the foreground. A pang of worry filled her.

It looked like him... It looked an awful lot like the feathered being she got to make acquaintance with; however, she had such prior knowledge and Owen did not. It may be able to pass as a hoax photograph. Knowing the blond, he wouldn't accept that explanation—insisting that they roll with the extraterrestrial idea; the only traction in the investigation they pursued.

"What exactly am I looking at?" She flipped the photo over, hoping for something to be written on the back.

The librarian smiled confidently, "It may be the connecting factor for us."

"You're saying this is a picture of one of the **aliens**? It looks like a misshapen Christmas tree…"

He rolled his eyes, "I know the quality is not that great, it's from a police report from the Fifties. I'm just saying it's something we could be looking out for."

Avie felt her tongue involuntarily press against her cheek, she was trying to think of a way to steer the photo in question as anything other than the creature she had been trying to know. It may have translated as an unconvinced look, Owen continuing,

"Aves, I know it's not much, but really, what else do we have to go on? None of the actual science we have come up with or tried has stuck. It's all fallen flat. This is an actual **photograph** someone took; I want to keep following this rabbit hole."

She was torn.

On one hand, she wanted to find answers, she had to when it affected her so much. Their Dewey Decimal team were the only ones working on questions no one else was interested in. But on the other hand, she needed to keep a secret.

If she fought back too much with this, it certainly would be suspicious…

"So, if it was photographed looking like this, there's probably a fair chance that it knew that it was. If there were no other images like this, it may have changed form. Like, what if it could shapeshift? What if it could turn into what suited it in the moment? Here, it needed to fly so it made wings… If it needed to hide, it could disguise itself as any one of us?"

"Damn Aves, and you say my theories are crackpot," he said, laughing. "I'm just speculating! Wouldn't there have been more sightings or reports than just this one if that was its only form? Bigfoot has tons of sightings as the same figure."

"But you want to explore this winged man alien—winged man shapeshifter with me?"

She sighed in a small relief, "It's like you said, it's the only thing to run off. Let's look for other buried cases due to peculiar claims. Maybe we can find a logical progression of what forms it likes to take."

Owen was over the moon, lifting her up and twirling her around in a tight hug, "Hell yes! Avie, you are such a creative mastermind! I never would have got this far without you."

It wasn't as if she outright lied to Owen, but she did withhold information to get him away from the topic. The woman felt terrible for keeping such a secret from him, but Rhulle only started to open up to her. Avie couldn't imagine he would be very keen on having another human thrown into the mix so soon—let alone how Owen would even react.

She hid the photo once again, taking care to make sure no corners jutted out this time. The blond would know eventually, the situation couldn't be kept secret forever, especially if she could find more answers from Rhulle and how he was tied in.

Cleaning up the mess she left in bed, Avie crawled back into the covers, switching off the T.V to focus on her book for the time being. It was getting late, the red numbers on her alarm clock reading out a fairly high number. She didn't care, the numbers marched up as the book kept her under its spell.

Awaking a few hours later, she came-to still clutching her book, venturing into consciousness as the dreaded sensation of harsh drumming palpitated throughout her body. It sang severely, making her teeth clench as well as her fists while the force hit. The woman couldn't think clearly in the state of mind, but a muddled thought raced through her brain; maybe if Rhulle sees it, if he sees what it was like when the attacks came on, then maybe a connection could be drawn, and he may know something more—something that could help stop the assault.

Once more she ventured in her state, pain ringing throughout her body and centralizing in her head. Holding her cranium to stabilize herself, she traversed the streets in a stumble, clinging onto the bark of a birch once she reached the tree line. She did this once before, she could do it again.

Damp snow fell off the trees above her, landing in her hair and down the back of her coral coat. It caused her to squeak, as if she didn't need more discomfort. Finally, after taking multiple breaks to gather herself, Avie held her sight on the manor in the woods, a small relief, all things considered, washing through her.

The woman tripped over her own feet, them refusing to cooperate while she explored the rooms she had been shown, calling out for the feathered cryptid, unable to find him—becoming more and more frustrated as every room she cleared, he was nowhere to be found. Her body reacted to something that was here, Rhulle would see that and help find the source of the mysterious power. He knew this place better than anyone, he's sure to have seen something that could explain the sensation now that it reverberated in its strongest form.

The clenched fists left small crescents from her nails into the skin, they shook uncontrollably as Avie opened them back up to inspect. Hands were turning pink from the frigid temperature, the frosty snow unforgiving to her exposed skin while she walked back outside.

If he wasn't in the manor, was he in the shed seen beforehand?

With all her might, she commanded her body to walk there in great strain.

"Rhulle! The vibrations, they're back... Where are—?"

The woman turned the corner of the building and was cut short by the air in her own lungs. Her eyes fixated on Rhulle, hunched over not far off from when she first saw him. His scarlet eyes were back, matching the blood dripping from his sharp teeth and down his face and body. Said teeth were just previously ripping open an older woman's neck; her laying on the cold ground under him, eyes lifeless.

Avie focused back on Rhulle, seeing him simply wiping away the copious blood around his mouth with the inside of his forearm, looking at her like a child with his hand in the cookie jar.

Fight or flight didn't kick in this time around. Instead, she backed away in shock, her mind wanted to look back at the person on the ground, confirm it was real. She fought against the instinct, it made her light and fuzzy, eyes blurring as she kept her stare with Rhulle.

Was he saying something? She couldn't tell, stumbling back in a daze. It wasn't processing properly, her thoughts in a limbo while they jumbled over each other, auto pilot taking over.

The pain eventually stopped.

Her mind came back to reality, realizing she now sat in the living room on a covered couch, staring ahead at the grand fireplace. Avie didn't know how to react, she knew this was what he did, but seeing the act was something else entirely—solidifying the experience as something real. Real death.

With her racing thoughts starting to subside, the shock tapered off, leaving her shaking cold. She wondered how long she had been sitting there, when Rhulle had entered, a timidity about him.

He took in her appearance, gazing over her form up and down, cautiously moving across her to begin a roaring fire, striking flint rocks together in the pit. In the new light, she could see that he was no longer covered in blood, his chestnut plumage as pristine as she's always seen it. The redhead didn't want to know what happened in the interim—but it did help set her mind at ease seeing the norm.

Avie watched him sit across her in a plush chair by the fireplace, assessing her.

"I didn't think I'd ever see you do it. I'm not really sure why, it was rational in my mind that I just wouldn't."

"It feels more real now, does it not?"

The woman nodded, "I know it's so normal for you. I really only saw someone... I mean someone that was..." Avie still couldn't say the words. She tried again, "I came here again because of the vibrating that messes with me. It came back and I thought that if you could see it or knew what I was talking about firsthand I... I don't know what I thought. It made sense at the time."

She watched him look away, "I am sorry you had to see it in this way. Do you view me differently now? Will you no longer want to see me?" he asked, voice low.

"No, Rhulle, I still want to see you, that hasn't changed. It's just that, I have to process this; I wasn't sure exactly how it was that you... Uhhmm..."

"Fed?"

She confirmed, face pale, "Yeah, how you fed on humans." Exhaling, she let her head hang. A silence filled in the conversation, her hearing the whisper of his feathers as he readjusted.

"Tell me about your feeling, when did it start? When did it end?"

Hiking her head back up, a different topic to discuss was a welcome one, "I was sleeping when it started, I'm not sure how long it was going for or when it really stopped. I feel like I keep missing the answer, like it's here somewhere but I always stop short of it."

Rhulle held sympathy on his features while she explained the sensation, how the world stopped while she was amidst the throes of pain caused by this unknown force. It got to the point where she was worried about going mad from the distress.

He changed the subject, steering the conversation to talk about her favourite book; asking her to explain the characters, what her favourite part was, how she came to discover the novel in the first place. It was a much lighter conversation, Avie pleased to participate in this discussion more than the previous heavier ones. If he was trying to distract her, Rhulle did a great job.

"I want to help figure what is affecting you. This affliction causes you so much pain. My friend should not be in pain like that."

Jade eyes lifted, searching out his. She paused, gauging his facial features, feeling warm by his words. "You really mean that? We can be friends?" she asked, voice hardly over a whisper.

"Yes, Avie. I have been thinking it all over, and I found consistently that I would consider you a friend. So long as *this*... will not affect too negatively, I hope." A gentle hand placed itself over hers, solidifying the endearment.

Avie felt light at the words, it was exciting to hear a reciprocation of comradery from Rhulle. She could see the shift in him as soon as it happened—the initial harsh rejection due to pride, sliding into the realization of loneliness. It was incredible to earn his friendship; it was all she could think about. Wanting to get to know him and learn more, she wasn't concerned with finding answers to only help her, it was always deeper than that. The woman was drawn to him, sharing a passion of reading and similar viewpoints in stories and characters. Rhulle was the impossible orphic being that only she knew of.

The redhead's face broke out in a giant grin, overjoyed at his words.

"I would love to be friends," she said, nodding passionately back, "you would really help figure this out too? I can't thank you enough! Could I—can I hug you?"

He raised a curious eyebrow at her, possibly expressing the how or why written on his face, instead Avie took the initiative to stand and step over the short distance to be in front of him. She smiled briefly down at him, collecting his hands in hers to get him to rise as well—embracing him in a split second. Feeling the umber feathers against her face as they caressed her skin, they were cool and slightly damp, but they were so soft, as soft as she imagined as she sighed and closed her eyes.

This human… she kept surprising him. It was as if she did not think half of the time. Avie had just bore witness to one of his feedings, and yet here she was smiling and holding him only moments later. She didn't regard him as something out of this world, instead as a friend and wanted his kinship—ecstatic when he returned the gesture.

Yes, he would help find out what strange condition had its grasp on Avie, his new friend, his only friend. Rhulle felt her nuzzle slightly in the plumage as he was encompassed in her sign of affection. How long had it been since he was held?

How bloody long had it been since he had *any* warmth like this human offered?

Rhulle wrapped his long arms around her torso, completing the hug, a small smile tugging on his lips.

CHAPTER 10

Blacken's police department sent out an official statement October 8th about the death of Garret Kipper.

Due to overwhelming evidence left on the body and lack of any outside motive, the coroner and deputies ruled his death a suicide—much to his widow's dismay. Mrs. Kipper fought against the statement, begging everyone involved to go over everything once again. She would have seen the signs if suicide was the case, insisting it was not. Imploring them to check again but was met with recommendations for counselling for her tragedy of sudden loss, many people meeting her queries with claims that it's never the ones they expect.

Avie wondered what could have happened that night that made him take his own life, talking over the scenario with Owen. She went over everything with him, tucked into the corner of his sofa. Everything that happened that night when she saw him, running over every detail once again, trying to express the lingering guilt she harboured.

"I'm sorry I didn't believe you, Aves. But don't beat yourself up over this. It was a suicide, we may never know why or what happened, but it wasn't like you killed the guy."

"Please, Owen… His name was Garret. If he was out there to do that… I wish I could have done more, called the police or something as soon as I got here, would that have even been enough time?"

Conflicting emotions ran through her as soon as the topic was brought up, any of the missing people, any of the deceased; that's when the reality struck her. The weight of a human life occupied her mind, having wanted to do so much more to stop what was occurring out in the woods.

Yet, that shouldn't mean that the creature, whose only crime was eating to survive, should be killed. Avie knew there had to be an alternative—something to keep people alive and have Rhulle sustaining.

"You were in shock Avie, as most people would be. It's terrible what happened to Garret, but he had his own reasoning to do what he did. If it didn't happen then, it may have another time. He was sick, Aves."

"I know, I just... I wondered, what if he was out there trying to follow the call too? And I—shit, I did nothing while he probably laid there in the dirt."

Rhulle wasn't the one to kill him, she had to remember that. But he did have to seek someone else out in order to feed, a victim that could have been anyone unsuspecting, anyone who potentially did not even go into those woods that night. She didn't even know who that woman was the last time she traversed out there.

Had she been overlooking the importance because of special treatment?

Owen hugged her, "You don't know that for sure, it was probably only coincidence that you even saw him out there. Would it help if you talked about it to a professional? There's a group therapy session that the town is putting together."

Avie closed her eyes, sighing at the gentle strokes on her back, "Maybe I can check something out, it may help put the pieces together. I don't know about group therapy though."

"Of course, I'm still here if you need to talk it out. What are friends for?"

Friends...

Her eyes opened. She thought of Rhulle and the friendship they started. He was alone, for who knew how long, feeding on people only when necessary, never going out of his way to harm someone. If he did, the woman wouldn't be here today.

No, she still did not view him as inherently wrong in his actions. He even admitted to trying alternatives to humans, unfortunately, farm and wild animals couldn't be tolerated. Rhulle drew every inch of her captivation, she only needed to think of him, and the disposition fell away. If she could know more about him, it was a long shot, but perhaps there really was a way to keep everyone alive.

"Thank you. That means the world."

He broke away slightly, "Do you need a distraction? Or do you need to keep venting?"

"Distraction, definitely."

Owen's eyes lit up under the mop of blond bangs, "Want to get your blood tested?"

"... *Excuse me, what?*" She blinked, taken aback at the question.

"They didn't take your blood at the hospital, right? Maybe it's not your body as a whole reacting, maybe it's something in your blood that can help lead us in the right direction."

Holy. Shit.

"Yeah, I mean—hell yeah! Let's check it out," she said, enthralled in the new topic.

Owen grabbed a small box of supplies, sitting back down beside her—pulling out tuning forks, magnets, hertz meter, a small radio, and a blood type kit.

"Wow," she snorted, "you pulled out all the stops for this."

"It hit me like a ton of bricks the other night, we needed to find the effect too, eh?"

Sanitizing her index first, with a prick of her finger, they started the home blood type kit, smearing the samples onto the card, then pooling extra droplets onto a petri dish. Over the course of an hour, Owen tested different frequencies, pitches, magnets and radio waves with her blood, seeing if anything would react dramatically, with no success.

"Another dead end," Avie sounded a little defeated.

"Well, not quite. There is something off about your blood, it's not matching with any of the blood types."

She spun her head, "What do you mean," taking the card from him, she examined the results, "did we do it wrong?"

"No, it's right, the test is just inconclusive. You may have some sort of mutant blood there, Aves!"

Her interests peaked, explaining that she would book an appointment to get it properly tested. Another puzzle piece added, yet no picture in sight...

Owen pitched the idea to watch a movie, that it would be a better distraction, and they were spending a lot of time on research. Avie agreed wholeheartedly, helping herself in the kitchen to bring out wine and snacks.

⎯⎯⎯⎯⎯

Turning to look at her, Owen heard her laugh translate into the most dazzling string of melodies. Taking a sip of his wine, the blond returned his gaze to the television, watching Avie from the corner of his periphery, taking in her better mood.

Everything about her was beautiful to him, the dark freckles, the curly hair that frizzed even on a good day, the hook of her nose... She had been the only person in town to try to get to know him when he was the social outcast. Whether it was from asking too many questions or his overbearing nature, he still wasn't sure. One thing that he was sure of, was that she came to him and matched his passions, not bothered by his energy or obsession.

And now, here they were, best buddies with a mystery that tied them together.

What would she think if he said he harbored *other feelings* for her?

Owen never had much luck with dating, let alone girls in general. But the way Avie made him feel, so accepted as a person... He could only think about the 'what ifs' if she also felt something for him. He was the only person that she spent time with, and a lot of their free time was spent together.

How would he go about seeing if she felt the same pining burn as he did?

The redhead laughed again, himself joining even as he was caught in his thoughts. He dared an arm around her and was met with no resistance—a blush hinted at his cheeks that could have been passed off as the alcohol.

⁂

Elongated fingers drew indents and small scratches into the trunk's wood.

Rhulle watched from a perch, hidden in the dark and away from the streetlights. He observed the pair inside laugh and have fun, Avie giving out smiles he only seen given to him.

His feathered self attempted to seek her out at her dwelling, proudly wanting to show off improvements and cleaning done to his own, only to find her residence empty. After waiting to see if she would return after a while, he became bored and decided to look elsewhere. Seeing her take up space at the *annoyance's* home.

He travelled there, finding Avie no problem, but also finding the male human in close contact. Rhulle felt weird at seeing that. It *irked* him. Crawled under his skin akin to a parasite and itched there as he watched, growing further evident as the seconds ticked by.

Rhulle already didn't like that Owen character for poking around his home so many times in the past, but now, seeing him together with *his human?*

… His…?

He shook off the thought, she took the time and patience to be his friend, to extend a hand in alliance and new opportunities. He simply just didn't like that it came so easy to the annoying creature as well. That was all.

Flying off in a huff, he tried to forget the sight of her so close, paying attention to that *human* instead of himself.

He nearly threw a hissy fit when he got home, pacing around his room. He thought, well, he couldn't place his thoughts about the female in that situation. She worked so hard to earn his friendship, doing the impossible, he wanted them to have that bond now that she ended up intricately placing herself into his life. Yet Avie was so close to that *irritation of a human.*

It was unfair that she gave her friendship bond to another male. He should be the only one!

Rhulle knocked over a stack of books, looking at the mess of a pile he created and seeing the copy of his new favorite book right away.

"But she was still scared of him because he wanted to control her," her voice echoed in his mind.

He sobered, bending down to take the novel, catching his thoughts. It wasn't right of him to control who she could and couldn't see. If she expressed friendship with... *him*, then he would have to learn how to deal with it. But he could still not like Owen, he figured.

Avie asked so many questions in the span of a few days, getting many of them answered in return. It was exciting figuring Rhulle out, his kind, and how he all sort of... worked.

She learned that he didn't need to eat the flesh of humans, only the blood—which was interesting, if not a little stomach churning. The young woman had been able to learn much more interesting factors, such as his species were called; *Truxen* or *Truxi* pluralized. Rhulle spoke an entirely different dialect, learning English from various reading techniques and books that were for learning said language littered around the collective. Stars glimmered in her eyes when he demonstrated a simple sentence in his native tongue.

The redhead found the length of just one of his wings was one... two... two and a half times that of her own arms span! She had measured by stretching out, palms touching the long feathers, before turning in toward his body, counting how many times her arms could fit. For how he came to Earth, he was here because he wanted to be. Technology of his planet integrated with the cosmos in a way that probably made sense to him, but left her with some confusion—boiling down to a gateway of sorts and how he arrived here.

She didn't want to ramble off too many questions all at once, after all, she didn't want to make him uncomfortable or overwhelmed by her intrusive nature. Avie did ask about the similarities and differences between how the truxi and humans danced, seeing as it became a new passion of his.

Rhulle demonstrated in the cleared-up space, hands placed differently, palms together between them rather than on their dance partner. Stepping differently yet, still in a swinging and simple motion. It was fun to dance with him and hear his laugh while he spun her around and around—learning new dances that were similar along the way. He enjoyed movie nights; she had shown him so many other movies that kept his attention more than he would admit to her.

In the quietness of the late hour, he gave painting an enthusiastic try, enjoying creating little details on a canvas, a skill he seemed versed in. Avie watched him in fascination, every stroke with his brush calculating and planned, bathing in the light of the fire. Eventually he turned and caught her staring.

"No moving," he said, a light-hearted affronted tone matched his side smile.

She laughed once, returning to her original pose and holding the position for a while. In the light of the fireplace, Rhulle handed her the completed work, leaving her mouth to hang open while she studied the incredible canvas.

A portrait of herself sat in profile, the fire that crinkled in the background blazed around her in the paint; blossoming into flowers that bore striking semblance to her fiery hair. They weaved into the strands, adorning a crown of intense chrysanthemums, roses and lilies, adding to the serene expression and distinctive red lips. It felt so… alive.

"Oh my gosh… You've done this before, haven't you?"

He shrugged where he stood, "I picked up a few skills awhile back."

It was the most beautiful thing she ever received. Even her own family could never put in this much effort… Her fingertips squeezed tighter around the border involuntarily, a question burned in her mind that she had been wanting to ask but danced around because of the heavier, more personal theme.

"You have another question?" The smirk stayed as he moved to sit beside her on the ground.

"Did… did you have a family that you had to leave on *Celisc*?"

Rhulle stiffened, his smile dropping, "I have n—I have not thought about them in a long time… What brings this all of a sudden?"

Avie looked down at the painting once more, "This is so beautiful, so much thought and talent went into making it, my own parents never took the time to think about me like this. I left them as soon as I could and moved far away, even farther now since I'm in Blacken," she laughed nervously, "I guess I thought of how far I am from them and I wondered about how yours must be in comparison."

He drew in a loud breath, having it essentially roll in his lungs before he responded.

"I see… I had a mother; I lost my father while very young; I do not remember much about him. I also had a younger sister, born of our mother but her father was unaware." Avie's head picked back up at hearing him explain,

"My mother could not defend me; I was betrayed by her in every sense of the word. It is… *difficult* to explain, but I needed her good word, pleaded for it, yet my words fell on deaf ears. She would not protect me, her own son. My sister, however, was only a child, she could not help. I cannot forgive my mother, but I miss my sibling dearly… I suppose we are similar in escaping them."

Her hand placed on his, "I'm sorry, that sounds terrible."

A lock of her hair fell from its place, Rhulle reached with his other hand and gently placed it behind her ear, "Sentiments are the same for you, how could those who should raise you not treasure the sunshine you bring?"

Avie felt her eyes water, a swell in her throat as her breath hitched. She didn't even tell Owen about her parents, trying not to think about them as Rhulle had with his. Rhulle made her feel special, they shared parallel events in their life and for the first time, she had someone tell her that her parents were not right.

His hand lingered there at the side of her face for a pause longer than normal while they sat, the truxen finally breaking the silence.

"I want to give you a gift."

"But I," she looked down at the portrait, then back up at him, "I just got one?"

"Then it is not a gift." He moved upstairs in a flash to retrieve it, coming back with her violet coat draped over an arm.

"My jacket! You kept it safe this whole time? I owe you a huge thank you, you really helped me," she laughed in a staccato, previous emotions threatening to break through with her elation.

"I did?"

"I could have been in trouble when those policemen were lurking around here. If they found my jacket so close to Garret, it could have tied me to the circumstances... Thank you, Rhulle."

He would not admit aloud that he didn't think he could befriend another human ever in his lifetime.

Avie was special, the first of her kind. No one else in the town would dare do what she did. Rhulle found himself enjoying her company immensely, she was the incandescent rays beaming through catastrophic clouds—brought with her each and every interaction.

He found a bond with her that was completely unexpected, them sharing much of the same wavelengths, even calamity through parental figures were understood. Rhulle could see that she had not talked about her own to anyone else, he had been the only one.

Even now as she smiled holding the purple coat, thanking him over a simple decision that caused him so much strife earlier, it led to an opposite reaction upon seeing the gratitude.

Something stirred in him that he couldn't place. His eyes washed over her and felt... different, unlike the usual feelings of inquisitiveness and joy, it had felt almost—sad? He mentally shook his head, that couldn't have been right.

How could he feel sadness when he sat across her, enjoying her company?

Rhulle could be reading it wrong, she did after all, bring out a plethora of new questions and emotions since the first time they unofficially met.

It would just take some time to sort out officially.

CHAPTER 11

The prick of the needle nestled itself in Avie's arm, drawing vial after vial of blood.

She wanted a little more than a simple blood test if her type didn't match up on a standard placard, if she had rare blood, Avie wanted to donate just in case. It was peculiar that she didn't fall into the standard blood groups, and while she understood that it was far more complicated than antigens measured and reacting with substances, there shouldn't be anything alarming just because it didn't show up with a main blood group, right?

The nurse placed a cotton ball on the puncture mark, taking only four containers of her blood, fixating labels on all the tubes.

"You're all done, Miss. Conrad. Now, these can go out asap, but the results may take a few weeks."

"That sounds fine, do I need to do anything?"

The nurse wrote down a quick script on a clipboard, not looking up, "No, we will call you. You're all done."

The woman excused herself, deciding on grabbing something sweet to eat from *J&K*'s. Even if she didn't have that much blood drawn, having something with sugar couldn't hurt.

Sandra was working again, Avie caught her eyes as soon as she entered, giving a little wave to the waitress in the quieter transition between bustling times. Her cleaning rag stopped mid swipe, coming up to the young woman with a grin.

"Avie! You're never gonna guess what, sugar!"

"What? What's going on?" she laughed, joining in on Sandra's excitement with a hug from the taller of the two.

"They approved me for a promotion! I'm going to be making way more and working less!"

The pair split apart, Avie's jaw dropping in awe over the waitress' good news, "That's incredible, congratulations, Sandy! You're the only one that deserved it, I'm so happy for you!"

They hugged again, caught in the moment, "C'mon, I've got the best seat in the house for you." She was led towards the back, sitting in the baby blue seat, taking in that herself and only one other patron occupied the diner. "Sugar, you want the usual?"

She reached for the dessert menu instead, "No thank you, I'm trying to stay away from poultry. How did you get the job, anyway?"

Sandra sat on the other side of the booth with her, leaning forward, "Elaine left. I think she was one of those that come in, stay awhile and leave again folk. I don't know why she left, but I sure am glad she moved on," she drawled in a whisper.

Avie got a flash of an older woman covered in her own lifeblood in the middle of the woods. "… This was just recently?"

"Couple days ago, just under a week. Which means no more cleaning tables for this gal as soon as Monday!"

Sandra deserved the big break more than anyone Avie had met. She was so elated and relieved with getting the new job with an increased pay grade, no longer having to worry about her financial struggles. The only thing that peeved in the back of the redhead's mind was Elaine had to disappear for the promotion to happen.

She had a funny feeling that Elaine was the anonymous woman she stumbled upon just days ago.

"You're going to have it so easy then, would I get to still see you if I loiter in every week?"

Sandra wiped small tears of joy with the back of her hand, "Probably not as much. Gonna miss all your visits though, sugar. You'll have to stop in early in the mornin's if ya can manage. Wanna try the new cinnamon roll?"

Looking down to see her hand resting above the picture of said confectionary, she nodded, "Yeah, it looks amazing." The waitress nodded back, getting up from the booth, "Wait, Sandy," she turned back to look at Avie, who paused with an admission on her tongue, "... I'm really happy for you."

She couldn't do it.

"Thank you, sugar. Let me get you that 'roll. S'on the house."

Conflicting emotions run through her as she watched Sandy leave; could she truly feel happy for one if misfortune had to befall another?

———⚬⚬⚬⚬———

The mystery Dewey Decimal team finally hit a wall.

Avie saw Owen become visibly frustrated, throwing down items as he slouched back in his seat, "It's like one step forward, then two steps back," he said with a grunt.

They were up late, running over anything they could that came close to what the woman experienced with the blood samples in the comfort of his home.

"We will just have to wait for the blood test to come back, then it may reveal more?"

"I don't know, Aves. I'm starting to think this is another false lead. You're the only one that has this, it might not be important to the overall mystery."

Her grip tightened, upset to hear those words coming from Owen.

"It's damn important to me, I wish I could shut this off. It's still intense, I need to find out what's causing it."

"Maybe it's psychosomatic?"

Looking at him, a frown plastered in discontent for his suggestion, "You're kidding, right?"

Avie knew that he was frustrated, but so was she. She was the one that had to deal with the afflictions every odd week, if anything, the redhead wanted to find the answers more than he did.

She rationalized that he was just speaking out of exasperation while he shrugged off her question.

It was only a matter of silent hours later, while invested in a microscope, that the feeling started back up again. Owen looked up to see what was going on as her fingers tensed in the back of her skull, a soft whine coming from her stooped figure.

Clutching at her head, a muffled ringing blurred out all of Owen's worried words. She wanted to vomit, it washed in, taking up all her attention. His words came in gradually, he was asking something, but not about the sensation.

"Give me your hand!"

Avie's face scrunched in pain, "What? What for?"

"I'm going to look at your blood." He took her palm, flipping her hand face up.

"Again? Owen, we couldn't find anything about it since last time!"

"You weren't vibrating last time, c'mon we may not get a chance like this again," he said, voice teetering on the edge of rushed desperation.

Her vision swam, but she focused enough to see the blond pricking at the end of her finger, observing the scarlet drops float out of the puncture. They hovered and bobbed in the air, rapidly dashing a second later across the room and splattering against his window.

It really had been trying to lead her all this time.

"Whuh—what? What the *fuck*? What was that? What did you do? What the fuck does that *mean?*"

Owen only watched with a smile on his face as the droplets bled through the muntins to the outside air. "It's a lead!"

He stood, hurriedly throwing on winter clothing, tripping over clunky boots and throwing open his hall closet door, "Get your coat, we have answers to find," he continued, grabbing a small box at the top of the shelve, opening it to reveal a small gleaming handgun.

"… Owen, c'mon, why do you need that?"

It was shocking to see him own such a thing. Avie never agreed with the concept, it was scary to think that he had ownership and was dangling the thing around wildly in front of her.

"For protection, whatever is at the end of your blood trail, it could be dangerous." He haphazardly pointed the extension of it towards her general direction while gesturing at her hand, making her flinch.

"Please, put that away. S-shouldn't we call someone? An exorcist maybe? This is freaking me out. It's not normal. And it sure as shit isn't normal to chase blood around town!"

He looked out longingly past the street, the door opened only a crack, before closing it with a grunt, coming back and kneeling in front of her.

"Avie, this has been our mystery since day one of you coming to the library. We have been met with blocks and dead ends, even after throwing everything at the wall. And now you may have an answer… *We* might have an answer to this *something*, and you don't want that now?"

She thought of Rhulle, her vibrations led her out to his manor before, it's where the blood would inevitably lead them if they went. Avie was desperate to not have him revealed to Owen. Owen could talk, he could get the media and a mob involved. While she did trust him and had high hopes that he wouldn't do anything to jeopardize a secret, she didn't know how he would handle the situation, *if* he could handle it. She warily eyed the silver revolver.

Would it mean his life? Either of theirs?

"I do, I'm just scared."

"Don't be, I've got us covered! Who knows how long we can follow the trail for though…? I'm asking you, please? I can't do this without you."

Shaking, a war raged in her mind. Her mouth opened to say something, but couldn't find words, only a defeated breath escaped. What could she do?

Her head hung, eyes darting in thought. Avie nodded her head in an almost imperceptible movement of affirmation, but that was all it took for Owen to jump for joy, throwing the pink coat over her body.

Outside, the wind blew a flood of snowflakes, disrupting the ones already fallen onto the ground. The woman shivered at the negative temperature; her hand was held in Owen's as he pricked the tip of her finger once again. They watched the blood rise and take off, showing them the way to follow. She felt sick, a combination of trepidation and the vibrating emanating from her blood. Yet, they had to move, they had to move fast to keep up with it.

For past treks under the circumstances, Avie could hardly muster the strength to walk normally. Here Owen was, yanking her by the hand to keep a fast pace through the town and towards the trees. Her legs gave out a few times, without rest, the blond raised her back up, hauling her onto her feet via their connected hand.

The pair kept going, reaching the woods.

Avie had been trying to think of a way she could change his mind. Make them turn around and return home, yet she also wanted with every fiber of her being to continue and find out where the blood led. It terrified her of what would happen should they run into Rhulle. Would he think she betrayed him?

"Owen, please! I can't go any further, we should head back and try again next time!"

He was silent for a moment, still moving forward, "Do you know where we are going? We're coming up to that abandoned manor! I knew there was something about that place!"

"No! Anybody could be inside of there, we can't! Let's turn back!" desperation rang through her voice.

The librarian was now practically dragging her along, his hand held to hers tight, causing the blood to constantly drip to see where it led, and keep her beside him. She was weak from the stress it put on her body, unable to break away or get him to stop. Even planting her feet in place was fruitless, she would just stumble and fall, being yanked up by him again.

"We can do this, Avie... Just a little further!'

The manor came into their sightlines, her eyes wide as she panicked.

"I can't. I can't, Owen, take me back right now!" He didn't respond, continuing to lead the way to the manor, "Hey! Owen, let me go. Owen!"

The blood stopped mid-flight, and it fell to the ground in front of them as her mind cleared, relief flushed over her body, senses returning to normal. She was so thankful.

But that was short lived.

In the breath of that same moment, Rhulle dropped from the trees, his dark figure standing intimidating—blood littering his upper body, as he landed a few feet in front of them.

"Oh shit—!" The blond reached for his gun, tucked into the back of his pants. Avie had strength now, seeing the movement, she rushed, shoving his arm away, stepping in between the both of them.

"NO!"

The gun flew out of his hands in an arch, gleaming in the pale moonlight before buried—lost in the field of snow. Owen turned to watch it fall, Avie using the moment to hurriedly approach Rhulle.

"Please-please-please, *please* don't hurt him," she begged, face virtually pressed into his chest, hands also buried there, gripping the scarlet plumage in an attempt to hold him put.

There he stood under her touch, immobile, shaking his mighty wings and glaring down the man in green. Rhulle wouldn't look at her, keeping hard rust eyes on the man that drew a weapon on him.

The two males observed each other, the woman caught in the middle watching each breath and twitch. Refusing to break eye contact with it, the librarian quietly called out, "Avie, come back here, get away from that thing."

"Owen, please, don't. It's bad enough you were going to shoot at him." She took a step towards him, one hand staying on the feathered chest, the other outstretched in his direction, stained red.

"Excuse me? That thing is a monster! What the hell else would I do?" Rhulle was growling in an undertone. But he still had not attacked…

"He is not a monster! Stop it, the both of you and just listen for a moment, alright? I can explain everything," her head swiveled back and forth to speak to both of them, frantic to get them to listen before acting.

"Avie," the blond called in a low voice, "what the hell is going on here?"

She looked once again at them from where she stood between. Both parties had their eyes on her instead of on the other. Avie let out a shaky sigh.

"You were right, Owen. There really is something in the manor."

CHAPTER 12

Inside the dwelling may have been out of the wind, but it was just as ice cold in the space. Rhulle and Owen gave Avie the benefit of the doubt and agreed to listen to her, heading inside to talk things through as civilized beings.

It was unnerving to still see the truxen drenched with blood. Before they walked through the threshold, he took scoops of the snow, using that to preen the grime from his feathers. In a matter of seconds, he was done, washed away any evidence of a meal on himself.

Avie did the same to the stains on her hands, walking into the frigid space, sitting with Owen on the old chesterfield.

"I will start a fire," Rhulle spoke just as coldly. The blond cast a confused look at hearing him speak, still very on guard with the whole situation.

She stopped the man from retrieving his gun, absolutely refusing him the opportunity. Already intruding on Rhulle by bringing an unwelcome guest, best friend or not, Owen shouldn't have come here until she had the chance to smooth things over at the very least. He expressed his concerns about being defenceless, Avie assuring him that they would just talk, everything would be alright.

The fire crackled to life, warming the guests and the atmosphere. In the light of the blaze, Rhulle took a seat as well across from them both.

The woman didn't know where to start, rather *how* to start. A silence filled the gap instead.

"So... How long?"

"I'm sorry?" she asked, unsure what he was referring to in this instance.

"How long have you known about this, how long have you been playing ignorant with me and this investigation?"

He was frustrated to say the least, keeping an eye on the feathered being, cerulean eyes flicked between Avie and him.

"It is not like that; this whole thing was accidental. That night I came to you freezing and a little roughed up… that's when I first met him. I didn't actually get to know him until later, he came to me, we were both curious about the other and it just so happens that we have become friends."

"*Friends?*" he laughed incredulously, looking back over at the copper coloured stare that bore into him, "Avie, I need to have a word with you before this continues, alone."

She wanted them to talk, having all of them present in the area to listen and understand. Already the librarian wanted to separate, uncomfortable with occupying the same space as Rhulle. She knew it looked bad, essentially lying to him for the better part of a month, however this was the chance to explain everything. It didn't feel right to speak in hushed whispers excluding a member.

Avie also didn't want Owen to turn and run, if she had to clear a few things privately, so be it. She looked over at Rhulle, he nodded in agreeance with soft eyes.

They left to the adjacent kitchen and subsequently into the dining room, murmuring out of range of hearing.

"Aves, what the hell do you mean 'friends'? That thing isn't even human, it's killed hundreds of people! It's the one causing people to die, you're smarter than this!"

"He doesn't do it just for the sake of it, he needs to eat just like all of us. I agree, it's terrible that he needs to feed on us, but I can't condemn him for it. I thought you might understand that too…"

A few seconds of silence fell between them, Owen holding back with saying something, uncertainty and hesitation evident across him.

"He could be saying *anything*, how do you know that's the truth? He could kill you at any moment, you know that, right?"

"Of course I know that, you think I haven't thought about it too? I don't know if it's an *if* or a *when*, and I certainly don't know if he has even thought about it… but I trust him. I trust him not to, just as much as I have certainty with you. All I'm asking is that you believe me on this."

Owen scratched the back of his neck; caught in the middle of a situation he never saw coming, "I do believe you; I just don't know if I can trust him."

"He is part of the mystery, we almost have all of the pieces, we just have to line them up."

"And then what? What do we do when we have the answer? We know why people are dying now, how many people have to keep 'disappearing' in the meantime? I don't think I can remain quiet on that, Avie."

Her heart skipped a beat as it dropped to her stomach, for whatever reason, she couldn't picture the future without Rhulle. She hadn't thought very much about what exactly would happen, but it was never 'he was caught or killed' scenario. The truxen became a close friend as they bonded in secret—a completely different connection than what she had with Owen. There was a way, she knew it, a way to keep everyone alive.

"Owen… You *can't*. W-we-we would—we just need some time. We might find an alternative for him."

"It's not right, if I can stop an innocent person from dying, then I can, and I will."

She could almost feel the anger bubbling in her body, why did he not see that it was still unfair to Rhulle? His only crime was staying alive. Avie's words expressed themselves, coming out before she rationally thought about them, "If he goes then I go too!"

"Aves, c'mon, this is stupid. Think about what you're saying please."

"No! It would be the same for you. I don't want anyone to get hurt, believe me, I don't; but that doesn't mean he should either."

"Don't compare his life to yours, you shouldn't even have to think about this! He's changed you in some way, brainwashed you into thinking like this, you need to wake up!"

"Owen, I'm serious. I **won't** let him be caught... I need to know; can I trust you?"

She felt awful in that moment, manipulating the blond into staying quiet. But she couldn't let him out Rhulle's existence, this whole situation wasn't fair to either of them. She hoped, maybe, Owen would be as excited as she was to discover an out of this world being, but all he could see was a monster, not who Rhulle was, not his mind or soul—just what was, to him, a killer.

Avie knew that Owen didn't want to lose her. He knew she was serious. *How serious?*

He sighed, low and through his nose, "Yeah, Avie, you can trust me. We'll figure this out, together."

Relief coursed through, her temporary stern face melting back into a smile, "Thank you, Owen, thank you, thank you!" She wrapped her arms around his shoulders, embracing the lanky man.

They returned to the sitting area, finding the truxen sitting patiently and reading a book.

"I suppose you have some questions for me," he stated without looking up.

Sitting down, they returned to their previous seats, "I suppose you should have some answers," Owen said, eyes meeting Rhulle's as he finally looked up.

Despite conversing in another room, his feathered self could hear the exchange, taking in every word. It seemed that they did not even try to be as quiet in some parts. Avie may trust him, but he would be keeping his eye on Owen.

The tension would not budge in the room. She knew him, this male did not. And Rhulle most certainly did not know or have an interest in the annoyance. The stars above knew how long it took for himself to warm up to her, and then in came this male to his property; interrupting, cutting a feeding short and waving a gun at him... Not the best first meeting.

Owen asked about what he was:

"By your terms, I believe it was 'alien'?" His cool, smug tone was back, having a bit of fun while Avie observed the conversation. She asked all of the basic questions previously, already knowing each answer. Her eyes never wavered while locked with his.

Why was he here:

"Just felt like leaving, and this was the place that I could function on that was the closest."

What he was called:

He looked over to his friend and half smiled, "Only a select few I deem worthy may have that privilege."

What he does here:

"Reading, mostly. Painting, sketching, creating. I have found a pastime in movies that I also quite enjoy. Oh! And dancing." That earned a doubtful look cast to Avie, with her shrugging in response, a light nod accompanying.

Why he doesn't need to eat every day:

"I do not eat as you would, I only need the blood. My system is a bit more complex than yours, but I too need to feed for energy to keep my body going, much in the same way."

Owen turned green at the thought; it was an amusing sight.

Avie interjected, changing the subject, "You know, Owen, he actually really helped me out a few weeks ago." She fiddled with her ring; an eyebrow raised from him for her to elaborate. "When the police were scouting the area, he kept my jacket hidden. If they found it, there's no way I wouldn't have been viewed without partial involvement."

"But you *were* involved, *he* was using that man as a meal when you got there, wasn't he?"

"No," Rhulle interrupted, "that man escaped, I never got to him."

"He was found dead, bled to death," Owen spoke coldly, his head snapping in his direction instead.

His friend piped up, "We discussed this, the police didn't find a struggle, you know he had nothing to do with it."

They both looked at Avie while she continued, "We don't know why Garret did what he did, and I can't speak for him, of course, but maybe he felt it like I do, every time. And if he was experiencing anything like this, his mind and body would have been exhausted from the constant drumming inside. If he was out here to do what he did, he must have been terrified at what he accidentally found. He didn't know if you were going to chase after him, if he was going to have to be on the run, if his body would even carry him any further... It's just a theory, anyway."

"So, what you're saying is that Garret was so scared of what was chasing him, he would rather *die instead?*"

Rhulle shuffled, "No, he could not withstand the pursuit, unknowing if his pain would ever stop. It is probable, I have read about humans doing that."

Owen turned back to him, "You can't possibly understand humans or what we think and go through. We aren't your kind."

Rhulle laughed once, a coy smirk gracing his features, "Then you could not possibly understand mine."

The male stood up with intent and he was quick to follow.
"Stop it, stop! Hey! We were just getting somewhere!" She blocked Owen, moreover, used her body as a buffer between them once again, "Look, it's late, we're all tired. Why don't we get some rest and pick this up another time?"

They both agreed without hesitation.

<hr />

Owen went to leave but hung back in the doorway when he realized Avie was not following him. He turned to watch her interact with the creature, she was smiling up at him with the expression mirrored back at her. They were close, talking about something he couldn't hear, seeing the sight caused a pang of disgust to twang in his core.

"Aves, we should go."

She turned to him, looking sheepish, "Could, umm, could I have a moment? Just to say goodbye?"

It rubbed him the wrong way to see her so friendly with what was essentially a serial murderer. But he nodded regardless, crossed his arms and leaned into the door frame, watching intently. If that thing tried anything to hurt her—well he may not be a fighter, but he wasn't a coward.

The creature straightened up; eyelids lowering, brows raised with his stare locked in his own. The blond recognized that look… it was almost a challenge, an act of superiority. It was waiting for what move Owen would make next.

"Uhm, I was hoping for a moment alone."

His eyes snapped back to her… Damn it… On one hand it was fair because they had conversed alone, but on the other, he couldn't trust the bastard-no-name.

"Right, right, yes I'll just wait in the other room," he said, speaking slowly.

Owen did his best to make it sound as if he moved far away, absolutely certain that thing had super hearing. But he remained a few steps away after backtracking nearly silently, hidden by the pony wall, intending to listen carefully.

"Thank you, oh my gosh, thank you so much," she gasped, relief flooding her voice. "I'm so sorry, I know this was sprung on you so suddenly and I never wanted to have this situation come out like that. Just… Thank you for trusting me."

Her words were muffled at the end of her sentence, Owen imagined she was hugging him, she was affectionate in that way but the worst also filled his mind… What if it wasn't the case?

"You sounded so distressed; I feared you were in trouble. I am partly to blame for the unwelcome introduction… Do you really trust him as well?"

"Yes, I do, I know it was a bad meeting, but I think he will come around. We were both trying to solve the mystery that seems to interlock with you after all."

Owen heard her speak again, which was great to hear, however that did confirm her being *affectionate* with the monster. He felt slightly nauseous.

The thing hummed in agreeance, "He will not always come with you, after this, will he?"

Like hell he wouldn't!

"No, there can still be times where it's just you and me."

The librarian almost spoke out, she shouldn't be alone with the monster, who knew when it would use Avie as a meal instead? He knew deep down it was only a matter of time… Couldn't she see he only wanted to protect her from it?

"I would like that, Avie."

Silence passed. He was almost worried they would be walking out and bump right into him.

"I should get going now, Owen will be coming back to see what the holdup is."

"Yes, go and rest, and come back to me whenever you would like."

"Goodnight, Rhulle," she sighed.

Rhulle… So that's the thing's name?

"And goodnight to you, Avie."

She started walking, Owen hurriedly moving towards the open dining area where he was supposed to be. Her rounding the corner just in time for him to pretend being busy browsing various items collected amongst the book piles.

He turned, thinking she may have known and was about to call him out, yet she smiled.

"Let's go home."

CHAPTER 13

"So, what exactly brought the both of you here the other night? It could not have been to just see me," Rhulle asked with a charming smile, expressing his ease to see Avie without company.

"Shouldn't this be a discussion that all of us should be present for?"

He sighed, leaning back, "I suppose we could, but you are already here."

Thinking with a smile, she pulled her legs down from where she sat, "You're right, I should go get him, he wouldn't want to miss out."

She watched amused as he straightened in his seat, hasty to decline, "Oh no, not necessary. I had figured; it would be easier to talk with you about it. That man does not want to be around me, let alone communicate."

"Owen is… Owen is pretty eccentric. He's a man who gets answers and plays to his strengths to find them. He wasn't expecting you, and he certainly wasn't expecting me to know you."

"What was he expecting when he came here?"

She laughed, about to explain the blood that they had followed and the absurdity of it, when she paused. The blood brought them. The blood that leapt out of her body and raced against the night air to the manor… to Rhulle… The blood that drummed in her veins seemingly whenever Rhulle fed, or was it only when he *needed* to?

Her eyebrows creased, observing her hands and falling silent as she started putting pieces together. The people who went out into the forest…

"It is not in my best interest to kill for the sake of killing."

"I have never had two show up at the same time before."

"Some humans tasted wrong."

"You may have some sort of mutant blood there, Aves!"

She stood up, Rhulle immediately following while holding her arms in concern.

"Avie? What is it? What is wrong?"

"The blood types... Why didn't I think of it before...? It makes so much sense!"

"What do you mean, types of blood?"

She looked up at him, "When you need to feed, I think, that's when my body starts to vibrate, I've always thought it had to do with the blood because that's what it felt like. Other people affected must have the same type. That night, Owen looked at my blood and it flew—right out of the house! He used that to find this place, to find you. My blood wanted to find you; I know that sounds so crazy, but I don't know how else to describe it."

His grip tightened slightly around where it held, "You were supposed to come to me."

"Yes! I think all this time, you've been inadvertently calling people to you. First to the town, then to you... All this time... I've only been lucky someone was here first."

"But this is just speculation, Avie. You do not know that for sure."

"I took a blood test, that should come back soon; I can test the theory out. It just makes so much sense, Rhulle."

"I would like to see it happen, your blood in motion, I mean." Her eyes widened, worried at the implication. "We are friends now; I would not do anything to harm you. I may be able to help your hypothesis."

That was true, he possibly saw everyone with the same blood type, he would know how it looks, and if hers did the same while he... fed. There was just one worry in her mind. The look he gave when he had torn open the throat of that woman... In the brief fleeting moment before he realized she interrupted... it almost looked like *desperation*.

Avie shook off the thought, "Okay, okay, Rhulle, I trust you," she really did, he hasn't given a reason not to, "uhhm, do you ever... know? I mean when you need to?"

"Yes, sometimes I get the feeling a day or so prior. Worry not, I do not lose control to hunger, I will be as calm as ever and will simply observe."

"Do you think we could fix it? If it really was about the blood?"

"If it comes to that, then we can worry."

The woman hugged him, resting into the soft texture of the dark feathers with a fractured inhale, "I'm scared."

"… Of me?"

She shook her head, still buried in his chest. "That it won't stop, no matter what we do."

The tone in her voice was filled with helplessness, after so many leads and speculations—trials and experiments, nothing led them to decrease the losses or the pain she felt.

Hearing her, Rhulle expressed his own shaky sigh, holding her tighter, "This is coming from the one who was not afraid of the thing in the woods confronting her?" Avie laughed once, returning the squeeze. "We will find something, Avie. There is always something."

"Right, there's always something."

She wanted to tell Owen; the redhead couldn't wait, in fact. The blood test would be back any day now and she finally had a hypothesis, and a strong one too.

After spending hours with Rhulle, her next stop was Owen's front porch. Knocking on his door, energy raced through her body. He answered, and immediately, she entered while going off on a rant about the similarities with her theory and different blood types.

"It really could be the link that brings it all together and—!"

"You went to see him alone, didn't you?"

"... Owen," she smiled awkwardly, "he's my friend. I visit you alone."

"That's not the point!" he exclaimed, wiping his face and pacing a full circle in frustration, he tried again with a calmer tone, "That's not the point. Avie, I'm worried about you. If you're there alone with him, then I can't protect you if he decides to eat you one day. I don't trust that *thing*. Would you come and look at something? I've been doing some research…"

Striding over to his desk, he pulled open bookmarks that lead to texts about demonology, and the occult in various books. He even had his computer on beside them, a few websites hyperlinked for further information.

"I think he's lying, especially to you; I think he's a demon or something of the sort. They're known for lying to their victims or exchanging favours for souls… seducing them to drink their blood and devour their essence. It's all here and it lines up with what evidence we have."

She looked at the pictures, read brief paragraphs before turning away, eyes clenched. "I know you mean well; you just haven't spent enough time with him. You'll see that he is not like this—he's really amazing and considerate. He just, inopportunely, needs human blood to survive."

He only stared at her; she's lined up pieces of the town's mystery with him from far greater leaps of logic. Owen would always see eye to eye with her, however, this seemed to cause a disconnect.

"Hang on, what's this?" Avie grabbed the mouse and clicked on one of the pages that caught her eye, Owen trying to stop her as soon as she clicked. She read Rhulle's name pulled up on the screen, a search in literature trying to connect demons presenting themselves to humans under his name. Her body ran cold.

"How did you get this name?" She turned to face him, only to be met with a deer in headlights look, him facing dead-on to the betraying screen. "How did you get this name, Owen?!"

"I didn't, I mean it was…"

The woman scoffed, disappointed, "You were listening in to our conversation, weren't you? After I asked for a moment alone?"

"C'mon Aves, I was just looking out for you. Don't you trust me?"

She paused, thinking over her words, "It's not that I don't trust you, I don't think you trust me. I know you're trying to look out for me, but I'm not a child. If I'm making a mistake, then I need to come to that conclusion on my own." She was worried, Owen just broke a strand of faith with her.

He readjusted his glasses in a nervous manner, "I'm sorry. Really, I am. I'll back off, I promise. I guess he can't be all bad if he didn't kill me on the spot."

Avie reached over and hugged him in his seat, thanking him, "That means the world."

Owen wanted so desperately to go back into the woods and fetch his gun.

But knowing that the thing would be on him instantly if he was not there with Avie, he dare not go alone. He decided to ask and see if the redhead would be the one to get it for him, watching her all but roll her eyes at the inquiry.

"I think it's better if you don't have that thing, there's nothing that you'd need it for as protection anyway."

"It's not just that, what if someone else got to it? Someone that wasn't the best person, or even a kid! It should at least be back in my possession so I can keep it locked up."

Owen lied through his teeth, coming up with an excuse on the spot to try and get the revolver back on his person. Like hell he wouldn't be caught without it if he had to keep protecting Avie from whatever the monster's plan was.

She mulled it over, agreeing in maybe that was better, it was just laying there under layers of snow waiting for whoever to grab it. Unless bird brain Rhulle already picked it up for storage...

"Why don't you go and get it? If you're still worried about Rhulle, I can come with you and explain."

"Yeah… I guess… I don't want him getting the wrong idea if it was me asking for it or looking around."

She hummed, "It would be good for both of you to talk some more, why don't we meet up soon? Say, tomorrow since we have some time off?"

He nodded, the sooner he got that fucking gun back, the better.

"Yeah we can do tomorrow," Owen stated, exasperatedly rubbing his face before sinking into his armchair.

She could see it in his eyes before Rhulle said anything.

"It is beginning, you may want to come over for the time being." His usual amber eyes had a red tinge around the narrow pupils, similar to the design seen in the past when he fed on the people of Blacken. It was unnerving, but fascinating that a physical change was present.

"So soon?"

"I was interrupted the last time…"

Avie nodded; goosebumps littered her skin. Only a matter of days ago he went through the same process, stopped short of getting his fill. She was nervous, not sure what would happen, but the uncertainty of the unknown also caused anticipation to burn alongside the uneasiness.

There went the plan to meet tomorrow…

With the truxen needing to feed, there was no way Owen would be so much as looking at the forest. God… What would he even say if he knew what she was doing?

She packed a few items in an overnight bag, as well as some bottles of water and entertainment in the form of movies, books, a puzzle and a notepad, just in case. While she was there, she could also ask about the gun. But she didn't want to retrieve it for Owen, he could collect his property and talk with Rhulle like a big boy.

If they could only communicate properly… Avie knew eventually Owen would jump at the chance to get to know an outer space creature.

Rhulle waited for her just beyond the sight lines of the trees. There, he offered his arm and they walked together until they arrived at the manor. The wind had picked up during their walk, Avie needing to pull up her yellow scarf to warm her nose, snow desperately trying to pummel her.

"I don't know how you can stay so warm; do they have weather like this on Celisc?"

"Almost, although it does not come with wind like this, the snow simply falls to the ground."

She practically moaned, "I'm jealous, that's when it's the most beautiful."

They walked in, met with a fire already burning inside, warming her skin as she sighed. Shedding layers, Avie relaxed in front of the burning logs, watching Rhulle shake and brush off any lingering snow in the doorway before joining her.

"So, the feeding, is that going to happen tomorrow?"

He shrugged, "It may, I only get a feeling before it starts to become full blown hunger, it may be longer, it may be shorter in time. I did not want you to miss it if it helps stop your sickness."

"It will help, I'm sure it will. I also wanted to ask about the gun Owen kind of just, left here. Is it still out in the snow?"

Rhulle grimaced, rolling his head away in a show of revulsion before returning, "Of course it is! I would not touch that if it were a last resort!"

"I don't like to either, he just doesn't want it getting into the wrong hands, he may pick it up sometime soon."

"To be expected, but not alone I presume?"

She laughed, "He is still a little wary of you, Rhulle. I might have to tag along."

They both shared a laugh, the noise dying down to silence while Avie stared at Rhulle. She rested a check on her knuckles, imagining what he must have gone through on his own planet under the feeding circumstances.

He shifted under her gaze, "What is it?"

"I was thinking, would you tell me more about your home?"

"That is all? What would you like to know?"

Avie smiled in an unsure manner, "It's a silly question, but when you fed there, did they look like us too?"

Rhulle threw his head back, a hearty laugh following before shaking it in dismissal, "Not in the slightest. We had creatures, nearly entirely full of liquids that contained everything we needed for sustenance—they were abundant, always coming to us when we had the need. The things not even sentient in existence, they were small and nude in colour, perhaps the size and likeness of one of your vermin with the fur and the long tail?"

Her eyebrows shot up into her hairline, "Rats?" she asked, incredulous.

"Ahh, yes, a rat; about their stature, but exoskeleton akin to your insects here. They were the only thing we needed, but we had other foods.

Although those were only to sample the taste, the more affluent one was, the more access to these other foods we had—"

She had been giggling, turning into full blown laughter as he was cut off.

"What is so funny?"

Avie still laughed, trying to take in oxygen as she waved at him in an attempt of an apology.

"I'm sorry, I... It's no wonder you viewed us so lowly, we were just *rodents* to you! Larger versions for you to feed on!"

The laughter bubbled out again, leaving Rhulle looking a little flabbergasted... He started to laugh too, joining her in a thought process put so bluntly.

CHAPTER 14

"You know I do not view you as one of those vermin, right?"
The pair were watching a movie, cozied up in the chesterfield residing in Rhulle's bedroom, conversations since then had come and gone. Avie turned to him, half thinking he was referring to the kids in the movie, before she realized what he meant.

"Of course. Rhulle, you've done everything to show me that."

His eyes were serious, "I used to… Before, I mean."

Still, she smiled, "I know, but that was before I had the privilege to get to know you, get to talk with you, spend time with you. Who else has done that?"

Rhulle took in her words, thinking over what could have been their conversations, or even conversations with others before her, "Only you. My view on humans has shifted. I would never want to hurt you, what if there are others that I do not want to either?"

"Then that is up to you. Yes, there may be others; you do still need us to stay alive though. I don't know what else could be used yet…" she trailed off, looking down. Avie felt selfish, in that moment a spark of envy filled through her at the mention of others meeting and knowing Rhulle as she did. She wanted, in a way, the chestnut truxen to be her secret. What if others had the opportunity to create the same bond with him?

He tilted her chin so she could face him, a gentle smile meeting her, "One thing at a time, dear Avie. We have to figure your mystery first. I only said my view has shifted; I am not ready to be the talk of the town."

She smiled, letting out a small laugh in relief, all she could do in reply was watch his eyes glow in the dimly lit sitting area. The hand migrated to her cheek, a gesture of affection. Could he tell she was wanting to be the only one who knew him on this level?

And what then of Owen? Did Rhulle dislike him in any way because Avie was also friends with him? Was it fair to keep pushing both of them to meet if that were the case? The thought of Rhulle and Owen perplexed her in a way that wasn't quite making sense.

Rhulle dropped his hand, and as if he read her mind, he continued, "In further regards, I do not think I will be able to view Owen as a friend, Avie."

"I don't know what's going to happen. I thought if he could see you as I do, then he wouldn't want to…" She grew irritated at the notion.

"What is it?"

"He wants to tell people about you. Sure, I don't want people to keep… I mean they will… You know what I mean, but I don't want you to either."

Rhulle shuffled, a curious tilt of the head accompanied, "Might I ask something of you?"

"Sure, yes, ask away."

"Death seems to be a difficult subject to you. As it is with many others naturally, yet I have not heard you even mention the term. Why would that be?"

Her jaw dropped, the question hitting from left field. She was aware of the limitations of her speech, the word caught in her throat of its own volition. Rhulle caught a glimpse of the story—the ballad of her parents she previously never mentioned. However, there was more to her history.

She laughed nervously, a tight smile stretching over her face. In a flash of a moment, the laughter stopped, tears filled her eyes while a hand came up to cover her own mouth.

No, she needed to. No more stopping.

"I had a sister too. She was seven years younger than me, she had the same hair, although a lot shorter. And her eyes, they were gorgeous, like ice water; piercing blue."

Her hand came away to talk, Rhulle quickly held it within his own. "You do not have to talk about this if you wish."

"I haven't been able to before. It's been five years since… I've never told anyone about it, but I feel comfortable talking with you."

"Then by all means, continue at your own pace, I will listen to every word," he said, tone soft and smile reassuring.

Avie took a deep breath, letting the air travel out with a shake.

"Her name was Aubree; she was born with a lot of problems. She couldn't speak, couldn't walk, she had very limited mobility overall. Mentally, the doctor said she was like that of a two-year-old, Aubree probably unable to progress further than that. Our parents thought that there wasn't anything inside her at all, but I knew there was. I could see it in her eyes. When she looked at them, they were dull, when she looked at me, they were bright. You should have seen her smile… I loved her with all my heart.

"We didn't have a lot of money in the first place, and it took a lot of it to pay for my sister and her needs. I dropped out of school to become her primary caregiver and I was working a few jobs to try and help every way I could, but my parents still fought a lot about the financial issues and their increasing debt. Aubree just turned fourteen, they never celebrated her birthdays, but that night… I woke up to a loud noise. I remember seeing my father in Aubree's room, a gun in his hand. He smelled so strongly of beer and whisky… And the way he was standing, I couldn't see her fully, but I knew he had shot her, I could see the blood. I think I was screaming, my mom was called, and she dragged me out of there, I heard three more gunshots while I was being pulled out of the house."

"What happened afterward?"

"I ran. I left with the clothes on my back, and as soon as the next day I found a city far away from them, far away from memories of Aubree. I couldn't take it. I couldn't deal with the fact that they… That she was… *dead.*"

It had been the first time she acknowledged the reality, even the first time since Aubree that she dared to say the word.

Rhulle squeezed her hands, "Dear Avie, my deepest sympathies are with you and your sister at rest. Thank you for honouring me with her memory."

Tears streamed down her cheeks, "Thank you for listening, I don't know if that would have ever come out until you."

"You have not told Owen?"

Feeling a little guilty, she knew there were times that she wanted to, but felt like he wouldn't understand. His parents had loved him; he didn't have any siblings... He didn't take many situations seriously.

"No, I mean, he never asked either."

Rhulle wiped the tears away, "You are very strong to carry this with you, but it has caused you too much pain. I am glad you have expressed it; you should tell your friend too."

Avie nodded in agreeance, "I was also hoping we could all talk again sometime soon. At least if it goes better than last time, I want Owen to see what I do."

"He trusts you with the circumstances. You have expressed this to him?"

"Yes, he's at least willing to try to understand, but he also doesn't know if there would be much... goodwill from his half."

"I am used to that. I do not mind," he smiled, soothing her, "will there be any ill will towards you for continuing to see me?"

She blinked in surprise, "No... No, Owen... I mean, he understands, but he won't do anything to stop or convince me otherwise now."

He hummed, "That is good then. I do not want to stop seeing you, dear Avie."

She smiled at the new nickname, "I don't want to stop seeing you either, Rhulle."

In the dim light, she focused on the illumination of his eyes. They played with the contrast of fire and moonlight, red seeping in more as the hours ticked by, taking over. There was such power there, in his eyes. Avie found herself falling into them more often than not.

"Would you dance with me?" His statement came out of the blue.

"Right now? The movie isn't even finished…"

"We were not watching it anyway, besides, I know you enough to realize when you would enjoy a change of subject."

A quick glance to the television, she saw a scene that made no sense with characters she didn't recognize. He was right…

"Yes, I would love to."

His eyes lit up, standing to prepare and move furniture. The boombox she left in his space started up, its soft music playing while they settled into a rhythm. Still entranced by his eyes, her own could not leave his face, drawing over the quills that surrounded the alabaster skin.

For the better part of the music's duration, Avie's gaze kept on the features, tracing over them with her eye's trail, wanting desperately to touch and explore them. What did they feel like? What was the texture of his skin like? Would it be silly of her to ask?

"Avie, I see the questions on your face, I do not mind, if you would like."

She smiled sheepishly, taking a moment before raising her hand that previously clasped in his; tentatively brushing the small silky feathers. His eyelids lowered, the dance slowing to a crawl while Rhulle's hand replaced itself on her hip.

Her fingertips traced the outline of tufts, the other hand caressing down the plumed bridge of his nose and brushed against the pale skin of his cheek. The skin there was soft, much like velvet—contrasted against his coarse and dark hands. It surprised her, her thumb caressing over the feel of him before moving, fingers starting to shake while her index touched his lips. She didn't mean to, her hand followed her gaze, pausing there in her realization.

Their bodies weren't moving now. In a standstill, soaked in the attention of each other.

"So bashful?"

His smile and voice caused her fingertips to briefly touch sharp teeth. Avie's eyes flicked up, caught in his amber elegance. She watched the colour swim, mixing together, drinking in heavy breaths as she focused on them.

Rhulle unfurled his wings; fluttering them in a gentle grace as her hand dropped to his chest.

Perhaps it was the way the moonlight danced across his feathered wings—the flex of muscle demonstrating power against gentle light trickling in through the darkness. A juxtaposition wherein beauty, power, command and caress all joined in one fleeting moment, causing a sharp inhale of realization from its observer.

She was shaking now, a hot band burning in her chest, constricting and squeezing, as all she could do was stare. Avie should not feel like this; it was taboo, it was outlandish—it was something she had to stifle down. Rhulle only gazed back, features cooling down to a serious look, increasing the apprehension, those heavy eyes filling her attention.

He grasped at the hand that still attached to his face, pulling her astride to the sofa where they had been seated only moments ago. Rhulle sat, grabbing her hips to place her atop of him. Avie gasped in surprise, his action causing that constricting feeling to tread lower.

She felt the plumage, soft and caressing on her legs where the hem of her pajama shorts had ridden up, hands instinctively going to his shoulders. Rhulle was bathed in moonlight, shadows from the tree outside waved on his face as he stared at her. At this moment, Avie found him so incredibly... *beautiful.*

What was he doing? What was *she* doing?

A hand went back to his face; thumb stroking the side, a soft crooning could be heard from him. His hands stroked up and down her back, eyes rolling back and closing as her hands massaged his nape and neck. That sound increased to a staccato of sighs, croons and warbling, the pleasant noise he emitted because of *her*. He held her legs now, absentmindedly kneading the flesh there, opening his eyes to find hers.

There he sat beneath her, sighing and gasping, trying to keep eye contact despite his eyes fluttering closed periodically. He looked nothing like the cryptid she first met, full of power and malice... He looked, he looked...

Like he needed a kiss.

She leaned down, lips meeting his. Avie felt him stiffen, his eyes snapping open and casting that amber-scarlet glow. Even though her eyelids the radiance penetrated, the kiss only lasted a second before a soft moan escaped him. She deepened the kiss, that sound bringing molten lava to burn wildly in her abdomen.

The burning made her bolder. In the rush, the stifled feeling finally came out and she let her emotions race, feeling him enthusiastically kiss her back.

God... It felt... He was...

Incredible.

The wind blew harshly outside, causing a loose bough to snap and hit the side of the manor with a *crack*; the noise caused them to startle and separate.

Heavy breaths filled them both as the adrenaline wore down. The woman still sat on top of him, hands curled in long feathers while his encompassed her back and thigh. They just stared at the other, unsure of what to say over their actions.

The front door slammed open, alerting them that someone had broken in.

"Avie! Avie, where are you? I know you're here!"

She threw her head back towards the door, "*Owen?*"

Jumping off, a quick apologetic glance was cast to Rhulle resting there on the sofa before she rushed towards the lower level. Sure enough, there he was, standing and observing the items she bought over, finally catching his attention.

"What the hell are you doing?"

For a moment, it felt like he knew what had just transpired upstairs, before shaking off the ridiculous thought, "You can't be here, Rhulle is going to feed soon, I don't think it's wise if you're here for that."

"Why are you here then? Avie, this is crazy! You're going to get yourself killed!"

"What are *you* doing here? What do you need so desperately at this hour?"

"You weren't home, I had to come and find you."

"Look, I know it looks bad on you end, but please let me explain!"

As they spoke, Owen was collecting her things, grabbing her coat and boots in a silent action to get her to leave, "No. We're leaving, the both of us."

"Just hear me out for a moment—!"

"What is going on here?"

They looked up at the direction of the voice. Rhulle stood on the stairs, watching their interaction from above.

Owen promptly tugged her behind him, "We are getting away from you. How dare you? What exactly made you think your plan would work?"

"I can assure you; I have no idea what you mean."

"Owen, stop it," Avie harshly warned.

He continued, "You led her out here to feed on her, right? Well you aren't getting the chance. She's coming with me."

"Why not ask her what she wants to do?" The chestnut-plumed truxen started to descend the steps.

"D-don't come any closer! Avie, get your coat on! What the hell are you waiting for?"

She shook her head, "I want this pain to stop. It's excruciating and it keeps happening. If there's a possibility he can help, I'm taking every chance I've got. Owen please, it's nothing like you think will happen, he's only going to look at my blood."

The blond turned to her, placing both hands on each side of her face, "But what if that wasn't the case? What if you were one of the ones who didn't come back? Aves, I couldn't take it if that happened. Not to you."

Rhulle raised an eyebrow, taking in the interaction, "Why not also spend the night, if you are so keen on protecting Avie?"

She took the hands from her face, holding them, "Owen, I want to stay, I'm sorry, but I won't change my mind."

He looked between her and the feathered being, almost glaring death at the latter. He spoke through gritted teeth after much consideration, "Fine."

"Are you sure? I don't think you'll-"

"I'll be fine. You're my number one priority, Avie."

"Okay… Okay, Owen, if you're sure…" She looked over at Rhulle, a silent thank you exchanged.

They sat in the same living space with the fire burning to keep warm. Owen had his arm wrapped around her back; she was shaking. He may have thought it was from the cold, but she was worried. She knew the librarian was going to try something, she just didn't know what or to what extent, absolutely sure Rhulle knew it too.

"So long as you are here, you must have more questions for me. Anything you would like to ask?"

"You're going to feed on someone soon, right?"

"Yes."

"When's that going to happen?"

Rhulle sat back in his seat, "Typically, I can tell when the feeling is coming. But I cannot tell when the hunger will show up."

"And Avie, do you want to feed on her?"

"*Owen…*"

The truxen waved it off, "No, I would never. Humans often come to me; I do not lure them or hunt them down."

Owen looked frustrated at that answer. "The blood inside her led us to you. Isn't that what you do to your victims? What you'll eventually do to her?"

The woman squeezed his arm, concern exaggerated on her features, wanting him to draw back. She wasn't really sure how to jump into the conversation.

"I have not seen any other blood do what you describe. I was hoping to see it myself."

"Never, huh?" he asked in disbelief, "Let me ask you something else… When the blood is around you, are you sure you won't go into a frenzy?"

Rhulle leaned forward, a stern look plastered on his face, "When it comes to Avie, you can be *completely* sure." He looked over to her, their eyes meeting as he leaned back.

Avie knew the way he expressed himself had been different, she knew Owen noticed it too. He turned to her, but her eyes still caught with blazing ones before them, unable to break away just yet. With the kiss they shared, the woman understood the dynamic of their relationship changed, yet she couldn't make that abundantly clear around the blond.

It was another secret she had to keep.

Owen stood suddenly, "I need some water. Would you have any, Avie?"

She broke out of her trance to look up at him, and simply nodded. Leading him to the kitchen where she placed a few bottles, once they were out of ear shot, he turned to her and started whispering.

"Has he done anything? Anything to hurt you?"

"No, absolutely not! You don't have to be here, but if you are, you're going to have to behave a little better."

"I didn't like the way he looked at you just then. It was predatory, especially with what he said. I'm sure he's going to try something, something to hurt you!"

"Rhulle wouldn't do that, there's more to him than you know. He really is remarkable; he's so smart and caring; an incredible being… Astonishing, really. I just wish you could see that too," she beamed, looking back down the hallway in his general direction as she spoke his praise, fiddling with her hair.

A strange look washed over Owen's face, "You're blushing…"

In the dim light, because of her pale features, the pink flush could be seen with ease. It took her by surprise, a hand reaching up to feel the hotness in her cheeks, "Yes, I suppose I am."

He scowled, "Is this what it's all about? What it's come to?" He scoffed, an incredulous laugh falling from his lips as pieces lined up, "You have feelings for that *thing*? When he-he's not even human, Avie!"

She tried to shush him, "Owen *shush*! Look, I'm not going to lie to you—"

"Why him? Hmm? Why him and not me?"

She stopped, "What?"

He grasped her face in his hands, leaning down and pressing their lips together. The kiss only lasted a few seconds, Avie pushing him away.

"We were always supposed to be together, Aves. It made so much sense; just tell me it's not real. Tell me the real Avie is in there still."

She reeled, distressed at his actions, "I think you should leave. You keep saying I've changed but you're the one who's changed. I've been defending you and making excuses, but this draws the line. I don't like you in that way; I never will."

"What, you wanna kiss the *monster* instead?" She looked down, away from his sad eyes. "You don't… Avie, you *haven't*!" He stomped toward her, causing the woman to flinch backwards.

Rhulle appeared behind her, his hands falling lightly on her shoulders, a wing blocking Owen's path, "Avie has asked you to leave. I suggest you do."

She watched through the gaps between feathers as the fearful cerulean gaze locked to Rhulle. Avie stared up at him, his eyes that were once seen a tarnished gold, now completely encompassed in a threatening crimson. The blond fell to the ground and scuttled back, finding the strength to stand up, run for his coat, throwing open the exit to flee into the night. She was heartbroken. A sob escaped her; Rhulle turned her to support while she cried over the transpired scenario.

"What just happened? I thought… I thought he was my friend. He kept saying he would try. He would at least try… We have been through so much, but he just… He didn't," she hiccupped through the sobs, grasping his feathered chest.

"He did not view you as an equal, but a prize. Come; let us go back to the fire." She could only nod, sniffling and sobbing getting the best of her.

CHAPTER 15

S he finally stopped shaking, a blanket draped around her shoulders and a water bottle in her grip, Rhulle drew light patterns on her back over the hour.

"Did I overreact? Did he deserve any of that?" Avie asked.

"I do not know him as you do, but it may be something that needed to happen. He tried to change you. He tried to use you. He had tried to claim you. A friend does not do that."

She nodded, craning her neck to look back at him, "What do you think will happen now? What will he do?"

"He can try to gather humans to search for me, I have been here a very long time with no luck on their part. He may try to come after me alone, however."

"You won't hurt him, if he does?" He was silent. "I don't want him to die, please promise me that you won't."

"… I promise, Avie, he will not die by my hand if it ever came to that."

"Thank you…" She rested her head on his chest, "Rhulle, how long have you been on this planet?"

"I do not know years in specific, I have lost track. But it has been numerous, at least."

"How old are you?"

"Truxi live for a few hundred years by your cycles of the sun. To us, it feels a normal life span. If humans live to be one hundred years old on average, I suppose I would reach around the thirty years mark, simply speaking, of course."

Avie laughed, "Of course…" She turned to face him, "I was thinking about it… and I'm wondering why the call came to me now, why didn't it affect me later? Same with the other people who come here, it's all different times in their life. How does that work?"

"We still do not know what goes on in the bodies of them, let alone yours. Are you certain you are okay to keep going?"

She nodded strongly, "It just keeps getting worse. This will help, I know it will."

"You are very brave, dear Avie." He brushed hair out of her face, taking in her features. The look was gentle, eyes drinking in her being. She glanced over him in turn, lingering over his lips… Lips that she kissed moments ago…

The redhead changed the topic, "Maybe we should talk about something else. It's tough to think about."

He hummed, "We could talk about what happened earlier between the two of us? I rather enjoyed that."

Was it just her, or did his tone sound flirty? She blushed brightly, not really expecting him to bring the kiss up. "O-oh? I wasn't really sure if what I did was appropriate, do you do anything similar?"

"We show affection in this way," he cupped her face, kissing her chaste on the lips and rubbing her jaw line with both thumbs, "it is for *vovii*. But what you had done… I have never experienced that before."

Her body flushed with heat, thinking about how her tongue danced in his mouth, she still had her face so close to his, lust filing her gaze, "… Vovii?"

Rhulle smiled in that soft way that made her heart flutter, "I like you, Avie. It took a long time, but I like you a lot. I do not know what your customs are, but if I get to kiss you like that, they must be similar."

"Would you like to again?" she whispered, her breath hitting his lips just inches from hers.

He crooned, a whisper barely funneling out, "Yes."

The pair talked about complicated feelings that built in between them both, kissing into late hours all the while. He spoke about reciprocating the same affection Avie had, unsure how to break the barrier that separated the two physically, or whether it was proper of him to even dare try. Thankful that she took the initiative after sending so many signals to her that he wanted more, but too afraid to try anything else.

His species moved faster, falling in love was easy once compatibility was established, then when a couple was declared vovii, his word for partners, a ceremony was held shortly after to solidify their union, not too unlike a marriage. But marriage often took years to get to, theirs took a matter of *weeks*. Rhulle expressed that once two are together, they typically are for life, whereas Avie explained humans come and go sometimes in a relationship.

She fell asleep in Rhulle's nest, awaking with a start only hours later while the night still loomed. The thrumming feeling washed over her, budding and building as she came to her senses.

The woman sat up, clutching at the waves inside her head, growing stronger with each pulse. Looking over to see Rhulle stir where he lay beside her, he awoke, seeing her sitting and staring back down at him. Nervous, she was not entirely sure what was going to happen next. She felt it even before he did—the hunger to be fed.

The chestnut truxen simply smiled, "It woke you up, did it?"

She sighed in relief, happy to hear that he was, indeed, in control as he had said, "Yes, is it still alright if you see it?"

He sat up as well, those eyes so blood red, essentially symbolizing the need, "It will be okay, you can show me whenever you are comfortable."

She nodded. "It's probably better to show you as soon as possible, I mean before someone wanders in," she laughed awkwardly. Grabbing a penknife from her bag nearby, she hesitated upon sitting back down. "Should there be better light?"

"I am still able to see it no problem."

With a prick, the droplets rose from her skin, rising into the air between them and floating idly. Rhulle looked at them in fascination. "*Incredible*. I have never seen this before."

"It—uh—didn't do this last time; it flew so fast I almost couldn't track it. Any idea on what it means?"

He started to move around, finding that it followed him wherever he tread, even as new blood steadily dripped out to join the others, "Your blood is drawn to me, but others must also have the same attraction if it brings them here, yet I have never seen this happen with them. Perhaps yours is just a stronger case?"

"It explains why it's more intense for me, I wish I knew why no one else had it this bad. Why just me?"

Rhulle played with the stream of droplets in and around the talons, thinking it over, "May I?"

"What, *taste* it?" His expression was still soft, reassuring her, "I-I… Yes, that's fine."

Avie watched Rhulle gather the blood on his fingertips, smearing some of the liquid on the pads before leading the puddle to his mouth, licking and tasting her blood. His face scrunched up, before eyes snapped open, a small gasp leaving him.

"What is it? What's wrong?" She was concerned, his eyes connected with hers still in surprise. Then she felt it.

"I no longer need to feed."

His eyes receded the dark shade, revealing his natural tawnier colour, Avie looked on just as in shock as he was.

"Just from that? That was a spoonful at most!"

"Whatever is in your blood, it has given me everything that I need in that small dose. I have needed *liters* just to get by every other time."

The words he stated beforehand raked through her.

"A stronger case…" She started to laugh, Avie laughed before it transitioned into a cry, "We can make it stop almost as suddenly as it comes… Rhulle, I'm so happy! People will live—*you* will live! Now, we only have to figure out what's in my blood."

She tucked into his arms. "You have a result on the way, yes?"

"It's been taking a very long time, but it should be soon. I hope they found something. It feels amazing to at least have an answer after so long."

The pair retreated back to the nest, Rhulle more or less pulling her half slumbering body with him, ready to sleep soundly for the rest of the evening.

⬥

Sweat dripped from his body in a cold flash.

That thing's eyes were filled with pure evil—red as the fires of Hell. Owen stumbled back, unable to break away from its vision, finding the strength thanks to adrenaline to leave the confined space. He ran home, a difficult feat with how much the snow had piled up onto the ground; the cold embrace helping itself to the inside of his boots.

Finally falling into his own doorstep, the librarian thought of Avie. She rejected him. Her face blanketed with repulsion once his own emotions flew off the deep end—kissing her in the heat of the moment rather than passion.

He only went out there to find her as she was not home, panicked at the thought of her becoming another one of the thing's meals, Owen set off trying to stop the feeding. Finding her perfectly fine and even stating that Rhulle would feed soon sent him into a frenzy of worry, yet Avie took the monster's side.

Owen shed his outerwear, heaving heavy breaths as he began to sob. The love of his life had *feelings* for that demon! The thing in the woods that lured people to kill them, and Avie *kissed it?* He should have gotten to her first, she was supposed to be his.

Nobody else in town was able to look past his odd energy and obsessive personality, Owen had no friends besides her, yet here he was alone again! He was lost. The entire time he had been swept up in solving what could have been the biggest discovery of humankind to really stop and think of the effect it truly had on her.

He made a mistake. But that creature… He would continue killing the people it brought into Blacken, it was only a matter of time before it got to Avie. Something was wrong with her; she was normally very thoughtful in scenarios. The blond thought for sure she was under its influence of some sort.

This problem had to stop. People needed to stop dying. Owen was the only one who knew the truth, the only one not brainwashed to be able to do the right thing—the heroic thing.

Avie couldn't stop him anymore.

A soft caress roused Avie from a dream, the feather light touch fluttering her consciousness towards the sunlight streaming across her eyelids, drawing her awake. A padded thumb drew across her cheek, her vision focusing on Rhulle as he lay there beside her, smiling at her slumbering figure.

"I did not mean to wake you, you just looked so serene."

She mirrored the smile, realizing that she was curled into him and had been sleeping in the nest, so to speak, along with him throughout the night. It didn't even register when she woke up in the middle of the night that she returned to slumber there alongside him.

"Don't worry, you didn't. Did I really fall asleep here?" she asked, a little embarrassed.

"Twice in the same night. Though, I do not mind, did you sleep alright?"

Avie laughed once, her mind still foggy with sleep, a hand that was placed on his chest lifted to rub at her eyes. "Very well. Did you?"

"The best in ages," Rhulle's hand moved from her face to brush red curls back, dipping in to place a small kiss on her morning glow, "I like having you sleep next to me, it is very comforting."

She stared into the amber eyes, Rhulle was very romantic, whether he realized it or not. He was comparative to the moon, mysterious, always under the guise of dusk yet beautiful in its glow. Illuminating through the dark, creating a path with iridescent silver rays.

Perhaps the comfort of having the truxen beside her while sleeping mingled with the ease of knowing how to fix her painful afflictions led to the restful sleep. Either way, Avie felt peaceful for the first time in years.

"I don't think I've ever fallen asleep that fast before, what time is it?"

Looking around, eyes scanned over the familiar setting, attempting to locate her watch. Memories of shy touching, gentle kissing, and confessions to feelings more complex than that of just friendship caught up in her mind.

It also brought forward the events with Owen prior.

Dare Avie share the news of what they discovered with her blood that night?

"It is still early, were you needing to go?"

She turned back into him after checking the time, "I can stay for a little while longer still. I *really* like this."

Her arms wrapped around the long neck as he smiled, returning the hold, "You do, do you? Care to show, dear Avie?"

The rest of the morning and well into the afternoon was indeed spent showing.

Returning to her abode after time spent with the incredible truxen, she dropped her keys next to the blinking answering machine, pressing play on the recorded message. Avie started on a pot of coffee as she listened, humming out a cheerful tune.

"Good morning, Miss. Conrad. This is Dr. Monroe's office calling about your blood test results, we have them ready for collection if you want to book an appointment. Please call us back at your earliest convenience—"

The woman rushed over to listen intently, hovering over the machine as soon as her blood test was mentioned. She could wait for coffee, jolting down the phone number, she called back immediately, able to get in straight away if she hurried.

Clutching the keys once more, Avie ran out, excited for even more answers. It was a short distance away, scarcely a twenty-minute walk, but the excitement squirmed in her abdomen with every step.

Finally, she was seated in the patient's room, "Hello, Miss. Conrad! How are you? You've got something remarkable here, would you like me to go over from the start?" Dr. Monroe greeted her, handing her a manila envelope filled with doctor script, confusing terminology and charts.

"I'm fine today, thank you. I was hoping to get my blood type for right now."

"Ahh, yes, exactly what I was eager to discuss. You see, your blood is quite rare. The test came back saying out of the sixty-one Rh antigens in blood, you are missing all of them. Now, that's not necessarily a bad thing, you still have the other makeups of blood that allow you to function with no problems, but because of the rarity, I highly urge you to donate blood just as a precaution. If an emergency does arise, there's only a handful of other documented cases, you may not get an organ donor if it ever came to that situation. I don't mean to sound scary, it's just a serious scenario should it come down to it. You're healthy now, so keep up the good habits."

"Is that why the home test wouldn't show me what blood type I was?"

He laughed, "That's a possibility, they're done wrong all the time, the important thing is that now you know."

"And there's nothing wrong with me? I don't need anything like supplements?"

"Your blood type was with you since before you were born, there's nothing wrong with you. It's unfortunate that it's so rare, it could be dangerous if you needed an abundance of blood or a new liver!" he chuckled.

She dismissed the comment, "I couldn't just get another blood type if that happens?"

"It's very unlikely that it would ever come to that, I'm just being precautionary as doctors should be. Good to have your bases covered, Miss. Conrad. Your blood type wouldn't accept any others, only the same one, and out of about *forty ever reported*, it's just good practice to donate to yourself. You were in a car accident a few months back, right? I'd say you've already had the worst of it, it's lucky that it wasn't serious enough to warrant any of that."

The woman nodded, "Right, yes I should do that. Thank you, that pretty much answers what I had wanted."

Avie shook his calloused hand and left, setting up an appointment to donate blood on her way out, the envelope tucked firmly in her grasp.

Reading through the test results as soon as she arrived back home, a cup of coffee clutched in her grasp, her mind spun over the rare blood and how it fit in with everything. This *must* be it... The reason so much had been happening to her...

She looked over the results again, finding that there were other blood types that fell into the category of being rare and having Rh antigens missing, a handy chart thrown into the printed documents showing the list. It helped explain how other groups classified the missing factors and what the rhesus element was; drawing conclusions that the ones who had most of the missing Rh antigens were the ones following the call to Blacken.

But how did it line up with the truxen who fed on the liquid?

She tried not to think into the schematics of something beyond her knowledge, but her blood lacked other components that more prevalent blood possessed. Maybe that was what made it taste so wrong to him; the antigens filled out the liquid more so he couldn't absorb what he needed in small doses. It was just filler for Rhulle, and he needed more blood in order to get the proper *nutrients* that were required. He only needed a small quantity of her, in his terms, purer blood to feed properly.

She was ecstatic at a revelation of sorts, but then a wave of sadness came over her. Avie should tell Owen about what happened... about what she found out and discovered earlier with Rhulle.

Showing up at his doorstep, nervous and hesitant, knuckles knocked with heavy raps on the wood. She stood there, waiting for some time before he answered, opening the door to reveal him looking more disheveled and worse for wear. Meeting her in the doorway, Owen's eyes were puffy and red, supporting an old house robe.

"I thought for sure I had lost you forever," he sighed in a small relief.

"I only wanted to tell you what I've found out," Avie flashed the envelope full of her bloodwork, "about my results, and what Rhulle discovered."

He visibly stiffened upon hearing that name, the small smile that graced him, slipping into nothing.

She continued; "I figured you deserved to know, I mean, after everything."

He nodded, before moving, "Come inside?"

They sat in an awkward tension in the living room, she fiddled with her ring on her pinky, staring at the manila envelope while he stared at her. She didn't really want to meet his eyes. It felt so weird now.

Why did it have to get so weird?

Avie stood to spill open the contents onto the coffee table, the papers forming a messy stack in front of them both, Owen taking initiative to pick up a few papers to thumb through.

"I have a rare blood type. I'm missing all of my antigens in the Rh system. When I was in my car accident, I think the medication they gave me affected my blood enough that I couldn't register this whole thing. When it started to leave my system, that's when I felt the vibration more and more intensely each time. Rhulle needed a filtered form of blood in order to feed. Only people who have an absence of those factors may be the ones who are lured. But mine is unlike anything he has ever seen, it's in its strongest form for what he needs, it only took a little bit—no more than a spoonful! It's incredible. No more people have to die, Owen."

She paced as she spoke while he just stared at her, in disbelief.

"... You let that thing *feed* on you?"

"Did you not listen to anything else I said?" She felt anger pulse through her. Avie never imagined she would still be so angry with Owen, but even yesterday, his behavior... Her fists curled, thinking over his reluctant need for people to stop dying, but was only ever outraged when she was in the center of the topic of feeding. Her mind constructed the building blocks together.

"You were never worried about the people in this town..." Avie laughed sombrely. "Of course, you weren't... You never cared for them because they never cared about you. You just wanted to control me. To stop me from interacting with someone else I consider close."

"Avie, that's not true, and you know it. I've only ever tried to protect you."

"I didn't need you to protect me, I needed a friend. I needed support. I was in pain every few weeks, but you just wanted to solve a mystery at my expense."

"Don't you dare say that!" He stood to match her height, "I am in love with you; I want everything for us. It was supposed to be me, you were supposed to be mine!"

Avie shook her head, tears filling her eyes before she laughed coldly, "I don't know how you don't hear yourself, Owen. This isn't you. I don't know who this is, right here, right in front of me. I used to like a version of you, but now I see he's gone. I thought *maybe* if I shared these results with you, or even saw you again, then the old Owen would show himself. He might apologize. He may want to still be friends. But I don't think that could ever happen."

He said nothing, a stunned silence occupied him while the redhead gathered her things—stopping in the doorway one last time, she turned to take in his figure.

"Goodbye, Owen."

She left him standing in his living room with a distressed look. Avie would no longer contact him, unless he could prove he changed, but she still would not want to see him for a fair amount of time.

Her first friend in this town. Her comfort. A home was made with him, but he was not that anymore. The cold wind freezing at her eyes, she wiped at them with the dry side of her scarf. She just had to get home, then she could let her emotions out...

CHAPTER 16

Avie felt as though she lost him forever.

She really thought that everything they worked through, all of the mysteries they were trying to unravel, how close they were because of it all… She believed Owen would keep his word to try because it was important to her. Yes, it was important to him too, but Avie was dead center in it all.

The woman walked into her apartment, throwing the stack of papers onto the floor, a loud sob following while she bent over at the waist. She cried distressed, never imagining Owen to react in such a way, changing as a person in what felt like the flip of a coin. Avie lied to him about part of the mystery in the past, she knew it had been wrong, but she apologized for it and never denied anything else. It was to protect Owen, and to protect Rhulle.

But look at where it ended up.

She wiped tears from her blotchy face, thinking about Owen was painful, but he said twice now that it should have been him, how it always should have been him to be the object of Avie's affections, not Rhulle. What exactly did that mean coming from him? The redhead hadn't done anything to hint she was alluding to more than friendship, sure she was affectionate, but never anything past platonic.

Avie figured it was because he didn't have anyone else, which she pitied. She only had Owen when she first came into town. Even before while she lived alone, she struggled to make friends, and he came in like a breath of fresh air. She imagined it was much the same for him.

In the time she grew closer to Rhulle, it was very probable Avie channeled that energy to express something other than a friendship to Owen. She thought back, wondering if it was maybe her own fault that this situation came to the climax it did.

The woman shook it off, rather tried to focus on the elating information found instead. It did no good to dwell on all the negatives.

They found a way to stop the people of Blacken, new and old, from dying. If it weren't for Avie befriending Rhulle, who knew how long it would have been before the situation would occur—even if it would at all. She mulled over it all as she started a shower.

Relaxing in the hot water, it helped in slowing her racing thoughts.

On the topic of Rhulle, something very unexpected did come out of it all. Emotions and feelings that surpassed that of kinship had developed. It was the mystery of him, the way he was, that initially drew her. Things may have started as a friendship, but she was not exactly sure when deeper feelings started to linger.

It may have been as early as the instance he admitted being confused by her actions, instead of running away.

It may have been when she first danced with him and he held her so close.

It may have even been there the whole time, growing, evolving while she learned more about him, without her realizing it until just last night; all her passions breaking through, coming to a head.

And yet, there was so much more she wanted to know about him and the planet Celisc he came from.

The thought of even kissing him drew butterflies to her stomach, as if she were a teenager with her first crush, the memories creating the ghost of a feeling of his lip's touch. He said once a connection was established, the relationship was announced and then celebrated; but was she his partner? Were the two of them vovii? Did being vovii include *mating?*

What did mating, itself, include?

Avie thought of the taboo scenario, a coil winding tight inside of her.

She sighed, the heat getting to her as she got out of the downpour. Grabbing a fluffy towel to dry herself and the dampened hair, the redhead moved into her bedroom and began styling; attempting to get the curls to fall just right with her hairdryer.

With the towel still wrapped around her body, she threw on her shorts and tank top once the hair had been tackled, fully intending to lounge around. She flicked on the small tube television on her dresser and left to grab a snack from the kitchen. The woman returned to see Rhulle in her bedroom once again, fixing the black out shades on her window himself.

"I almost want to get you a bell," Avie said with a smile.

He turned, happy to see her in proper lighting for the first time in her apartment, "I am like that of a bird, not a cat."

Laughing, she went to hug him, her face once again brushing into the soft plumage of his chest, inhaling the scent of pine sap and firewood, "What brings you here, Rhulle?"

"I wanted to see you again," he lifted her chin so she could meet his eyes, "it seems that you wanted to see me too."

"Of course, I wanted to tell you about my blood, and I was hoping I could maybe ask something... About what you said earlier?"

Rhulle affirmed with a hum, her breaking apart to sit on the bed. He strolled over, joining in the action; sitting just across from her in the armchair with their knees practically touching, "And what was it I said?"

Nervous, she fidgeted with her ring once more, "Well, it was when you were talking about partners, sorry, *vovii*, and you demonstrated how they kissed. I guess what I wanted to know more about was... umm... what qualifies someone as one?"

A sly grin broke out on his face, seemingly entertained at her question. "Are you so keen? We have compatibility, are you certain you would like to follow my customs?"

He was teasing her, making Avie blush. God, yes, she wanted to be together with him in a sense of a relationship, learning to blend the two customs could be the easiest route, however in order to do that, she needed to know more.

"I would really love to know everything about your customs."

Rhulle's smile faltered a fraction, then pulled down as he contemplated over something. She was worried she had said something wrong.

"Dear Avie, I am afraid I have not been entirely honest with you, but I would like to clear a few things up about myself, and my being here."

A fiery glow sat high in the sky, mid-morning shone the brightest and signalled the time to take a well-earned break from tending to the crops.

Rhulle and a few others in the fields were the first to notice them: the army from the city marching into their small village with intent. It was only a matter of time before their colony would be discovered and integrated to the larger structure, the joy of living independently being short lived.

All dropped what they were doing once alerted, attempting to flee with loved ones, Rhulle quickly finding his mother and sister in their hut to run with them.

It had been no use, futile even through the chaos of scrambling truxi. They were captured, locked away to be taken into the closest city's monarchy to be decided what their fate was. Of course, it would be some variance of forced labour, it always was. Rhulle remembered how hard life was before the escape into independence.

The high council composed of elders had indeed sent his family to build the grand brick intricacies of their homes and buildings, a labour compulsory with heavy lifting and hauling—working just to survive on meager earnings.

Enough had been enough. After tirelessly working down to the bone for weeks, Rhulle rose out of his seat in their shack, shouting the injustice of being mistreated and desire to escape once again, being shut down by his mother in worry that guards would overhear. After arguing for quite a while across the table, he angrily dropped the topic after getting nowhere. Rhulle only wanted something better, for himself and his sister; his mother clearly did not care.

Early next morning, guards raided their home, arresting Rhulle and placing him on public trial.

He was entitled to a statement from any truxen of his choosing for any final word in an attempt to sway his public appearances or even the High Council. He cried, on his knees as he begged and pleaded for his mother's testimony, for her to *say something, **anything** to keep him alive. Yet she couldn't even look at him, even as he was dragged away.*

Rhulle stood in the raised stone pillar, surrounded by his peers, and his trial runners, awaiting his fate.

To his surprise, and also dismay, Rhulle was given a choice. He could be executed publicly or banished from his home world—a rare option for a long drawn out death. Either way, his fate was sealed.

His claws gripped into his palms, drawing blood that fell as his tears did, staring blankly ahead.

"I choose banishment."

Appalled murmurs and gasps littered the crowd at his decision, and he was escorted away. The last thing he saw was his sister's sad eyes and his mother's indifferent ones.

"We are fiercely loyal; I spoke out against the system, as most held the belief that labour was an opportunity to move up and only a temporary position. Those generations of truxi were not the same ones that sought refuge away from everything like my father did—like I had. Banishment was an unheard-of choice. But I took it. I was a coward."

"No. You are a fighter, you saw a chance to keep living, and you took it. I am truly sorry for what you've been through, I couldn't imagine what that must have been like."

He smiled, genuinely, "That is why I like you; you see the better parts of everything. Thank you, dear Avie."

"I can't picture how intimidating it was to come here and not know anything, learning an alien language just because it was something to do."

Rhulle laughed, "Yours is so simple in comparison." He looked back to her face, his own sobering into softness, "Listen, Avie… You make me feel very complicated emotions, I cannot help wanting you to be mine. As a vovii, we would do everything a couple would do in your regards, even—ahh—*coitus*. I understand this is a very odd situation, and I will not ask anything of you, but I had the thought of us together, even in that sense."

He grasped a hand in both of his, lifting it to hold between them. Rhulle sounded almost embarrassed at the confession, causing her to flush warm at his words and actions. At least she wasn't alone in her thoughts…

"How would it—would it even… *could* we even…?"

A nervous laugh escaped, "I was hoping to find this out too."

Avie bit her lip at the implication, the blush deepening from dusty pink to cherry red. She wanted to find out, if just to know and understand tonight.

"We could *explore*… If you wanted."

His breath hitched, Rhulle's usual calm demeanour breaking for a moment as he fumbled, "Right, just explore a bit, no harm in that." He rose, extending his hand to help her rise with him.

She stood in front of him, not sure how to take the first step. The truxen stroked the side of her face with the back of his hand, delicate fingers tracing there before moving to the lace through her hair, tilting her head as he leaned in to kiss her. Her heart drummed in her chest, heavy with anticipation, breaking away slightly to remove her shirt, her chest lay bare before him. Rhulle looked down at her, his hand moving to her shoulder, massaging the collarbone there as he drank in her appearance.

With a brave hand, she moved his lower, allowing him to touch the flesh there, enjoying him gasping at the sensation.

"They are soft, I was not expecting that."

A light, nervous laugh was shared between them, he brought his other hand to play with her chest, tracing over every inch of skin, finding that it felt good for her. He ran his hands down, drawing over the stomach and the beauty marks that scattered there. Avie watched as his lip was caught in his teeth in desirable concentration, discovering that he too could blush.

She took his face in her hands, gripping each side while bringing his mouth to meet hers once again in a quick kiss. The woman still supported the patterned shorts, deciding to use his hands as a guide and led them to the fabric, hooking his thumbs to allow him to shimmy them off her hips while she watched his face. Rhulle in turn glanced down, watching as he was the one to remove the clothing, having it hit the floor with a wide-eyed look.

He took his hands off of her, stepping back while his wings draped over him, "I… I am used to wearing something to cover certain *afflictions*. I am afraid that is not the case this time and I wanted to be sure it was alright before I… I- uhm…"

Oh…

"I would like to see…" her voice was airy, slightly dazed at the arousal positively dripping in the room.

Rhulle's breath was shaky as he was met with her soothing smile. *Was he truly that nervous?*

The deft wings parted, revealing a pale member parting through a slit. It had a slightly pinkish tone, the shape coming to a point at the tip with a wide base. It was covered with ichor, having been stored inside of him and writhed slightly at the cool air.

Avie let out a breath in holding, staring at the new revelation that showcased itself for her, "It's… *incredible.* May I?"

He nodded, and she reached out, feeling as though the movements were in slow motion as she touched, resting a single finger at his base. It was smooth, warm, and wet. Following the length of it up, her other digits joined in the trace—cupping the smooth texture further. Rhulle moaned, his knees buckling slightly at the touch.

"That is… quite sensitive. I—uhm, could I see you first instead?" his voice was strained, eyes locked on her connection to him.

She released her hand, "*Of course.*"

Settling back down on the bed, the woman leaned back onto palms, timidly parting her legs enough for Rhulle to observe. He leant over her, placing a hand on her thigh, brushing up until he touched the lips, playing and exploring the sight before him.

He hovered, eyes fixated while the pad of a finger stroked her most sensitive bit, a gasp leaving her. Rhulle's head snapped up and looked at her, his narrow eyes watching her reactions as he repeated the act, applying more pressure, his own quiet pant slipping out as he drew more sounds out of her.

"That feels good," Avie sighed as her hands gripped at soft sheets.

The hand disappeared, both of his moving instead to grasp the back of her torso under her arms. He stood her up with him, flush up against each other while he kissed her deeply.

She felt the erection squirm on her bare stomach as they kissed, tongues locked in an erotic dance. The feathered being let out a breathy gasp, his voice husky, "I want you, Avie."

He sat in the armchair, pulling her down onto his lap, much like the first time they kissed. In the same motion, he wrapped his wings around them both, blocking out a majority of the light in the room, keeping her close to him. Only his eyes casting a faint glow allowed her to see. The crooning was back in full force, his member now slick against her.

"I have never felt like this. I want you; I want *this*," the claws brushed into her scalp once again, the other tracing over her bottom lip with a thumb, pulling it down slightly.

Avie pant in anticipation. *Was it too soon?*

"I want you too."

His features lit up, akin to receiving the most amazing gift.

With his hands on her hips, Rhulle moved her closer, his own rocking up towards her to create friction. It felt *amazing*, electricity shot through her and pooled into her core, hands curling into his feathers while her eyes rolled back and closed.

The crooning intensified; she could feel it rattling her body from where she sat. Avie opened her eyes, reaching a hand down to grasp him, reveling in the sound he made. He watched her ministrations, small noises escaping whenever she increased her grip, his bottom lip clenched between sharp teeth.

He was panting, stopping her hand and letting her release her grasp, "I want to make you feel as good as I do." Rhulle kissed her again, raising her up with his extraordinary strength.

Caressing his face, she felt the small tip of himself make its way inside of her.

She moaned into the kiss, feeling him lower her onto it—getting her accustomed to the shape as it got thicker the further down she got. He had to break away with an inhale, his claws gripping into her hips while she was fully seated.

"Tight…" his voice was strained again.

Avie looked at him to see his eyes clenched shut, breath laboured. She let out a questioning noise, not sure if she heard him correctly.

"It is so tight… I-Is-is it *supposed* to be like th-that?"

She never heard him stutter before, he had always been so eloquent with his speech, but here she was, ushering it out of him…

"Does it hurt?"

His eyes snapped up to hold hers, "No. It feels good. It feels so *fucking* good."

Swearing… Another first.

The burn she felt began to subside, hearing the way he was talking made her feel hot and bothered, ready for more. The woman rocked her hips, earning her a low hiss. His hands still encompassed her hips, that flick of friction sending him in need of more. Rhulle lifted her up, and then back down with power. A loud moan slipping past her. His grip tightened so much; she thought the digits would bruise her.

The pace increased; her following the tempo, feeling him squirm inside the entire duration. It drove her over the edge, she could feel herself orgasm around him, her grip tightening in the tufts at the nape of his neck and wanton moans flying free. He must have felt the difference, strong legs lifted them both while arms supported. The dim lights flooded her vision before she was on her back, the lights blacked out once more by truxen wings spread out over them.

His pace was unmerciful, muttering something low and unintelligible. The pleasure wracked through her at such intensity she couldn't bother to ask him to repeat. He continued; the words almost stringing together, Avie finally realized what was going on…

He was talking in his native language.

With the thrusts and his moaning language, she came undone, holding on for dear life to the figure above her.

Rhulle bit her shoulder; the sharp teeth meeting the junction of her clavicle, she knew that he had broken the skin. The pain mixed with her pleasure felt incredible. She realized he was also climaxing; his hips stopping their intense pace to pause and stay inside her—whimpers and groans escaping around her flesh.

He finally released his grip, lazily lapping at the few strands of blood. His breathing coming out in heavy puffs. A softness filled his eyes as they took the moment to just bath in the afterglow with the other, his hand coming up to caress her cheek with long fingers.

"I am yours."

She had a compulsion to mimic the action, "I am yours," she whispered back.

He smiled, showing teeth still tinted with her blood, it was an odd contrast against the serene expression. Rhulle looked at the mark he left her, and then down to their connection, "Oh Avie... I am terribly sorry; I did not mean to. I do not know what came over me."

"It's alright, this felt amazing just then," she touched below the mark, "and I think we were both caught up in the moment," the redhead beamed. The sting simmered down at his exit while he shifted, lowering his forehead down to hers.

"I have been alone for such a long time, forgive me for my time to adjust. I am aware of how much I have been asking of you."

"You have nothing to worry about, I wanted this too. I-I've never felt like that before, I don't want you to leave... Can I stay with you tonight again?"

"My dear Avie, I would love nothing more."

CHAPTER 17

Bundled up in her favorite purple coat, Avie walked together with Rhulle through the forest, his wing hanging over and shielding from the falling clumps of snow as she tucked in close to his side.

They strolled, hand in hand, caught in the enamor of the other. The woman noticed the truxen had a slight bounce in his step as he walked, reinvigorated from their time together moments ago. He was all smiles and soft glances, so very different than anything she could have imagined, it truly was amazing to see the real Rhulle.

Reaching the threshold, he picked her up, carrying her through the manor and up the stairs to the bedroom, setting her gently down onto the elegant sofa. Avie squealed out in surprise, having the noise dissolve into a fit of giggles at the action.

"Rhulle! What was that for?" she asked with a light laugh upon being sat down.

"You were not close enough to me," he said, as if the answer was obvious.

Setting a fire in the far less intricate wood burning furnace as he spoke, he grabbed from the miniscule pile that lay beside it. Avie pictured him ripping the trunks apart, shaping them into the wedges before them with his strength, no doubt how he collected them in the first place. In the light of the glow, he sat beside her, the woman reaching to play with the quills resembling the long hairstyle. She smiled, leaning up to reach his level to gently kiss his lips.

"Avie, I... I did not realize how truly lonely I was until you. You put in so much effort to get to know me, to want to spend time with me. I could not imagine going back to how I was now." Her hand rested on his face, his own coming to hold there, turning into the affectionate touch. "I regret that I cannot show you an evening properly, I have read in great detail about date night activities between two humans, and I wish that I could show my affections in that way."

"Rhulle, we don't have to do anything fancy out on the town, we can do so much just in the comfort of your home. Dates like the movies, the dancing, even dinner can all be done here."

He laughed, "Almost as if we have been dating this whole time, dear Avie."

"The activities would be more special now, why don't we plan one? I can make dinner, bring candles, dress up?"

The feathers perked up to the idea, "Yes, that would be incredible! I would enjoy a date with you immensely."

She blushed and chortled at his straightforwardness, "Then we will do one soon."

"Tomorrow, could we do a date night tomorrow?"

Avie thought about it. Tomorrow was her birthday, initially she made plans with Owen to do a simple night with wine, gifts and generic party activities. But that idea changed rather suddenly this morning. She didn't even know if Rhulle knew what a birthday was, if he would want to celebrate that alongside the date... The woman digressed; the evening spent with him would be all the gift she needed.

"Yeah, tomorrow then."

He crooned, matching the smile.

They lounged in the nest, moving for her to be in front of him in a cuddle while they express tales about their home, stories of their life as they grew up, common fairy tales, myths, and even rules for grand orders and the higher-ups.

Learning of common children stories told when Rhulle was growing up, they were similar to some of the ones she heard; always having a lesson for the children listening. She learned of their structures and buildings; made from brick and glass forged from the sand surrounding half of the world. They were built tall and spiral in most cases; Rhulle sketching a picture in front of her for better reference.

It was commonly bright on Celisc with two suns, even at night the light never faded fully—Rhulle struggled with seeing details in the dark even with his illuminated stare due to his biology. He could spend days awake due to the time change between two worlds; something Avie figured but now had confirmed. It was a blessing he was a light sleeper in that case…

Avie also learned their monarchy was similar with a king and queen ruling. She learned in that discussion some truxi viewed the harsh labour only as an entry point, but moving up ranks could take *years*. Instead of that route, truxi gathered in small groups to try and live free, by their own rules—seeing the construction often sentenced out as a punishment, a way to keep them under the royals' thumb.

The conversation moved onto the topic of gestation periods for women and how childbirth worked for both species, even Rhulle having questions.

"The mother carries the child for a short period, about two months on Celisc, having the fertilized egg spend the rest in incubation with mother and father, eventually hatching."

"That sounds much easier than what we have to go through. It takes about nine to ten months for women to carry around a baby, pushing them out under immense pain or cut open to welcome them into the world."

"That sounds very painful, why do women keep having children if they know how the process is?"

"Because it's worth it, two people came together to create life—a gift to pass on. It's very beautiful in that way."

"Very interesting, and it is just the child that comes out? No shell?"

She laughed, "Just the baby, the mother has to be the shell."

Rhulle joined in on the laughter, "What a silly thought."

"When the baby is born, the date is called a birthday, and we celebrate it every year. Do you have anything similar?"

He thought over his words, "In a way, yes. We all have a celebration of life that happens every cycle of the suns, it is for everyone."

Enamoured with the difference, she asked, "Tell me more?"

They talk about childhood memories, celebrations shared, and triumphs won, bringing up a few idioms passed along that stuck out alongside them.

"Truxi always had a saying: Exist as a whole or exist not at all. I have heard that phrase drilled in over and over even from such a young age. I have always hated it."

"We have 'treat others how you want to be treated' and it hardly works outside of childhood."

The pair laughed at their own sayings, enjoying the learning experiences.

"Is that what ran through your mind our first official meeting? Even in the face of danger you had expressed friendliness."

"I don't know exactly… But I thought, while my brain was on autopilot, that it was more natural."

"It was definitely abnormal. I think that is why it took me so long to process it. You made me think, for the first time, differently about a human."

"I'm glad it was me," she whispered, eyes locking with his.

"Your eyes…"

Confused as to what he meant, and before she could voice her question, he began playing with her hair, continuing his thought,

"You looked at me the same way, even in the beginning. The look confused me, I could not place it, it made me feel small—*unsure*. But now, I can see what your eyes expressed; it is *adoration*. Never have you viewed me as something to be feared, but rather someone to know and learn with. I cannot thank you enough for taking the time, dear Avie."

A kiss was shared, feeling her heart swell from his honest words. She never knew she expressed such a powerful emotion towards him, all the times she felt curious, enthralled in his mystery, her expression could have changed without her knowledge, having left lingering traces with him.

"I would also like to be sure—I have seen you look at *Owen* in much the same way. Would you consider the both of us, ahh what was it, dating… exclusively?"

Avie laughed at hearing the term put so formally, before a somber thought held her, "I said goodbye to my friendship with him today. I have no interest in even looking at anyone else." She smiled looking back up at him, "We are exclusive, Rhulle."

"Oh, I understand that would be very hard on you. Are you wanting to talk about it?"

"Well, yes and no. I wanted to tell him about my blood test, you too actually, but he was more concerned over proving something. He couldn't be happy in finding an answer. He isn't the same person as I knew him, it hurts, absolutely, but it would have hurt more if I kept going with him."

"That is wise of you. Perhaps he needs some time by himself to think things over. What was it you discovered about your blood?"

"I'm a rarity, the doctor said only a handful of people have the same blood in the whole world. Parts of my blood are completely absent. There are other variations of the type, and I figure, it's the reason why it affects certain people. It also makes sense that I have the vibrating more intense for that reason, you needed a filtered form of blood, and I have it."

"Very interesting, can you confirm if others that feel the same vibrations have similar blood?"

"I was going to see if I could find anything out, but it's the strongest theory I've got so far!" Avie spoke with excitement.

Rhulle hugged her tight from where his arms lay on her torso, "Then I am excited for you, my dear, exclusive, Avie!" She giggled, loving the hold and words that came from Rhulle. "And to be clear, you do not celebrate until later in the relationship, when vows are exchanged?"

"Right, there are different levels in a way, until it's regarded the same as a vovii union for you."

"Would you like to celebrate a level? There must be something to signify that you are in a relationship. Something that other humans would recognize and not *try* anything."

She thought for a moment, "Well, a ring is an easy indicator if you're involved with anyone if it's on a specific finger."

"May I give you a ring?"

Avie blushed, the hot pink flushing her neck and cheeks, "Is this going too fast? Rings are regarded pretty seriously in any case."

He simply smiled, "This is customary where I am from. Please do not let me pressure you into something you are uncomfortable with."

"No, you're right, it's not like we're getting married. I'm worried about messing something up. I really like you, and I really do want to show that I'm with you."

Rhulle smirked, eyeing the mark he left on her collarbone, "That mark will fade in time, it is almost a shame, no one would dare approach you with my marking on you so prominently."

She looked down at the light bruising that began to form around the puncture marks.

"Thank you again for that," she jokingly berated, "I didn't think you would be so *passionate*."

He stirred, "I could not help myself. I have never lost control like that before; all I knew was that I needed to mark you—have a part of me with you."

"Is that what you were saying during?"

"I… no, actually, was I that unintelligible?" He looked away, evidently a little self-conscious.

Her eyebrows raised, incredulous that he didn't register the switch, "You were speaking in a completely different language."

Rhulle balked, "I was? I spoke Truxen to you?"

"I've never heard you speak so much of it. It was incredible," Avie spoke with a nod, eyes sparkling at the recent memory.

He ruffled his feathers in response to her praise, his smile coming back full force and causing him to glance off to the side in a rather shy manner.

"Would you like to learn it?"

Her eyes doubled in size, "Could I? Really?"

"Yes, I think you would pick it up quite well."

The next few hours were spent learning vocabularies and pronunciations. Simple beginner words presented with examples written down for her to absorb, his alphabet resembling braille and odd loops. Even basic introduction sentences and questions were grasped in the short time, reciprocating the words well, but struggling when reading to translate and sound out. It was all very fun to teach and be taught.

She started a sentence, being interrupted when Rhulle grabbed her chin, turning her to face him while pressing his lips to hers.

"It is incredible to hear my language flow from you, but we should get some rest. It has been an *eventful* evening."

Avie agreed, head light from the mix of drowsiness and the rush of kissing him.

She slept cozy and warm while the harsh winter wrapped around them, Rhulle kept her warmer than any blanket could with him practically radiating heat. She sighed, content, while falling into the bliss of sleep.

Rhulle wanted her to feel the same as he did. His heart sang with every glance in her direction, dancing in his body when she smiled, those glorious green eyes illuminating in every sense of the word. It was a shame Avie could not see what he did.

This human really did capture his heart, he thought his life was over, that he would be alone forever, doomed to be confined on a planet in his punishments... Yet, here was a ray of sunshine that cut through his darkness. She wouldn't give up. She wanted to see him, to know him, despite everything... Everything he said and done. They were even compatible! Each viewing things in a similar fashion, it was delightful to talk, learn and teach with her.

Rhulle never thought this day would have come. If he told his past self about these future events, surely, he would have killed the 'imposter' that told him grandiose tales about humans.

No, he still didn't like humans... just this one.

He wanted Avie to be beside him through whatever the circumstance, to be with her forever, symbolized as truxi do with their union, and humans with their marriage. He was hopeful that getting a ring for her would be that first step in having her accustomed to the idea he wanted her eternally, and that they could be just so.

But how would he go about getting one?

He couldn't very well march into town to purchase one. Rhulle figured he could make one yet had no idea what he could use that could be forged in a similar fashion. He needed to get one, possibly from another human.

The truxen had an idea on where one just may be.

CHAPTER 18

Owen was pacing, walking tight circles around his bedroom for what could have been hours, his gun clenched tightly in his fist. Every so often he would look at it, trying to summon courage.

Last night as soon as the sun started to dip behind the horizon, he headed out to the old manor, hoping the guise of darkness would help protect him from being seen searching. If that monster was there, he didn't want to linger for long, if Avie was also there; she could have at least explained away him searching for his gun. However, if she *was* there, Owen didn't want her to see him frantically searching through the snow. He couldn't stand to see her since that afternoon, hearing news that she let herself be victimized by the thing, having her blood taken, the creature no doubt had a taste for her now.

If she saw him feverishly digging for his revolver, the desperation clear in his movements, well, she used to be smart, she might put two and two together.

Finally, he found the silver handgun, its frame gripped within warm gloves. Taking no time, he got the hell out of there, not wanting to risk his presence; the snow falling would help fill in the disruption he created.

He looked down at the gleaming metal—could he really do it? Shoot to kill? Could he really end a life? Owen never saw himself as someone with the ability to do so... But he needed to now.

In the pacing, he plotted. What was the best way to go through with it? Would there be resistance or retaliation in different scenarios? In his mind, he ran over every possible outcome, finding one that had the best approach after much consideration.

Owen was dedicated.

It had to be him.

Avie bit into the chocolate chip cookie, sugar instantly hitting her tongue.

She finished getting her blood drawn, donating in a sense for insurance purposes as the doctor advised—a birthday present to herself in an odd way. Munching on the extra goodie on her way home, she enjoyed the soft crumble made possible only by extra butter, having the thought roll over her mind if Rhulle had ever tried cookies and if she should bake some for tonight.

Walking the sidewalk of downtown, her eyes spotted a beautiful black dress in one of the boutique's display cases, feeling an urge to go inside and take a closer look. Avie walked inside to the smell of cinnamon and marshmallow, a few decorative pumpkins and tacky Halloween decorations littered the store.

"Hello," greeted the store clerk, "how are you?"

The redhead smiled at the young lady, "Very well, thank you! Yourself?"

The blonde woman straightened up, "Been a slow day if I'm honest, I'm happy for a customer, anything catching your eye?"

Avie turned back to the dress in the display, "Well, this dress is beautiful, I've got a date tonight and it's practically calling my name."

The clerk gasped in excitement, coming around the desk to assist, "No kidding, that's bangin'! What's your size? I can check to see if we have them in the back."

This boutique associate couldn't have been older than eighteen at the most, full of enthusiasm even if it was just a fake front most employees had to put on for the customers. She felt that wasn't exactly the case here, however.

Avie matched her energy, "I'm about a size four, it must be pretty popular then!"

She laughed, blue eyes crinkling closed, "As if, we only had it come with a few sizes, it's really more of an exclusive dress. I'll be right back, help yourself to coffee or some water!"

The clerk bounced off, jade eyes following her path, choosing instead to turn back to the beautiful black dress, admiring the design as it formed the mannequin elegantly. The blue-eyed woman returned a moment later, looking thoughtful.

"So, there weren't any in the back, like at all, but I'm wondering what was on the mannequin—it's the last one in stock." The woman turned hopeful, watching as she stepped into the display, checking the tag at the back of the garment. Her face lit up, "Good news! It's a four!"

"It's my lucky day! Thank you so much, I can't believe it." The blonde handed her the dress, Avie admiring the silk slip sleeves, the soft material of matte black, "Can I try it on?"

"You have to! I've never seen that dress on anyone besides the display. Here," she led her towards the curtain change room, "my name is Kelly if you need a hand."

The redhead nodded in thanks, starting to change as soon as the curtain closed. The piece zipped easily on the side, fitting a little snug, but looking beautiful on her. The material hugged the shape of her body, sheer sleeves wore off the shoulder and looped around her upper arms, showing off more skin than she was usually accustomed to. Avie felt truly beautiful in the dress, spinning around; trying to see every angle with a smile on her face.

She came out, showing off the dress to an excited Kelly.

"Wow! It looks perfect, like it was made for you, how do you like it?"

"I love it, Kelly. It's a definite purchase, I almost don't want to take it off!"

"That man is very lucky," Kelly smirked, eyebrow raising in a coy manner at seeing the mark on her shoulder, "I'll get you rung up whenever you're ready," she said with a wink.

Avie almost wanted to cover it, having a wave of embarrassment, before she laughed quietly. It wasn't abnormal to have love bites and hickeys, and

Kelly was young enough that she acknowledged that. She was glad someone older was not working, they most assuredly would be looking at her in disdain upon seeing her mark.

She took one last look at herself in the mirror, the dress had a lot of power—that, or she herself willed it to look so beautiful on her. Either way, it was perfect for the evening she was planning, another birthday gift to herself! Grabbing the giftbox holding the dress, Avie thumbed over the periwinkle case.

"Thank you so much for your help, Kelly."

"It's no problem! I hope you have fun on your date!"

They both shared a smile, saying their goodbyes.

Arriving home, only a few minutes from the boutique, she started right away on a dinner to take to Rhulle's later. It would take a few hours for the pot roast to cook, wanting everything to be ready and perfect for the night, excitement vibrating through her instead.

She flicked on the television as background noise while she set off to work, the time flying by in her craft.

With everything finally prepared, Avie applied the umpteenth bobby pin into her hair, keeping the curls tucked into an elegant updo as she affixed some well-placed jewelry. Stepping into black tights and heels, she was about to slip on the little black dress, when a knock on the door interrupted her. Cursing, she threw on a silken robe, jaunting to the spy hole and peeking through; not expecting anyone.

It was Owen.

The woman still didn't want to see him quite yet; she accepted that he may no longer be a part of her life as her once good friend. Seeing him still hurt, she was not ready to let the person she knew leave.

Regardless, she opened the door, "What do you want, Owen?"

The man in question held up a small box, wrapped in purple and pink, "It's still your birthday, even if you don't want to see me, you should have this."

He was gruff, Avie speculated he didn't want to be here either.

"Thank you, you shouldn't have," she reached out, grabbing the small gift, eyeing its ribbon. It was truly appreciated, but Avie didn't want to come off as inviting or welcoming until she saw some actual changes.

She looked up, seeing him open his mouth as if to say something— mouth ready to form words with breath drawn, but before he could his eyes flicked down. There they sat focused on something, something behind her with a disturbed expression glossing over him.

The woman turned her head to look back, feeling the bite mark tense slightly from the movement.

Crap.

He had been staring at her exposed love bite. She turned back to him immediately, covering it back up the best she could with the collar of her robe.

"You still think he has the best interest for you? When that *monster* is feeding off you like *that?*"

Avie hated hearing how much Owen talked down Rhulle, he didn't even know the whole story. Yet if he did, it may only bring more reason to dislike him.

"Were you here just to deliver my birthday gift or was there something else?"

"I want to solve this goddamn mystery! But you can't accept me anymore, your partner, your friend. I've been replaced by that beast in the woods. I'm at least giving you the courtesy of knowing that I plan to do something about it."

"I've told you that no one else will be dying, if you kill him, you kill an innocent," Avie said, scoffing, her eyes hard.

"And all of the other killings he did, there's no moral question in your mind that you're okay with that?"

"I can not dictate whose life matters more, it's in the past. What matters now is that we have stopped it."

"You're crazy, Avie, absolutely crazy! If I asked anyone else, they would see I'm the sane one. He's controlled others through their blood and now he's done the same with you," Owen raised his voice, gesturing to the bite on her once more.

She had enough, he insulted her and Rhulle with no regard to see things from another perspective. She snapped, words leaving her quickly in her retort, "Actually, this was from when I slept with him. Thanks for the gift," she stated in a rather matter-of-fact tone, slamming the door in his face.

The redhead sighed against the door, getting back to work on dressing up for the evening, planning to enjoy the night nonetheless.

It didn't take too long for Owen to be heard banging on her door, shouting at her to open up and talk. She figured her words finally registered. It was curt of her to say what she did, but damn it felt good, after all, the librarian wouldn't drop any of his accusations. Becoming more and more insufferable each time. Avie hated that she was still closely attached to him, letting him get too far in instances such as this, then getting fed up, coming up short with her responses.

Really, she should just cut him off to stop further arguments.

Her dress finally slipped on, makeup touched up, and a silk shawl wrapped around her shoulders to complete the look. Avie checked herself out in the vanity's mirror, making sure she was all put together.

"You seem to have a visitor at the front door, I do not know if they will be going away too soon."

Rhulle entered through the usual window, drinking in her appearance. She was sure the noise Owen caused could be heard down the street at this point. A smile broke out while seeing the chestnut-plumed truxen perched there, walking over to kiss him.

"It's just Owen, for some reason he won't drop the mind control theory, or what's happened to me with you."

"And so, he is going to be there all night because of that?"

She paused, "Well no. He saw the love bite. He might know about my *intimate* relationship with you."

"You are no longer worried about how he may act due to that information?" He cocked his head, fully entering the room.

"If he wanted to do anything, he would have by now, we would have seen someone poking around in town or in the woods."

"This is true, you look ravishing by the way!" Rhulle twirled her around, catching her entire look, "If you can not leave out the front, then I will have to sneak you out."

"Sneak me out," she laughed. "How? Down the fire escape?"

He looked over his shoulder, unfurling his wings and flapping them once for good measure.

"*Better.*"

"No… You don't mean—!"

The truxen nodded, confirming her thoughts. Avie essentially squealed with delight, grabbing a coat to keep her warm as well of her bag of things to bring on the date. Rhulle cradled her in his arms, she balanced the fabric carrier on herself, one hand gripping onto the handles, the other holding onto the feathered body for good measure.

He jumped, her breath leaving her when his wings caught the wind, her stomach dropping and feeling weightless in the first moments of flight. The night air struck her, demanded her attention to the cold, yet she could only focus on the feeling of flying, wrapped up tight in Rhulle's arms, landing in the trees once they reached the forest in record timing.

Rhulle used the canopy of trees to leap instead of attempting to navigate through with his flight, the branches too close together for him to weave through. They arrived outside of the manor, Avie being kept in his arms once again as he carried her through the home, letting her stand once the dining room was reached.

"Rhulle… Thank you, that was astounding."

"I thought you would enjoy it. We had to start the night with a little excitement."

"I'm excited to have this night," she spoke while setting up the table, placing dinnerware, candles, the roast with veggies and red wine onto the rich oak. She lit the beige candles with a box of matches brought, showing off the ensemble to her partner.

"Dear Avie, it all looks so enticing, shall we?" Rhulle pulled back the chair at one end, gesturing for her to sit.

Sitting across him at the long table, the woman started to sip at the wine. The truxen copied her, staring at the glass with a wary look before trying the strange liquid.

"This is… different. I wouldn't say I particularly like it."

Avie smiled, "You don't have to drink it, I thought you may want to try it at least."

"*Thank the stars.*" He pushed glass far away from him, causing her to laugh.

With trying the roast, Rhulle expressed his approval of the food Avie had cooked, happy to try some Earth food at last. They conversed as two lovers would at any dinner, laughing, exchanging stories, in general getting lost in the other. It almost felt like she was at a fine dining restaurant with him. As they ate and conversed, the scene made it easy to imagine soft music playing, idle conversation chattering in the background, soft ambient lighting and even dreamy thoughts of him wearing a suit.

It felt so real. A real date.

After dinner was dancing, Rhulle held her close, her head resting on his chest as they swayed with the music. Her eyes fluttered closed, soaking up the affection.

"I couldn't ask for a better birthday…" The words slipped out in an appreciative soft voice, riding on the waves of joy.

"*Birthday?* Yours is today?" he sounded caught off guard, looking up Avie could see that his face matched.

"I'm sorry I didn't say something, I didn't think it mattered."

He paused their dance, "It matters because it is you. I am honoured you agreed to spend the night with me, I would like to have given you a proper celebration or even a… Wait here."

Rhulle suddenly broke away, strolling off to fetch something, coming back to reveal it in front of the firelight. A golden band caught the light, wrapping around a stunning diamond reflecting the flames tenfold.

Avie gasped, not expecting such a thing, "This isn't because I said it was my birthday? Where did you even get this?"

"I was planning on giving you this ring soon regardless. It has been mine for a while, lost in the forest, but now it is yours to show, or to think of me whenever you look."

He slipped on the ring, her finger accepting with no resistance, it fit slightly loose but sparkling while she played with it in the lighting. It was beautiful. He was beautiful.

"Rhulle, I—" She didn't know what to say, her throat tight with emotion from the grand gesture.

"*Delahara incu.*"

"Delahara incu…" she repeated, looking up from the ring to watch him bristle with excitement, eyes and smile wide. His hands tightened their grasp around hers with the ring. "That sounds familiar, what does it mean?"

Rhulle pulled her closer to him, making it easy to lean down. A soft kiss on the shell of her ear was matched with an equally soft whisper, causing chills to run up and down her body.

"*I love you.*"

———

Owen's fist still rapped at the door, it had been forever, he was tempted to just kick open the door and make her explain herself, possibly shake some sense into her.

A neighbor opened his own door, the old man short in stature telling the blond to piss off or the cops would be involved. He stopped the noise, questionably looking back at the door. There's no way she would be leaving without bumping into him, so he just would wait it out… or break in.

He decided on the latter, trying to pick the lock with supplies in his pocket.

To his surprise, it worked, and he was in. He closed the door behind him, locking it. Owen called out for Avie; searching the space before finding she was not there.

He must have snuck her out. Taken her to his manor in the woods.

The librarian was pissed. He could maybe rationalize that she was confused and thought she had feelings for the monster. But… *sleeping with him?* It was disgusting, an unholy thing to even imagine. It made him absolutely sick to his stomach to think about.

He needed to kill before it caused further damage to her, she really was gone.

Owen didn't have his gun with him. He cursed himself, wishing he brought it. He had to strike. It had to end. His hands balled into tight fists as he stood in the darkness of the apartment.

He had let it get too far—but things will be fixed.

"You do not have to respond now; think it over, take your time."

Avie was left speechless, hardly expecting a ring *and* a confession. She really did care for him, had been enthralled with him since the first time he decided to visit and communicate with her. He had every opportunity to kill her, but he didn't. It was a long shot, even then, but on that simple note alone, she felt that there was more to him and that the woman wanted to know as much as she could.

Of course, this wasn't a traditional dating scene, his species moving seemingly much quicker in comparison to humans. However, nothing really felt rushed. She never felt pressured to reciprocate his intimate feelings, only by her own ego pushing that it was too soon by society standards.

Rhulle was the most incredible being, he filled her with praise and made her feel so…

Two hot tears streamed down her face, catching on his thumbs. Instantly his demeanour changed.

"Oh no, Avie, I have upset you."

She shook her head, smiling, "No, I'm not upset. I'm so happy!" Avie kissed the palm placed on the side of her face, seeing him wash with relief.

"You make me happy too, dear Avie. So very happy."

He kissed away the streaks, landing on her lips. He kissed her individually, three, four, five, six, seven, landing in quick succession before bringing her in to deepen it. Keeping her in his grasp, her face was delicately held between his gentle claws, connecting her to him.

"I just. Cannot. Get. Enough of you," he spoke between more pecks, moving to lift her up above him, twirling her around as though she weighed nothing. Placing her back down, he finally let her break away from him. "Stay with me again tonight?"

Avie smiled, ready to say yes, but she had other responsibilities.

"I have to be up early in the morning for work," she answered sadly.

"Right, yes. It would be easier with your things at home," he sounded nearly as disappointed.

"I can still stay, for a little bit longer at least."

His feathers bristled in an excited manner, "Wonderful."

She yearned to stay, the hours falling away far too quickly as she spent passionate time with the orphic truxen. He was the one to comment it was time for her to return, needing a good night's rest. Rhulle flew her back home, hesitating in her window, leaving her a longing kiss goodbye.

"Goodnight, my love."

Her hands still caressed his face, reaching up to his height in the sill, "Goodnight, Rhulle."

They held a smile, before he turned and disappeared into the night. Her hand reaching out, similar to the fashion of the night she reached out after him, not wanting their first real conversation to end.

Avie didn't want this night to end either.

Her hand glittered in the low light of the streetlamps, her gaze finding the ring once more. She drew it back to inspect, twirling it around as she gazed over its beauty. Avie knew it, the feeling rushing in at full force, she knew that she too, loved him.

Nothing else could cloud her feelings, no worry about what others may think, no worries about the implications of the taboo—just Rhulle. Just his love. It filled her; the overwhelming feeling of needing to tell him. Should it wait? Could she wait until she saw him next to tell him?

No. She needed to tell him now, caught up in the feeling.

Regardless of coming from his place barely minutes ago, she decided to go back. To tell him, to say *fuck it* to the obligations of early morning rising. The woman needed to be with him tonight.

Her smile was wide still glancing at the ring, still looking it over and thinking of him, rushing, all but throwing open her bedroom door.

Her heart dropped.

The door opened up to reveal Owen on the other side, the barrel of his gun pointed straight at her.

CHAPTER 19

Rhulle found it strange that Avie had not come to visit him after her workday. He waited for hours, trying to occupy his thoughts as he huffed, wondering where the young woman was. The light of the sun eventually disappeared, leaving dusk and nightfall, yet still no Avie.

He could wait no longer, as the darkness came, he slipped out into the night, going out to see her instead. When he arrived at her place, however, he found it surrounded with a yellow ribbon, no lights on and the window locked tight. It worried him. It wasn't like her to not be home at this hour at least, and he would have seen her if she was on the way to him.

The thought occurred that she may have been over at the other house—at Owen's. The stars above knew *why* she would be there, but he decided to check as well.

Arriving, Rhulle saw the house dark, no warmth and no sign of anyone.

A sense of panic rang loud inside of his head. Something was wrong. Something happened and he needed to find where Avie was, right now. Rhulle returned to her abode, breaking the window in order to get inside. He felt bad for a split second, but he rationalized if he could just find something of hers that could help lead him to where the woman was, then it could make up for the damage.

Once inside, Rhulle immediately spotted the shawl she wore the evening beforehand, using the scent to find a trail. The scent was strong, it smelled overwhelmingly of her blood, a clear path drawn for him to follow.

Got it.

He followed it, anxious as it mapped the trail that led through town, stopping cold through the doors of a large grey building surrounded by bright lights. Rhulle couldn't get any closer, he surely would be discovered in an instance if he dared. At least he found where she was last, or possibly was still in.

The hospital.

Damn it. This wasn't good… What the hell happened?

———

It felt like she was dreaming, yet somehow had this one before.

Avie lingered in on the brink of consciousness, feeling reality sharpen and smudge around her. Muffled voices shouted around and on top of her, overlapping in hurried speech. Pain washed over her, coming in waves that dug scorching blades into her abdomen. She tried to move, tried to speak, but nothing came—just people trying to get her attention across blurred visions, poking and prodding her, adding onto the pain. Only able to register pain.

The dream turned into a nightmare.

"She's losing too much blood! We need to get in there ASAP! Clear out the O.R."

The doctor finished hanging a bag of blood, stating disgruntled that she would bleed the stuff out just as fast as they could get some in her.

He looked into her eyes, she was aware, just barely. It was agony, to be in this much pain but unable to black out to avoid it. A semi consciousness. Avie thought she could see the recognition of pity written on his face.

"Anything on the blood bank before we move?"

The nurse on the other end of the trauma room nodded on the phone, "They've got an ID, no medical conditions, but rare blood. She's only compatible with Rh-null blood, she's got one bag donated from herself."

Another voice joined into the conversation, *"We only have a half liter?!"*

"Nix the O neg! Get that out of here." A flash of blonde hair crossed her vision.

"Anything else she can get? Anything on file? She will bleed out at this rate without more!"

The nurse shouted back, over the cacophony in the room, "They're working on it!"

"What do we do, Fidler?"

The doctor in question hesitated above her, holding medical sponges tight on her bleeding body as he hurriedly ran through the options.

"Get her into the O.R, number one priority is to conserve blood and we gotta stop the bleed. Hook her up with the cell saver while we wait for word back. Let's move!"

A petite doctor stayed atop her as they moved, a beautiful young blonde girl, possibly her own age. She could feel her hands pressed into her stomach, no doubt trying to keep pressure on the wound to keep from bleeding as she was transported.

Avie kept watching her face, clear blue eyes the same colour as the springs of a mountain periodically locked with hers. They were so clear… She felt as though she could see right through them. They looked like…

"*Aubree.*"

It was a breath of air that passed through shaped lips, hardly a word whispered at all. Perhaps only a jumble of vowels and consonants that escaped, mixed through a sob with no proper function to be called a word at all.

However, the name drew the blonde woman's attention as she smiled down at her, Avie would have given anything to be able to smile back at her. In a way, it may have been a gift she passed on, because in the moment Avie was able to register it, she passed out, finally away from the pain.

"So, you've known this girl since she came into town, is that right?" Owen sat across from the officer, watching the gruff man take a drag of a cigarette, staring at it while it created wispy patterns from across the metal table.

"Yes. Her first few days into town we had met. She came to me in the library. She was still a bit beat up from her accident."

The officer leaned forward, the dark suspenders stretching, "Is that also when you decided you were going to kill her? Liked the vision of a battered beauty so much you wanted to recreate it?"

He finally looked at the detective, "She and I were best friends, you can ask anyone. I never did anything to hurt her."

"Really?" the detective chuckled lowly, "That's why it was your gun at the scene of the crime, and why multiple witnesses saw you fleeing the scene?"

Owen looked down. He wasn't looking at anything really. The disheveled man just stared off into an empty space, "I would never hurt her…"

"Right," the man chuckled again, "it was someone else that attempted murder, not you. Don't 'cha have difficulty making friends? You've been a social outcast by choice—or was it by chance? And then comes this young woman, occupying all of your fancy, but she didn't return the same feelings; making you mad. You couldn't have her so no one could. Am I getting close?"

"She was in trouble. I had to help her; it had gone too far."

"And what exactly do you mean by that, Mr. Zagorski?"

"Damn it, I can't clip the vessel, that bullet is still blocking the way!"

The line rang across him, his pastel brown eyes flicking up just as the attending nurse answered. "Fidler, the bank found a cross compatible match, they say it's still risky with the overall difference."

He grunted with sheer frustration, could the patient last long enough for a closer match…?

"We're talking about using *several* bags here! Can she handle that?" Miller exclaimed, her blonde eyebrows disappearing into her cap.

"We try anyway, she can't wait for something else. Get it here, now. I need another approach. I'm going to make another incision."

"Doctor, BP is dropping, whatever you're planning, it better happen quickly."

"It's her only shot. We're doing this fast once the blood is here. Dr. Zhang, get the bullet as soon as I cut, and then I'll follow to get the artery. We're gonna get this thing."

The surgeon nodded; determination set in the crease of their brow.

A nurse ran in, gasping heavy breaths within precious minutes, bags clenched in each hand. Wasting no time, the new blood was hooked up intravenously.

"Ready? Scalpel."

The instrument was placed in gloved hands, skillful fingers adding another element of difficulty to the situation. This was it, the make or break moment.

The cut was made, the surgeons held their breath.

It was not just the article of clothing that gave him the scent trail; there was blood present on the garment, it was the prominent trace that led him here to lay in wait.

Rhulle knew now because he could smell her blood taking up rooms before him. It hurt so much knowing that his love was in pain, hurt somewhere inside of there, currently bleeding or her blood pouring some time recently.

There was so much of it, everywhere, drowning out his senses. He couldn't even have the knowledge of what was going on, if Avie was okay, if she was even *alive*. He could only sit and stare at the building, out of the light and away from any onlookers.

He was at a loss.

Rhulle questioned if *Owen* knew anything about what was going on.

"Dear Avie... *please*... please be alright. I will be back as soon as I can for you."

The truxen searched, returning to the quiet house, finding no sign of the man. Grunting in hindrance, he too broke a window to gain entrance, needing to find something to get answers. He found a trail, leading him back to Avie's apartment, only to see officials poking around, taking photographs and collecting items, him watching from afar as they passed by windows. No doubt about it; Owen was involved somehow.

The trail faded fast after her home, Rhulle was unable to go back inside to look for clues to further investigate.

He was shaking, feeling true fear for the first time since coming to the planet, being left in the dark about the woman he loved. His hands came up to clutch at his head, his mind swimming with endless possibilities and explanations. Rhulle felt truly helpless.

Hours of the night passed as he returned to the hospital, waiting, still knowing nothing.

⊶⊷

Owen learned of Avie's death just moments prior, she wouldn't have to suffer anymore.

The shrill tone of the telephone cut through their conversation, Detective Arcand excusing himself before standing to answer.

With the news, the blond told Detective Arcand all about his former best friend, about the way her mind slipped, controlled and influenced by something else. She couldn't think clearly, constantly putting herself in harm's way. She was growing into someone who wouldn't listen to reason, no matter how hard he tried, someone who grew short with him every time he expressed concern. He was only protecting her. Protecting her from the bigger picture. Protecting from a creature in the woods.

The portly detective muttered a few things during the brief conversation over the phone, eyes never leaving Owen's glazed over expression, cigarette perched unsteadily between his lips. He smirked, thanking the person on the other line before hanging up, waltzing back to his side of the table once more.

"Well, well… Just got word that the lil' lady survived. I hope she shares the same story as you do."

Cerulean attention snapped back to his words, widening, "Avie is alive? But you had just said—!"

"Sometimes criminals are cockier when they think their victim didn't make it. So, anything else you may want to tell me? Anything you need to clear up?"

Owen remained silent, staring down at his cuffed hands resting in his lap as they curled into fists.

She survived. *God damn it.*

"I want a lawyer."

CHAPTER 20

Eyes blurred into a white out upon her first attempt to open them; the brightness and intensity causing her to squint them shut and try again.

Avie was at a loss, confused as to what happened, memory not able to recall her last moments of awareness. Looking around she figured she was in a hospital, but that didn't make any sense... Why would she need to be here? Let alone how she got here...

Oh!

There was a gun... It had been pointed at her face initially, Owen's eyes over the target. There was so much malice held within them.

"You're going against me. I've only ever tried to protect you." His last words to her echoed as she remembered the firing shot, his hands trembling while they lowered to hit an easier target.

The woman felt the discomfort in her abdomen, flipping the blanket with little strength she had to see the bandages. Hot tears fell from her green eyes. There really was no going back with him. The Owen she knew gone forever; this new one scarier than anything she could imagine.

She felt betrayal in its harshest form, pain washing in with each shaky breath.

Chills wracked through her body, similar to the feeling she had after her car accident, making her body feel light but stiff, shaking from the uncomfortable feeling. She tried lifting her arm, seeing how far into the air it could go, when a doctor entered, startled to see her awake.

"You're awake already? Let me page your doctor, how are you feeling; one to ten?"

Avie recognized her as she got closer, not entirely sure where from, only the blonde hair and icy eyes ringing a hazy memory.

"Eight on the pain scale, I feel sick."

"You went through a pretty traumatic event, we didn't have enough of your blood to replenish what was lost, your body is having an acute reaction to the new type. I'll get you something for the pain."

"Wh-what does—what does that mean? Am I going to be okay?"

She smiled, "A test was administered to make sure nothing serious would affect your body, we still have to monitor you, for now it's a wait and see to how you're going to react, then we can act if anything comes."

The doctor administered a liquid through the IV tube, feeling the effects almost immediately, helping the scorch from the surgery diminish into a dull burn. Shortly after, another doctor in lighter scrubs entered, introducing himself.

"Hello Avie, I'm Dr. Fidler, your trauma surgeon. I gotta say, it's good to see you awake and coherent. It was very touch-and-go there."

She laughed weekly, her muscles protesting, "Am I going to be alright?"

Dr. Fidler gave her charts the once over, checking her stats and dressings, "I'd say so. The surgery was a success, your blood will replenish itself over time, we will monitor you just in case complications arise. I'm hopeful for a full recovery after some physical therapy training. You've got a Guardian Angel looking out for you, you were very lucky."

Smiling, she spoke weakly, "I've been told that, thank you, Dr. Fidler. Has anyone tried to visit me?" She was half worried Owen would try to show up.

The doctor with blue eyes piped up, "Nobody yet, but visiting hours are from nine until seven, family can stay longer under the exception of two or less persons. Do you have any family members you would like us to contact?"

"No, my family is… too far away. I might need rest, thank you, Doctor…?"

"Audrey Miller. Get some rest, Avie." With their closing, both doctors left her room, shutting the door on the way out.

Avie lay there, waiting for what felt like endless minutes wrapped in her own thoughts. She wasn't sure if she had the strength yet, or if it was wise to attempt to stand, but she wanted to slide open the window. The woman wanted to see if he was waiting, waiting for her, waiting on any news, even a note, that he could find her here. She would be distraught with worry if similar circumstances happened to Rhulle.

No, she couldn't risk trying to get up, but she could reach a telephone.

The baby blue plastic rang once, twice, finally getting an answer on the other line, "Front Office."

"Hello, I hate to be a bother, but is it possible to have my window opened for me for tonight?"

A crackled voice on the other side paused, "I'm sorry, but it's policy to have them closed and locked at night, especially with the weather."

"I understand, but could I at least have it opened just a little bit? I can't even move to cause any worry."

"I'm really sorry ma'am, but like I said it is still a hazard."

"Listen, I get you're just doing your job. But I need this. I was in a serious car accident coming into Blacken, and now my best friend shot me in my own home. All I am asking for is a little bit of fresh air with my shitty luck."

A brief silence hung in the air, before a sigh filled her ears, "Alright, but just a crack!"

The nurse came and opened it in a pinch, having it cracked just enough that anyone could pry it open further, if the rather inconceivable circumstance should arise.

"Anything else I can help with?"

"You have helped so much, thank you."

The redhead didn't know what she really expected. Maybe others had been able to open up their windows, but she imagined, maybe hers was open in comparison to the other closed ones—and maybe Rhulle could at least use it as a sign.

She wasn't even sure if he could get close to the building, all she wanted was to be with him, to have his comfort. Avie cried; Owen shot her… tried to kill her! Wanted her dead, for what reason, exactly? Because she was in love with Rhulle and not him? Because she wouldn't help him expose Rhulle? Because she was involved more heavily in the mystery with Rhulle than she was with Owen?

How were any of those reasons enough to take someone's life? Eventually she passed out again, her mind a cacophony.

Avie awoke early in the morning, finding Dr. Miller checking her dressings and temperature, sharing that she had visitors.

"They're here on your case. Are you feeling well enough?"

"Sure, yeah that's fine," she said, still drowsy.

Two men in dress suits entered, showing off their badges, "Miss. Conrad, I'm Detective Arcand, this is my partner Detective Cooper. We would like to ask you a few questions about what happened, are you able to do that at this time?"

His voice was raspy, low as though he was a smoker. The detective was on the short side, potbelly protruding with dark grey hair slicked back. His partner was younger in comparison, thinner and taller with a beauty mark drawing her eye to his olive cheekbone, long jet-black hair styled in a similar fashion.

Avie adjusted her bed, sitting up more proper to join the conversation, "Of course. If you're looking for a motive, I may not be much help; I've been wondering what exactly went through his head myself."

The men sat adjacent to her, pulling up the plastic chairs beside the bed, bringing out pens and paper. "You're saying you know who did this to you?"

"Yes I… I thought the police would have caught him." Confused, she thought they were here to clarify her side instead of getting an incident report.

"Hang on, can we record this?"

She nodded, watching them set up the small grey device on her bedside table between them.

"Avie Conrad, can you tell us who it was that broke into your home on the night of October twenty-six?"

"Owen Zagorski."

She watched as they scribbled down notes as well, "Is Owen Zagorski the man that shot you?"

"Yes."

"Was there intent to kill? Anything they may have said or done to indicate such?"

"Owen said that I was against him before shooting."

Detective Arcand nodded, not looking up from his notes, "Were you two in any sort of altercation beforehand?"

"Yes. He was upset with me; I told him the same night that I was seeing someone."

A wave of his writing hand, "Dating, in that sense?"

"Yes, right, that I was dating someone. I don't think that's why he decided to try to kill me. I don't think he's actually that well."

"Can you explain further, Avie?" The detective tapped the ball of his pen a few times onto the paper, dark eyes watery as they looked into her own.

"His attitude has changed since I first met him. Before I really became a resident, he was my first friend. We were trying to solve the mystery that's in the town, like why it scientifically affects people, you know? It was something fun for both of us to do regularly. The more we got into it, more questions came up. I think he got frustrated, losing a bit of himself, caught up in it more than reality. I told him that he was changing, but he didn't see it that way. Owen tried to spin it on me instead, saying I wasn't dedicated enough."

Detective Arcand wrote a few things down throughout; he paused after scrawling more after her explanation. "Did you find him aggressive during this time?"

She looked away. Taking a moment, she stopped herself, she wasn't his friend anymore, he made that very clear. "Yes."

"Can you give an example?"

Avie looked to her hands, "I felt very sick one night, it must have been about midnight when it was the worst. I was staying at his house, and he had the idea to look in the woods to try to find clues for the investigation we were doing. He dragged me out into the snow with him, I protested several times, asking him to take me back, but he kept going. He had a tight grip on my hand and wrist the whole time."

"And what about the creature in the woods?" Det. Cooper asked his first question, earning him a hard look from his partner.

She quirked her head, "Like, an animal?"

"Mr. Zagorski talked about a monster that hid in the woods, living in a manor. Stating it was the cause of people dying, and that you were its next target."

Avie laughed, wincing shortly after from the strain, "I'm sorry, that just sounds so bizarre. I haven't heard anything from Owen about that, we looked through the house and couldn't find anything besides remnants from squatters. There would be some sort of evidence of a person or something living there, right?"

The young man licked his lips, "Just covering all bases. Thank you."

"I'm worried about him if he's like this. I really am worried…"

The duo closed their notebooks, collecting the tape recorder, "Thank you, Miss. Conrad, you have been a big help. We wish you a speedy recovery." Handing her a business card, Detective Arcand tipped his hat, "In case you remember anything else."

She smiled while watching them head out.

Owen's future was uncertain, but then again, he didn't care about hers. She at least wanted him to have the opportunity to be assessed, if there was a sliver of hope of him coming back to himself in a clearer state of mind, then she could at least give him that last parting gift. But she couldn't be around him any longer.

Avie had given too many chances and look where it left her.

CHAPTER 21

"Keep going, Avie! You're doing great!"

Pushing her limits, Avie worked with a physical therapist as she stood and took a few tiny steps; her body building its strength back through the motions after such a trauma. They told her it was beneficial to be walking around to help in the avoidance of developing a clot from her surgery.

She kept pushing through the needle pinpricks of pain coursing through her, the sight of the ring Rhulle gave her filling her with strength as her hands gripped tightly. She did not want to be on an operating table ever again.

Clutching the cold metal bars with shaking hands, Dr. Miller stood beside her, Avie found the will to take five steps, exhaustion catching up to her as she collapsed into the seat provided by the therapist who also followed her movements. She was distraught, counting the single steps aloud to keep her mind occupied on something else, yet she couldn't even make it very far.

"That was fantastic, Miss. Conrad! Most patients can only make it to standing their first time, make sure you're not pushing too hard. Are you having any abnormal discomfort?"

The news enlightened her spirits, "It's. Good. I'm. Good," she panted hard from the exertion, needing her strength back as soon as possible, Rhulle was waiting for her. "I'm good to go again."

Within a week, Avie was able to walk the length of the hallway outside of her room. She grasped the cool gel of the four-legged walker, having it warm under her palms while shuffling along, the days in passing making every step easier.

In that time, she picked out a pair of large purple sunglasses and a feather boa from a box of props a nurse handed to her. Halloween approached in the first few days spent at the hospital, the staff trying to make it as enjoyable for everyone with candy and pieced together costumes anyone could wear while they trick or treat through the hallways.

A parent and his child were stopped just before her room, the latter of which swished a tail while shyly asking if she was trick or treating too. Not very many people were, nor were they able to participate, but the staff had a lot of candy to give away if they wanted to go to each section. Avie was invited into the duo, excited to go along and work up the strength with her walker for support. Each door of those who wanted to participate was marked off with a plastic bat or skeleton hanging from the nob, the small group knocked on the wood and was met with a man in a wheelchair.

"Trick or Treat!"

"Hello! Here is some candy for...?"

The kid beside her piped up, "I'm a lion," they said, brandishing their drawn-on whiskers and fuzzy cat ears.

"And I'm a farmer," the older gentleman tipped his straw hat.

"I'm a superstar!" She flicked the white feathers and posed for good measure, earning a giggle from the lion.

"Yes of course, a lion, farmer and superstar at my door, how exciting!" The man gave each a piece of candy, having the goodies hit with a clunk into the empty carriers.

The lion, farmer, and superstar ended up collecting a decent haul, trading off chocolates and sweet treats after the night ended with each other, able to stack up their own favourites.

"I didn't even get your names, I'm Avie."

"My name is Penny, thank you for coming with us, Avie! And thank you for trading with me," she said while scratching smudged whiskers.

The father shook her hand, "Lance. Thank you, it really does mean a lot that you joined us, Penny was self conscious about no one else being out," he spoke in a lower voice, the end of their conversation more private.

"I was glad to, this was a lot of fun. Don't eat too much candy, little lion, you'll be up all night!"

She smiled, revealing a large gap, "I won't! Only most of it!"

Making her way back to the room, Avie collapsed back onto the bed, tucking herself in for the night. She sighed, exhausted at walking for that long with only a few breaks between. Her head fell to the left, catching sight of her closed window.

Just as soon as rounds are done...

Within two weeks, she was walking without assistance.

Only the doctor and therapist there at her side, just in case. Yet there she was, walking! It may have been stiff, it may have been more of a shuffle, but she was mobile! She could have cried from excitement.

A little old lady came into her room, sitting down beside her bed with a warm hand reaching out to grasp hers. "Miss. Conrad, dear oh dear, I'm so sorry to hear what happened!"

"Mrs. Harris?" Avie started to shift to sit up properly, a man walking through the door just seconds behind, "And Gerald? What are you two doing here?"

He carried a bouquet with him, his face stern yet sad. "Hey, kid. Here to see how you're holding up. Sorry to hear about what you went through, figured you needed some time to recover before we could come in. These are for you."

Gerald handed over the flowers; purple freesia sprinkled through white lilies and even a few peonies decorated the gift, "These are beautiful, thank you! I'll have to ask a nurse for a vase. This is such a nice surprise, thank you both for coming to see me. Anything interesting happening?"

Vivian patted her hand, "Business is doing better, took a lot of the junk out of the store, it's a lot more open now. Even took some of your advice, put in a coffee maker and an old arcade game for the kids to and from school, they clear out the stock in just a few days, I have to order more and more!"

"That's amazing news," she replied, elated, "you have too many customers to handle by the sounds of it!"

"Speaking of, customers miss you. They send their condolences and hope to see you back."

The woman looked up at her boss, happy to hear the job she struggled with in the beginning became rewarding.

"C'mon, step aside, I gotta see my sugar!" The pair in front of her turned towards the new voice, opening a gap for Avie to see through.

"Sandy! Oh my stars, I'm so happy you came!" Setting the flowers off to the side, she opened her arms wide to receive Sandra's incoming hug.

"How are you feelin'? You got the whole town a buzzin'." They broke apart, Sandra taking the second seat, sitting beside Mrs. Harris while Gerald offered his seat and stood behind.

"I'm much better now. I had a pretty big scare for sure, I had to learn how to re-walk with a physical therapist and I am getting better every day."

"Aww shit, no kidding, sugar. But I was more worried 'bout how you were coping with... you know... *Owen?*"

Hearing his name caused her heart to twang sadly.

"Oh yeah, he was your little friend. If you ask me, he wasn't well in the head to do that to such a sweet girl." Vivian squeezed her hand.

"Right, yeah... If I'm honest, I'm not doing too well accepting what happened. I saw the signs of him changing, he started to act differently, but I thought it was something he would get over."

"Don't you blame yourself," Gerald threw in his two cents, "he wasn't that good of a person if he did this to you in the first place."

Light lashes blinked away a few tears, "Right, you're probably right."

She chatted with her visitors for a few hours, happy to have familiar faces fill her in with their lives and entertain her. Avie always seemed to collect a distraction when things got difficult.

Six days later, she was discharged.

Heart knocking in her chest, she left the hospital in warm clothing Sandy gifted her, stepping from bright fluorescent bulbs and the scent of sterilization into the overcast November with crisp air meeting her lungs. Avie inhaled deeply, shuddering on the release.

Finally, she was going to Rhulle. The desperation consumed her, coursing through every fiber of her being to reunite with him as she clutched her winter jacket, boots crunching in the pillowed snow.

The woman could walk, and she could walk well, but she couldn't walk the same as she did before. Taking frequent breaks on her trek past the treeline, the snow caused her to take larger steps, levels coming up to her calves in some areas. It took triple the time to finally trudge up to the manor, all circumstances working against her.

Lugging the heavy boots, Avie reached the front door, tripping and catching herself inside of the dwelling due to the change of environment. Lungs gasped for breath, her body combing through the sitting area, dining room and kitchen, wheezing slightly and breaking a sweat despite the cold weather. The house was cold, no signs of a fire for possibly *days*, and absolutely no Rhulle.

She gulped in air, steadying her breathing, tackling the stairs to try and locate him upstairs.

"Rhulle?! Where-wh-where are you?" She was in his room, borderline hysterical at not finding him yet. That was until he swooped down from the rafters, capturing her in a flurry of his arms and wings.

"*Avie*… Oh, darling, I thought you were the officers again," his voice shook, relief filling his tone.

"Rhulle, I'm so sorry, I wanted to see you so badly, I wanted to tell you what happened, but I… I just… I couldn't…" her voice broke, letting out the welling tears while her hand came to cover the distraught sounds.

How must have he felt this whole time in the unknown?

"Shh, it is alright, you are safe, you are alive. That is all that matters now. Oh, stars above, I could smell your blood, it was everywhere in that building. I have been so worried!"

"I'm okay, I'm okay, I'm okay…" She kept repeating the words, face buried in his chest as they sank to the floor, wrapped together in each other, Rhulle stroking her hair as she held on tightly. They were together in the assurance that they were both alright after everything, reunited once again after all the pain and worry.

They sat in the other's hold through endless minutes, each needing the contact.

"I-I am sorry, Avie. I held it off as long as I could, but I needed to feed while you were gone."

Her eyes opened at his words, turning up to face him, "I didn't even feel it... I have different blood running through my veins. There was nothing else that could have been done. But I... I *told* him, I told him this didn't need to happen again but he—!" The sentence dropped into a disgusted grunt.

"... This all happened because of Owen, correct?" his voice was dark.

"He-he's really gone, not even close to the same person I befriended. He tried to kill me that night," she felt Rhulle tense, his grip tight on her arm. Avie continued calmly, "The police were asking me questions, I told them what he did. He will be locked up in no time; punished for his crime."

"How are you not angry at him?"

"I had a lot of time to think about it, and I feel sad instead of anger. I keep thinking that there was something different I could have done, situations I should have handled better. If I kept my temper under control... Would it have even mattered? Or would it have happened regardless of what I did?"

"It should not have happened in the first place! He put you in the worst situation imaginable, it is amazing you survived. I was losing my mind thinking I may have lost you, not knowing if I would ever get that answer. And he gets to, what? Sit in a cell for a few years of his life?"

Rhulle was, understandably, pissed. Owen had been a constant annoyance with him and now he tried to do the unforgivable.

"Yes, he will, I'm sure of it, and it will be hell on him. But he may also get some help and reorganize his mind. Right now, he sees himself as doing nothing wrong, Owen may eventually come to terms with what he's done, how he's acted. His old self may resurface with that knowledge. That will weigh heavily on him, that knowledge in his clarity. That will be his true punishment."

Rhulle looked at her in a puzzling manner, looking to possibly understand her logic.

Avie explained further, "What if... How would you feel if you found out you tried to kill me when you weren't aware of your own actions?"

His eyes lowered, thinking over the example, "I would be devastated."

"Owen will have an awful long time to think about it. I think that's a suitable punishment."

"You still want what is best for him, even after what he did," Rhulle's voice was soft, contemplative over her reasoning.

"I don't want him to be lost anymore, but I still want justice."

He brought her hand to his face, kissing it, "You will, most certainly."

They talk over events of their time separated, over her surgery; lifting her shirt to show the bandages, two long gauze pads taped down over her stitches to aid in healing. She stated how the doctor found her very lucky—all things considered. Avie went on to explain the process of re-learning to stand and walk after the trauma, why it took so long for her to come to him.

"I wanted to come sooner, I gave it my all, pushing to walk as much as I could, trying to get better faster. I had no idea what you must have been going through."

"I tried to distract myself, with reading mostly. Most of the time, all I could do was sit in silence and stare at the hospital. There was a window that was always open at night. I half thought it may have been you, it gave me hope."

"That was! I'm sure of it. I wanted you to see it so badly, and maybe you would know it was me and that I was okay. I tried to look for you, every evening, all of the time—I hoped I could see you in the distance. I'm happy you at least noticed my small signal."

The police were brought up again, they were prodding around his house during the few weeks she spent in the hospital. Rhulle had the ability to see them coming, able to hide all of the items Avie brought over up inside the plaster of the roof before they reached his dwelling. Owen spoke of his existence to them, that was evident by the question Detective Cooper asked. But since they couldn't find any evidence of Rhulle, it further didn't look good for the blond's mental health.

"I trusted you with my life, and you have kept me secret all this time. Darling, I do not think I can let you be alone tonight."

"I can't be alone tonight, I need to be with you, I've missed you. I've missed you so much."

He ran his hands through her hair, cradling her close and enveloping her in his wings. Avie felt his chest stutter on an inhale, before crooning in a bittersweet warble, his heart strung words making her own chest ache at the emotion behind them.

"Stars above, oh how I have missed you."

They kissed, the first one in weeks.

She was encompassed in the comfort of Rhulle, even after they broke from kissing, they still stayed close to the others face, taking in all details, memorizing all features. She gently caressed the feathers at his jaw once more.

"*Delahara incu.*"

Rhulle let out a shaky breath at her words, having his eyes fall closed, "Say that again."

"*Delahara incu, Rhulle.*"

His forehead touched hers, his hand cusping the side of her face, "*Again.*"

"*Delahara incu, Delahara incu, Delahara incu, Delahara in—!*"

The woman was interrupted by his kiss, his emotions coming to the forefront, she could feel what he did though the connection. All of the pain, the fear, the relief. All of his desperation and love. Avie was sure he could feel hers too.

They were two lonely souls in need for the other, despite all odds coming together and finding comfort and love in the other half. Avie was all Rhulle wanted and needed, Rhulle was all Avie had been missing. The two lost and desolate had found a home in each other, intending to stay forever.

After this, nothing could separate them.

CHAPTER 22

An information was handled by Blacken police, keeping Owen in a temporary holding cell at the jail until court proceedings could be set up. Almost as soon as Avie gave the statement to detectives, the criminal complaint was placed and accepted for Owen Zagorski's arrest.

Due to the nature of Blacken being such a small town, people began to gossip about the circumstances. Everyone knew of the eccentric librarian who spent all of his time with a certain florist, but to attempt to kill her in cold blood within a few short months? Rumours spread over what happened that allowed such an event to take place.

"I heard they were secret lovers. She was carrying his baby that he didn't want, that's why she was shot in the stomach!"

"No, no, no, you're wrong! She had to have been having an affair with another man, getting pregnant with his child instead. Once he found out—boom!"

"There's no way, have you met them? He must have planned it ahead of time, he was in her apartment and everything!"

Everywhere Avie went, she was hounded about what the circumstances were.

She chose, however, to spend most of her time in her apartment, worried that a gossiper would follow her trudge to the woods where Rhulle resided. After the first initial days, her alarm clock heavily blared this night at three a.m., a time no one else would be awake—she awoke to set off to his place for some time while the hubbub had a chance to wear down.

The woman triple checked that no one else was watching her, looping around some neighbourhoods before making off to the woods, just to be safe.

The howling wind blew a crescendo against her frame, it kicked up snow to pelt against exposed skin and between poor stitching of a coral coat. Exhaustion loomed heavy in her eyelids, whispering temptations to turn back and head home, collapse into a warm bed and try again another time... She persisted anyway.

What had once been a standard twenty-minute walk, turned into an hour affair, leaving Avie frigid to the core, a biting numbness radiating her face with a low dull hiss of a headache beginning to form.

The door to the manor opened, revealing a confused and concerned truxen inside of its frame.

"Dear Avie, this is no weather for you to travel in! The fire is going, go sit in front of it at once."

"What are you doing awake, Rhulle?" She wore a smile as soon as he appeared, passing through the doorway while sidestepping him as she asked.

"I could ask the same, and even why you try to traverse in this catastrophe, you will catch a cold."

The wooden door was closed after them, having allowed a small amount of the winter inside, melting as the fire burned brightly in its grand case. She sighed at the warmth, feeling as though the frosty cage around her was melting too.

Doing exactly as he suggested, Avie sat before the blaze, sticking out her hands to warm the pink fingers, "Well that's simple; I missed you. I wasn't sure if I would be able to see you for another few days. I've always been a risk taker when it came to you," the woman smiled slyly, happy to hear he cared so much about her to fret over such a small thing in comparison.

Rhulle sighed through his nose, joining her on the floor beside the fireplace, "I suppose we were on the same wavelength; I had been worried about your absence, I was thinking about coming to see you too. I could not fall asleep until I knew you were alright."

"I think you should lay low for a little while," her head dropped to his shoulder, resting on the upper arm, "it may be a bit before you could come into town, people won't leave me alone."

"Why is that? Everything alright?"

She looked up into his face, "Owen has been arrested. People want to know what the circumstances were for him to do what he did."

"That is good for him to be held accountable, what will happen next with him? Why do the other humans need to know your business?"

Avie chuckled, "They're setting up a court date for him to be judged, I will have to explain my half, he will his, then a jury will decide what will happen with him. It may take a few weeks and it's a big deal for everyone in town, I suppose this has never happened before. People are not sure what to make of it or what even happened, so they make up scenarios on what they think could have occurred. Others need to know as soon as possible and try to get information to clarify. Either way, that's what the trial is for."

"It sounds confusing. Why do the humans feel the need to bother you personally if the information is coming?"

"It's just nature, I guess; the need to know. It's what drew me to find answers about the town, and about you. Some people just run a little harder with their curiosity."

Rhulle hummed in thought, "And Owen, he will not be able to interact with you again, correct?"

"I will only be able to see him in a courtroom full of other people, or behind protective glass in the prison if I needed to. He won't be able to be around me like he was… ever again."

The chestnut truxen lifted her, cradling her in his lap with a gentleness in his embrace.

"He still hurts you."

Avie realized she had started to cry; she wasn't exactly sure when—her focus was deep into the flickering flames as she spoke. But Rhulle was right. Wiping at the few streaks, she sniffed once.

"Nobody wants to lose their friend."

"Owen lingers in there no longer with his actions; he was not the one who tried to harm you. Just as your father was not a father to you, but a man who murdered Aubree. Owen was not *Owen*, but a man who tried to murder you that night."

Rhulle's words hit her, blindsiding her with their impact.

A whole new perspective arose from her as she digested the words, thinking over them again and again. No, Owen did not try to kill her; the sweet fun-loving character she grew attached to didn't pull the trigger on her. A madman did. The two were distinctly different and it finally clicked for Avie.

She wasn't remorseful for her father even though the man raised her, he was viewed only as his change into the abuser underneath. It made sense that Owen mirrored the same viewpoint now with his own change.

"*Oh my stars.* You're right. I-I-I don't know how I didn't see it before. Everyone said he was awful for what he did, but I could never see it. I only saw Owen as I knew him. But that wasn't him that shot me, not even close."

"You had the reasoning already there; you may have just needed the push to complete it. I hope it helps you to heal, you deserve it."

Laughing into the hiccup, a sense of relief washed through her with the revelation, poignancy hanging heavy in her chest. "I think it will."

They stayed there by the fire's breath, Rhulle became a comfort for Avie, and she to him. All she wanted to do was spend her time here in the manor, it was away from the stressors of everyday life, it was with Rhulle. All she wanted was to be with Rhulle.

It pained her that she had to live a life in town while he remained dwelling in secret. She couldn't just disappear and live with him in the decaying abode, yet the thought of having to be living separate from him bothered her. She knew the visits couldn't last forever, but what would come after? How could they keep together in secret away from everyone when Avie was just…?

A human.

They were connected, made for the other, there was no way the pair could be separated now that they came together.

"Rhulle, I've been thinking. Owen was talking about this hideout; I'm worried people will flock here after the trial. You would have to hide more often, that isn't fair to you. I'm so sorry, I've put you in an awful situation."

"That is a risk I took on when I chose to come here. The influx is just a speculation, it may not happen, but if it should then I have the whole forest to call home. This is not your doing, Avie. We will figure this out."

"I don't want to have you in hiding," she spoke, cradling a hand to her cheek, "I don't think you deserve to, you should have your own home, your own sanctuary that doesn't have to be intruded whenever someone stumbles upon it."

He was ruminating, pausing a beat after the words left her.

"Then… let us build our own home, far away from here. Inside the border of the forest. We could farm our own food, make our own clothes, be away from society. I was raised in a small colony; I have memorized books on gardening; I have the knowledge to provide us with everything we would need. But that would also mean you would give up the life you know."

Avie stared at him, the vision of them inside of a small log cabin floating to the surface of her mind. Just her and Rhulle living off the grid together without worry, without bother. Without everything she had ever known. She had no family, no attachments to the rest of the world, Rhulle was her only constant, the only one she needed to be with.

"I cannot live without you now, Avie. This was a life I thought I could never return to, I never dreamed of having the ability while I resided here on Earth. But now, with you, we can be together, *really* together. Living like true vovii do, I would be able to love you every day. I want to love you every day."

He held her hand to his face as he pleaded the case, speaking everything she desired. She couldn't live the same life she had regardless. If there was no Rhulle, the future seemed bleak and dull, he was the colour that whirled in her vision, the light that made her want to start each day. Avie fell in love with the creature in the woods, she was as much his as he was hers.

Living a life with him, to see him every day, to love him everyday in return—it was all she wanted, all she could think about. She ran with the thought to live together, instead of the alternative of days apart, conflictions constantly keeping them spaced out.

"All I want is you, all I ever wanted was you. I've never been attached to anywhere, but you are my heart, Rhulle, you are my home now. I would love nothing else but to live together. Let's *fucking* do it."

His face brightened, widening in surprise as if he expected she would say no. Upon hearing the affirmation, glee took over and he laughed softly with a smile; drinking in heavy breaths, tears falling down the pale face and landing into the pink palm.

"Avie, I-I, I thought my life was over. I was only existing until I met you. I n-never imagined I could be this fortunate, that I had a chance to f-fall in love, and live happily... You changed everything by stumbling into this place. I think I had been calling out for what I needed, I do not know how, but I was. I needed sustenance and I needed someone beside me, to teach me. And this world sent me you. You are all I need, dear Avie. I love you. I love you so much it hurts thinking I could have... I almost... I almost *never* had this."

Her heart panged in her chest, feeling the love he shared for her. Avie never had this before, never had anyone to love her as Rhulle did. She was certain this was new for him as well.

"I'm going to love you forever," she whispered, "I've never felt like this before, I can't get enough of you. We were meant to be, Rhulle, plain and simple. There's no doubt in my mind that this was all supposed to happen. From the moment we first spoke, it felt destined, I don't know how else to explain it. I just had to be idiotic enough to try to get to know you."

"Meant to be... That is a human term, akin to soulmates, correct? I never believed in it when I read about those things. We do not have that belief on Celisc, whatever happens is the result in your own work. But you? Everything that has transpired is too coincidental to just be results of action. I do not know what I did to deserve someone like you, but you were sent to me, supposed to come to me. All I can do is thank the stars above."

He led her in for a kiss they shared. Rhulle always was filled with beautiful words, he sung her praise when all she had done was get to know him, falling in love a sequential event to the connection they shared. He explained the stars and sky and colours unseen the same way he spoke of her, she never felt such love. She had never been able to reciprocate in verbatim until she felt the true love he expressed.

Avie loved him with every fiber of her being, and now she was able to begin a life with Rhulle.

She also took a moment to silently thank the stars.

After spending a few days with Rhulle, she returned in the evening to find Detective Arcand and Detective Cooper standing at her door. Seeing her coming to meet them at the residence, they smiled and called out a friendly greeting.

"Good evening, Miss. Conrad, forgive the lateness of the hour, but we have something important for you," Det. Arcand handed her the slip of paper, outlining her appearance in court and when to attend.

Her eyes flicked over the paper, reading the capitalized and bolded words, taking in the information presented for her there. It was straightforward and made perfect sense on what she was supposed to do, but Avie was in the dark about proceeding in a courtroom when she had been a victim.

"It's alright, the night is still young... I, umm, wow. I didn't realize the date would be so soon. I don't know what I'm really supposed to do."

"Just bring that with you, and any copies if you choose to make them. Dress nicely, you will have a victim's management personnel assigned to you before your first appearance. If you are uncomfortable being in the same room as the accused, make sure to bring that up with them and they can make arrangements before you testify," Det. Cooper said with a calm grace, as if recited hundreds of times.

It reassured her, she didn't mind being in the same room with Owen, that wasn't the problem. She was, however, worried she couldn't eloquently express her words in a way that made sense to the judge and jury.

"Right, thank you, detective. Anything else I should know?"

"Don't communicate any details with anyone until the trial has ended, you could be viewed as coming in contempt of court," the shorter of the pair spoke curtly, Avie imagined that must have happened quite a few times if he needed to drive the obvious point home.

"Of course. This all helps so much; I appreciate the time."

"Ma'am," Cooper tipped his hat, following his partner as they left the apartment's hallway.

⊶∞⊷

The redhead sat on the hard-metallic chair, facing the ballistic glass with the empty seat on the other side.

Calmly, she waited, finding the security guard's stare, smiling awkwardly to him. The bright lights in the bleak room turned the atmosphere green with the hue it presented. It mimicked Avie's twisted stomach, full of nerves and making her queasy with trepidation.

She was here just for one purpose: to be sure. Just to be sure that Owen was no longer Owen, that she no longer needed to harbour intense guilt over his actions that did not come from the same person met those few months ago. Avie had to be sure.

The man she waited for dropped into his own seat across her, dark eyes filled with suppressed rage while he demanded all of her attention. Her eyes flicked over to the two-way phone, picking it up and awaiting him to mimic the action.

He looked, to put it quite simply, terrible. His usual dishevelled appearance increased tenfold, Owen appeared to have lost weight despite his already small size, it may have been the lighting, but his skin looked colourless, gaunt, drowned out by dark shadows swallowing his once bright blue stare.

Picking up his own phone with a huff, his shackled hands clinked on the countertop through the receiver.

"*Why are you here?*" Owen's voice was rough, short and ragged. He truly was a shell of his former self in this instance.

"Court date is set for December fourth, I haven't seen you since the night you shot me, I figured you might have some remorse for your actions. I wanted to know why you did it."

"You'll get to hear all about everything in court, I'm *sure*. Are you even allowed to be here?"

"It's highly ill advised, but I was hoping something of the real you still remained, that you may be in there, somewhere. You were once my friend, after all."

He scoffed, rolling his eyes, "That was over the moment you chose *him* over me. Are you going to tell them about your little secret? Hmm? About how I was the only one brave enough to step up and do something? First you, then *it*."

"You left something in my apartment after you shot me, I don't think you would have made it very far with whatever you wanted to do. Besides, I never chose anyone over the other."

He breathed heavily, "*Liar*."

Avie was not sure what he meant, exactly. Owen in this state was a different person with different thought processes and she couldn't read what he was thinking. She opened her mouth and began asking to clarify.

"I brought you to him with the team we built! You should be dead! He took everyone else, but not you. Why not you? Because you *loved* him? I could tell you loved me first. He stole you away, he deserves to be killed just for that. You can't protect him, Avie. You can't protect your *disgusting* relationship; everyone will hear about him. Everyone will know soon enough."

He still clung onto the concept that he was able to have possession over her, that she was brainwashed into accepting Rhulle as her lover instead of him. His words had been slightly different, it hung in her head as though he was almost angry at himself for being the initial person to guide her into officially meeting the truxen. As if he was to blame for all of it, despite her own choices and his disdain towards them. Was she reading too much into it?

Hearing him talk like this always got a rise out of her, the calm level-headed Owen usually handled facts and evidence. This new rash and hostile man no longer held her sympathies, temper or emotions.

Avie was in control of herself for the first time.

"I miss you, you know? You were my confidant; someone I could always come to and trust. I've never had that before in the twenty-six years lived until coming here and meeting you. I thought we would see everything through together until old age, and I did love you, just not in a romantic way. You were my family, something I never got to experience. And now, I can't even get an apology from you. I wanted to thank you, Owen, thank you for the best few months of my life, but also the worst. Thank you for clearing this up. I will see you in December."

The woman hung up the phone, turning to get up and walk out of the visiting room. She heard him shout something behind her, but she didn't look back. There was no more looking back at Owen. He was gone. Someone else entirely was taking his space, and she would only move forward.

CHAPTER 23

The floral top was no good, it bunched up in an awkward way, making Avie's figure look lumpy instead of professional. Smoothing out the fabric, she turned and observed herself in the mirror, trying to find a way to make it work, with little success. She huffed, annoyed, shedding the material before raiding her closet yet again.

"Damn it. What the hell am I supposed to wear now?"

She had been planning this outfit in her mind, having it play out much differently than how it actually looked put together. The woman didn't own dress pants, and only owned a few skirts that could pass as business—apparently, they didn't pair well with most of her other casual wear. Avie didn't think twice about planning a back up.

December snuck up on her, too busy spending her time in the manor with Rhulle, making plans for when spring weather would come, shining sun and green grass becoming a deep yearning while the wind and snow persisted outside.

Her attendance was in an hour, nerves taking the form of indecisiveness over attire.

Grunting, she stomped over to her phone, dialing the memorized number and listening to it ring once, then twice, three times... "Come the *fuck* on," Avie muttered.

"Hello?"

"Sandy, I've got to be at the courthouse in an hour and I am freaking the fuck out! Do you have a nice blazer or something I can borrow?"

"Sugar? Oh of course! Take some deep breaths and I'll be there asap!"
Thank the stars for Sandra.

She hung up, causing Avie to do the same while she started to pace, breathing deeply to calm her nerves with mixed results. Rationally, it had only been ten minutes until the knock came on the door, but it felt much, *much*, longer. She still hesitantly peeked through the spy hole, examining only Sandra on the other side.

"Okay, so, I can't even think straight, do you think just a white tee underneath? And I should have it open... No maybe closed," the redhead spoke in rapid succession while opening to let Sandra inside, she was met by a funny expression on the other's face.

"Sugar, you must be more frazzled than I thought. Talk it out a bit, you got time."

"What do you mean? I have no sense of business wear, you have more experience than I do," she was exasperated. Closing the door behind them, the woman looked down to see that she had forgotten to put a shirt on, a black bra making itself known.

Avie sputtered before laughing, "I'm sorry, what a sight I must be!"

The older of the two set the plastic covered grey suit down on the couch, coming over to place hands on shoulders, "You're alright, s'the nerves. Talk what you're feelin' out, it'll help."

The young woman swept the beading sweat from her brow, giggling in a nervous fashion, "I-It's just-I have-I-I..." She breathed, steeling herself, "What if I can't convey my experience properly? What if they don't have the evidence to convict? What if he doesn't get the help he needs?"

Sandra smiled, "You gotta do the best ya can and let them figure it out. The whole situation isn't cut and dry and there's a lotta gaps that you and the other witnesses will help draw together. Just tell the truth, speak from the heart, you're always amazing at communicatin'. People stop to listen to you, you have an ability to make them pay attention and they will hang on your every word while they draw a verdict," the brunette reassuringly stated, helping to calm Avie's hyper state.

It all soothed her, giving her strength. Shaking out her hands and legs, she released some of the energy, "Thank you, Sandy. I'll remember that when it's my turn, I should- I should really get dressed!"

The pencil skirt she bore was grey, pairing perfectly with the dark blazer Sandra provided for her. After talking out her concerns, she found herself to look professional and ready for court as she sighed with relief at her friend's words.

"Sandy, I can't thank you enough, I would have been a wreck the entire trial."

"Glad I could help, sugar. It will all be done soon with your testimony, I'm sure! You got this." Her enthusiasm helped pump up the redhead for the inevitable court arrival ticking away.

Smiling, she styled her hair back with a clip to keep out of her face as she studied the final look. Her ring caught her eye, feeling butterflies unfold throughout her as Rhulle filled her thoughts. She half wanted to take it off for the trial, thinking it would be brought up, Owen possibly reacting from the information.

She thought better, her ring gave her strength, drawing it from inside herself when she needed.

"You're gonna have to explain yourself!" Avie turned, seeing the brunette gesturing towards her ring. She brought her hand up to silently ask if the object was what she was referring to. "*Yeah*, the ring, silly! How long has that absolute rock been on your finger?"

She lifted her eyebrows, pulling an apprehension laced face while she twirled the band around, "Well, uhh, I received it the same night I was shot."

Sandy's face practically paled, "*No!* Aww sugar, I'm sorry, I was just thinkin' I didn't even notice it all this time and last thing you need is me pesterin' you about that night... Well, let's not talk 'bout it, you can explain this mystery man and why I haven't met him later. Right now, you gotta get going, I'll drive ya."

Being ushered out the door and hopping into the truck, Avie stared back down to her gold band while being transported through the streets, a sigh escaping her as she longed to be with him instead.

"You're in love with him, aren't ya?"

Her head snapped up, catching Sandy's brown side eyes and knowing smile, "I've never felt this way about anyone, I think he's the same way. I've been in love with him for a while now."

"You gonna tell me his name? I've met 'most everyone in town, I want to see which one took your heart away."

The woman smiled, "He isn't in town, I have to go and visit him, or he comes to me."

"Damn. That's rough, sugar. It must be tough having to leave and deal with the oddity that happens ta people like you."

Avie almost forgot about people essentially needing to stay in town. The vibrations plagued her even throughout her stay, wracked her body as she worked tirelessly to find the answer. She remembered what her first information source had said some time ago; about people experiencing the same feeling once they left Blacken for a period, always bringing them back in due time. She wondered how those individuals were affected now when Rhulle no longer needed to continuously call people to Blacken.

"I haven't felt the—uhh—*phenomenon* any time I have left. Then again, I'm only gone a few days, so it might take longer. Who really knows?"

"If anyone could figure this stuff out, I thought it would be you. I don't really know much about it, never bothered 'cause it sounded so made up. But how could people with no contact with each other all feel the same pressurized *'travel incentive'*? And why to our town?"

"I think I got a few answers," she laughed, "nothing interesting to warrant an end to the mystery."

"I don't know, been a bit since I've heard 'bout anyone skippin' town, you may have done more than you're lettin' on."

A shoulder shrugged, nonchalant, "I would love to know what I did then, this whole thing was only a passion project."

Sandra laughed, herself chiming in while they parked in front of the courthouse. It was small, like everything in town, only expanding outwards in a long shape with maybe two levels in all. Avie's stomach tied in knots while she sat before its intimidating form.

If she could stand before an unknown creature of the night, she could do this easy.

"Once you're done, I need to hear all 'bout mystery man. You still haven't told me his name, so I expect that at least. Call me when you're done, I'll pick you up." Avie huffed out a long breath while the brunette patted her back, "You got this, sugar. Startin' is the hardest, you just have to start."

She nodded, determination lighting behind her eyes as she gained confidence through Sandra.

The woman stood outside of the blue truck, drinking in the building that seemed bigger than it was, waving a small goodbye to the driver before walking up to the double doors—boots clacking on pavement and a purse clutched in sweaty palms.

"Just have to start," her mind repeated while opening the heavy door, walking in with her head held high.

Dappled grey stone made up a majority of the elegant hallways and flooring, gold intricacies laced throughout the stone and pillars as she walked through the professional building.

Despite the modern outside, inside of the courthouse styled a Romanesque fashion, older and more delicate areas showcasing its old age as it more than likely had been up and running with expansions added for numerous decades. Many arches and pillars lined the space where Avie walked, going through examinations and being directed to the courtroom.

The dark wooden doors opened, and she strode inside, placing a seat beside her victim service personnel.

She only met the man once before, introducing himself as Todd Harper with a firm handshake and soft chocolate brown eyes the night after she received the subpoena. His beard speckled russet and red while his long hair was sandy blond, clutches of freckles marked his tanned skin in a similar fashion to her own.

Todd smiled, flashing overlapping teeth as he ushered her to the reserved seat.

"There's a chance they won't call you up to the stand today, but still prepare to, just in case," Todd whispered as he leaned over, "you doing alright, Avie?"

"A little nervous, but I'm ready."

They nodded in response.

Owen had been brought in, adorning the bleak jumpsuit and hand-cuffs, his cerulean eyes finding hers immediately, as if waiting for her, seeking her and only her in the sea of people; watching only as he passed through the aisle before biting his cheek with gaze returning to the forefront.

Avie felt her heart squirm in her chest, unsure why she felt so appre-hensive upon seeing him. Chalking it up to the fact both of them would be the only true dancers in this turn, one of them would plead a case greatly compelling the other's life. She was absolutely sure he would bring up Rhulle, or the strange circumstances with her blood or others who per-ished in the unfortunate circumstances.

Could she protect the location and identity of her love in the court of law? Moreover, how would everyone take to what could be outlandish stories wove by a man driven mad by a conspiracy?

He was escorted to the defence table at the head of the room, sitting heavily beside his lawyer dressed in a fancy cranberry suit.

"All rise for Honourable Judge Neish," the court clerk's voice bellowed, catching Avie's attention from Owen in front of her, rising as the room did while the judge entered in black robes.

The material swished as he stepped behind the bench, sitting while inspecting the papers resting there. Judge Neish must have been in his seventies if she had to guess, wispy white hair combed over to one side with half-moon glasses perched precariously over the edge of his wide nose.

"The court recognizes the case of R v. Owen Zagorski. The public may be seated."

To her surprise, he spoke with strength, a smooth and confident voice that came only with decades of experience flowed from him as he spoke to the room. He commanded the authority with no questions asked.

"Court is now in session; Crown counsel please proceed with the prosecution."

Graceful in her movements, the Crown counsel rose and paced at the front of the room, long robes giving the appearance of gliding over the floor instead. "At this time, I will direct the witnesses to their allocated rooms before the trial is to begin."

Avie did just so, Todd leading beside her as they were escorted with a few other familiar faces. In a small side room close by, they filed in, taking seats in awkward chairs. She caught a glimpse of Owen sneaking a look at her as she left.

She had no idea what he was thinking, but she knew it was full of spite. After all, she survived his murder attempt and was about to testify against him, maybe he felt like she owed him not to—as if he didn't act out the most heinous crime towards her.

Inside of the room, they were instructed to wait until they were called, and to not discuss amongst each other details of their accounts or the case. The bailiff stood powerful at the door to watch over them, giving them freedom to watch television so long as it was not news or information stations. Avie made eye contact with a few of the other witnesses, recognizing her neighbour, her operating surgeon and even the detective that she had dealt with a few times in the case. There were also a few faces she did not recognize, more than likely there to go over evidence and testify on Owen's behalf.

Time crawled by as they all discussed pleasantries, deciding to put on a movie after seeing what was available on various programs. It was mostly background noise as all simply sat in anticipation for their own turn. It was even worse than being alone, to have people here and not discuss what they were all here to do.

She fidgeted, watching a scene take place that had something to do with Christmas, her leg bouncing. Det. Arcand left for his testimony, it felt like hours had gone by in his absence. Her chin jutted into her hand as she leaned over the dark table, she wanted to get this all over with, yet this could be how she spent her time for who knew how long?

He returned eventually only to have her neighbour leave shortly after for his turn. One by one they were going up, seemingly leaving herself for last. It was an agonizingly slow process, made worse by the fact that she couldn't even know what was going on. She wished it was possible for her to sit in front of the bar and watch the trial go down, it would be leagues better than sitting here in morbid curiosity.

The woman pondered about what Owen would say, how he could spin the situation into his favor. If she was him, she would try to make it seem like self defence, probably his only bet. Although it didn't translate well in her imagination, he was something the lines of six feet tall, she could hardly stand toe to toe with him.

And what of Rhulle?

Would Owen bring him up at all? Was that ill advised by his defence lawyer, or would it again be warped into having to do with herself instead? How would the mystery they worked on be discussed as it laced intricately with Rhulle?

She felt sick with boredom, conjuring up a hyperactive mind.

<hr />

"Ladies and gentlemen, I would like to open with a thank you for attending today. This has been quite a movement in Blacken's small community; the first of its kind in generations. A person had attempted to kill, to take the life of another, for an unknown reason. I would like to outline the defendant, the only suspect in this case, as that very perpetrator. Owen Zagorski is a man who was found fleeing the scene, his name is registered on the attempted murder weapon, and attached very closely to the victim. I implore you to carefully consider all evidence in your judgement."

The dark-haired woman smiled, flipping her loose curl strands in an almost exaggerated manner. It annoyed Owen, finding that she kept repeating the action even in early trial. It was distracting for him to watch; she should have just worn it back...

"My first witness I'd like to call can help us put some pieces together with what happened. I'm calling Santi Arcand to the stand."

In a matter of moments, the man who had toyed with Owen in his interrogation waddled in, the blond side-scowled, readjusting in his seat.

The short man was sworn in, settling down into the bench.

Crown counsel started up again, "Mr. Arcand, can you state your occupation for the record?"

He leaned forward, "I'm a detective for Blacken's police department."

"Were you involved with the defendant in any way?"

"I handled his booking and filed the information on him."

She talked to the detective as her body opened to allow the collected jury to easily see their interaction, hands moving greatly with her speech in inflated motions.

"Were you ever at the crime scene on the night of October twenty-sixth?"

"I was. Called in shortly after midnight and arrived about a quarter after then."

She nodded, approvingly, "Since you were involved, could you identify the weapon found at the scene of the crime?"

He chuckled, "Sure can. A Taurus Judge, silver, dark grey handle."

The Crown counsel woman brought forth evidence collected during the case, starting with the most critical piece that tied Avie and himself together as a crime.

She showcased the item and spoke high and mighty, "Ladies and gentlemen of the jury, I present to you Exhibit A: The revolver used on the night of the crime. The same handgun registered to Owen Zagorski, purchased in the time that he got to know the victim."

Passing around accumulated papers, the Crown described them as matching fingerprint documents and ownership records of the piece, "Now, the evidence presented here is pretty cut and dry, it very simply connects the defendant being in possession of this revolver. Detective, you said you were the one who booked the defendant, correct?"

"Yes, I was."

"How much time passed between the crime and the detainment that night?"

His face pulled down while pursing his lips, "I would have to wager about an hour, an hour and a half."

"I would like to ask, did Mr. Zagorski appear in pain or with any markings on himself at the time?"

He shook his head, "No, the kid had clearer skin than he does now. Nothin' mentioned during the interview neither."

She turned back, giving the jury all of her attention, "I'd like to show evidence, mug shots taken at the police station mere hours after the attack." Her confident stride presented the shots, showing the clear-cut V-neck blue tee shirt, showing off his neck and dipping enough to glance at the beginning of a chest.

"Detective, if two people are mixed up in a fight, what happens when someone is hit so brutally by an attacker?"

"Broken skin, broken bones, swelling, discolouration, bruising… depends on the severity."

"And how long does it take for any of those to show up after an attack?

"Usually? Immediately."

"What is missing on the defendant in this photograph?"

"All of the above."

Owen saw her smirk at the information presented by the detective, she was covering her ass for his own inevitable testimony. "Upon processing the defendant, he gave a statement to you, could you let us know what was said with the documents you have?"

Det. Arcand spoke about Owen being in a trance-like state, most likely due to the disturbance experienced. The Crown played the recorded interview, listening to his own confession played back for him. He only opened up about what happened once he believed Avie had died in the hospital. He explained about needing to protect her, from herself, that she wasn't thinking right or the same way she had been. Admitting, finally, to firing the very same handgun presented as evidence, but not the circumstances around that night.

"Thank you for your time, detective."

The trial went on, the prosecution called upon one of Avie's neighbors to testify as well. The older gentleman Owen only met in passing instructed to be called Buddy. Buddy was asked about the same night of the shooting, testifying that the only raised noise levels had been the blond at her door pounding for several minutes and shouting through the barrier. That, and the gun shot a few hours later.

His well-suited attorney asked permission to cross examine the neighbor, claiming the fact that Buddy had hearing aids, asking if they were turned down at the time.

"The man was making such a ruckus; I did turn them down for a short period."

"Could it have been possible that in that time, if Miss. Conrad and the defendant were both aggressive, a struggle could have been muted to you?"

"I… I guess it is possible."

Owen smirked behind his hand.

Afterwards, a Dr. Fidler was called to the bench. The pictures were presented at his testimony of Avie's torso that had been cut open, showing off the damage done by the bullet. Even the bullet itself was brought up, matching the gun record.

Dr. Fidler talked about the state his patient had been in on arrival, how tricky the surgery was with her extremely rare blood and how no other injuries were found on her person. The questioning woman asked about attack injuries once again.

"Typically," he went on to explain, "even an assailant would receive marks on their body from a defender. Things like imprints on the wrist from being held back, or a push or kick imprint on the skin if they were forced away."

"And you can confirm that the victim didn't arrive with or show any signs of those developing in their time at the hospital?"

"None. It would have raised concern from any of the doctors or nurses attending."

The Crown dismissed him as well after a few more technical questions, thanking him for his time while she turned her head to the jury, dark waves of hair tossing around in that annoying superior motion.

"From the information we gathered here, there casts reasonable suspicion on Mr. Zagorski. Only one other person had been there that night who can tell us their side of the story. The very person who, by all odds against them, survived a gunshot at close range. I would like to call to the stand, Avie Conrad."

"Avie Conrad, you are being called upon for your testimony, please come this way."

She sat up straighter, a chill running through her body, causing her to forcibly shiver. This was it. She felt as though she could throw up at any second, public speaking never being her forte. Still she made her way to the bench, the world around her feeling as though it moved in a slow-motion fluidity.

Finally reaching the podium, she heard the distorted voice of the bailiff recite the vow for her to plead to, the world coming in as a sharp focus as soon as his words finished.

"Avie Conrad, do you swear to tell the truth, the whole truth, and nothing but the truth—so help you God?"

"I swear."

The woman sat, staring at the Crown prosecutor with her raven hair and bright chartreuse eyes staring back. Here she was at last. All the apprehension building up for her testimony and here she sat, awaiting to start it.

It was time to tell them what happened that night.

CHAPTER 24

Miss. Conrad, could you tell us the date of the incident that took place?"

Avie had the whole courtroom's attention. She tried to keep her stare on the questioning woman in front of her as best as she could, the temptations of looking over the audience tickled at her sightlines, yet they remained fixed instead on the Crown counsel dressed in black.

"It was October twenty-sixth."

"That date is significant in another way, was it not your birthday too?"

She nodded, "Yes it was."

The Crown began to stride across the room, asking questions to her at the stand, but also gauging the jury's reactions as the testimony took place.

"How old are you now?"

"I am twenty-seven years old."

"Very exciting, birthdays. Especially for a young lady like you, you must have had big plans, with someone special?"

"I did, yes. I had gone out to dinner with my boyfriend."

"And this boyfriend, is he in the room today?"

Avie easily shook her head, "No, he isn't."

"Miss. Conrad, did the defendant ever know about this relationship you had?"

"Yes. The both of them actually met a few times, unfortunately, they didn't get along." The redhead laced her fingers, holding them in her lap, hoping it would help their shaking.

The prosecutor held her hands steepled in front of her chin, "Did the defendant ever treat you differently upon learning of your relationship?"

"He was very upset, trying to intervene and declaring his own feelings. Owen said it wasn't right, that I was with someone else. Like he was entitled to me."

Her brow furled, "Could you explain, please?"

She drew a deep breath, looking down at her ring before addressing her once more, "Two days before the incident, Owen didn't know of my relationship. We were all together and he quickly put two and two together. Owen pulled me aside and said that I was supposed to be his instead, he crossed a line and forcefully kissed me. I was mad at his actions and attitude, and I told him to leave, which he did."

"And did Mr. Zagorski try to contact you before the night of the event?"

"No. I tried to initiate contact in the afternoon of the next day, I was hoping it was an out of character moment, I've never seen him act so aggressively before. I stopped by his house, hoping for an apology. All I got was a person who couldn't accept the fact that I wouldn't be with him romantically. He accused me of being tricked into thinking I was in love with someone else. The logic just didn't make any sense and I thought for sure he was not himself."

"How do you mean 'not himself', Miss. Conrad?"

"Owen started to act a little differently for a few weeks prior, as though he was so wrapped up into the little amateur case study we were doing, that he couldn't focus on anything else. And then with the addition of my relationship, he came undone—a shell of the former man who was initially sweet and kind, turned bitter and accusatory. As I see him now, he's not even the same person anymore."

"This is the same attitude you had during the defendant's visit on the night of the incident?"

"Yes, it was."

Avie couldn't help it, she looked over, just for a flash of a second, to see Owen and his sour look. He couldn't be bothered to even look at her.

She went on to explain what transpired that night; how she had entered back through her bedroom window after sneaking out, having no idea if Owen still lingered outside of her door. Only to leave her bedroom to find that he broke in, standing on the other side with his gun drawn and pointed to her. Absolutely no provocation.

"Thank you, Miss. Conrad, that is all—"

"Permission to cross examine, Your Honour?" Owen's lawyer piped up, catching the attention of everyone, causing her to slightly squirm with concern.

"Granted, go head."

The Crown counsel returned to her seat as the man in the bright suit waltzed up the bench. His dark skin made his attire look chic instead of tacky. Fixing his tie, he leaned a nonchalant elbow onto the stand in front of her. He reminded her of one of those slick 1920's gentlemen with a no-nonsense attitude and dapper sense of style.

"Miss. Conrad... your father's name was Harvey Conrad, right?"

Her blood drew cold at the name.

"Yes, that's right," she spoke slowly. Where was he going with this?

He laughed once out his nose, "Quite the character, wasn't he? Murdered your sister in cold blood and is still serving time across the country, isn't that correct?"

"Yes..."

"Do you have a history of violence, Avie?"

"No! My father is unwell, that doesn't mean I am the same."

"Right, right... What about your late sister Aubree, she had some mental deficiencies, didn't she?"

Avie paused, she wasn't sure where this man was going bringing up her family, what could it possibly help serve?

"She did, Aubree was mentally at the age of two-years-old, even into her teens."

"And could it be possible that you suffer from some undiagnosed mental health issues too?"

"Objection, Your Honour! More prejudicial than probative," the Crown jumped up, voice projecting.

Judge Neish nodded, "Sustained, defence is allowed to rephrase their argument."

He rolled his bright shoulders, looking back at her, "Miss. Conrad, your sister had a lot of development issues, were you diagnosed with anything as well?"

She shook her head, "No, Aubree was born that way. Once my parents saw how she was struggling at birth, they worried for my overall well-being too and took me in to see how I was developing. I have a clean bill of health."

"So did Harvey until he reached his forties. He became very aggressive towards his immediate family, especially to Aubree with no provocation and it only increased as his alcohol addiction peaked. Now the apple doesn't fall far from the tree, you're almost in your thirties and haven't been examined by a professional since childhood. Can you be sure you are not showing the same signs as your father did? Lashing out at my client the same way he did to your sister?"

"Objection—!"

"I want to answer the question," Avie spoke up, looking up towards Judge Neish, who hesitantly waved at her to go ahead, the redhead leaning forward in her seat.

"I am nothing like my father. The man you represent is the one in the same boat as Harvey Conrad; I have been the one to see their actions, their attitudes, their mental state slip in very much the same way. I can assure you; I am not the one who needs professional help, I am not the one who tried to take a life," her tone was low and calm, getting her point across with poise at the lawyer trying to intimidate an emotional response from her.

"Did you have anything to drink that night?"

The question caught her off guard, ready to answer more loaded ones about her family, "I, well, yes. I had a glass of red wine at dinner."

"Could it have clouded your memory of the evening?"

Shit... this couldn't be good. "No, I remember the night crystal clear."

"This is a woman who came into town with no attachments, no friends, disowned by family. She had nothing left to lose, that level of isolation must take its toll on the psyche. She admitted to drinking that evening, leading to a reasonable connection with alcohol fueled irrational behaviour and clouded interpretations of events. I ask the jury; which is more believable? A woman with a family history of neglect, alcoholism and violence, running from her past and attacking someone close to her—or a man completely unprovoked shooting in cold blood? Thank you."

Judge Neish called for a recess, allowing people to stretch and use the washroom if needed. Avie stood immediately, making her way to the door, Todd following her at a rushed pace.

"Are you alright? Do you need some water?"

She was fighting back frustrated tears, a lump in her throat as she hiccupped out a response, "I j-just need the bathroom."

Pushing open the swinging door, she hovered over the sink, sobbing out heavy breaths while allowing a few droplets to fall. She wiped at them with the back of her hand, staring at her reflection. The woman was terrified she would look differently. Not once did the thought occur of being compared to her father—where he always was intimidating and cruel, she always tried to be kind and patient, never wanting to be anything like him. Even though bits of her temper flared and slipped through the cracks, she still tried.

There she was, staring back, the same Avie she had seen all her life. Not Harvey. She placed a palm on the mirror, solidifying that it was still her, that she was still the same person.

Even her mother growing up had been aloof, never being present in her years. Avie didn't have very many memories of her, Cecilia seemingly blending into the wallpaper throughout her life—constantly under the same stressors of having to take care of Aubree, muddling through on autopilot. It was never Aubree's fault that they had shown their true colours. They were never ready to be parents, having Avie and then Aubree a few years later with a whole slew of added on responsibilities made them resent their own children.

Avie only wished it never turned out the way it did.

"I hate to intrude," Todd knocked, peeking his head into the women's bathroom, "but when I'm upset, I have hot chocolate, I brought you some if you need to decompress."

She laughed once, sniffing and wiping away streaking makeup, "I'd love that, thank you, Todd. I just needed a moment to clear my head."

"You were very brave back there," he handed the Styrofoam cup to her as they exited the doorway, "you did perfect and left the room still very composed; rushed, but composed."

Sipping at the drink, it scalded her tongue slightly from the burning temperature, "I did? I was worried I messed up by answering that question."

"I don't think he was expecting that, he had to scramble at your answer. We should get back to the courtroom, the break is almost over."

They returned to their original seats, sitting in front of the bar as people began to file back into the room. She didn't know if Owen left at all, he still remained at the table, cautiously turning around to look back at her. For a moment, she could almost see a glimmer of the other Owen in his eyes. They were soft and apologetic, maybe even sympathetic at hearing her testimony involving her family.

She wondered if she even made an impact at all.

⸺⸙⸺

On the second day of the trial, Owen was finally called to the stand.

The blond gained a quick nod from his lawyer standing at the bench before he stood up and shambled over to testify. Handcuffs clenching around his wrists were released but the ones securing ankles remained. He rubbed at the carpal joint where metal chafed, the warm skin meeting his cold fingertips, placing it on top of a bible once it was presented by the bailiff, raising the other for his vow.

"Do you swear to tell the truth, the whole truth, and nothing but the truth, so help you God?"

"I swear." He sat in the rigid seat.

His attorney approached, a smooth fluidity with his stride, "Mr. Zagorski, you were born June fifteenth, 1970, is that correct?"

"Yes."

"Have you been in Blacken your whole life?"

"Yes."

"Good, Mr. Zagorski, could you state your occupation for the record?" He leaned over on bent elbow, asking easy questions for him to start out with.

"I was a librarian for Blacken Public Library."

"Thank you. Now was that also when you first met the victim, Avie Conrad?"

What the hell did that have to do with anything? A first meeting couldn't have anything to do with the correlation, and he didn't remember discussing this with him at all.

"That's correct."

"Can you explain in your own words how the first meeting went?"

He adjusted in his seat, talking over the first meeting, finding her at the front desk shaking and cold, still bruised and bandaged from her car accident. They bonded over the mystery; Owen explained how Avie interjected herself into the picture that was originally his private project.

"Sounds like the two of you got on pretty well initially. Would you have considered her as a friend at that moment?"

"I did."

"What about when you bought the Taurus Judge revolver six weeks later?"

"Avie was my friend then too."

"What, exactly, did you purchase the gun for, Mr. Zagorski?"

"Protection..." He sighed deeply before continuing, "I bought it because I had a feeling that whatever Avie and I were working on at the time, was linked to someone hostile and living outside of the town in the woods."

"How do you mean working on, and someone in the woods?"

"Both her and I were working on what causes people to come into town since she was one of them. Avie Conrad went out into the forest alone one night, she was chased out by someone, I thought they may have wanted to harm her in some way, and by extension me. I also thought at the time the two instances were connected."

"At any point, did the victim know you had the firearm?"

"Yes."

"Did the mysterious person ever make themselves known to yourself, or only to the victim?"

"Just the victim."

He followed his rehearsed script to the letter, changing the narrative. Hopefully, it could get him off scot free, it certainly painted Avie in a bad light, that's all he cared about.

Mr. Gabriele hummed thoughtfully, "That never struck you as odd?"

"It did, that's when I really started to notice her change in behaviour. I asked her the next day about it, but she relented that she was unable to even see what they looked like. I knew she was hiding something from me, but I didn't push."

"Did you have any altering opinions of the victim before the night of October twenty-sixth?"

"I fell in love with her. But the more time I spent with her, the more I realized she was acting differently. She put herself in danger by exploring the woods constantly in the middle of the night. I expressed my concerns over and over again, but she never listened. She stopped listening to me for everything, all my advice, all my declarations, finally breaking off the relationship on October twenty-fifth."

"She was the one to break away from the friendship... How were you after that date?"

"Empty. She was the only friend I had."

"And you wanted to continue the friendship even after her blatant disregard for her own safety?"

He shrugged, "I thought I could help. It's what friends do."

"Mr. Zagorski, were you present the night the incident took place?"

"Yes."

"Could you please run us through what happened that night?"

Owen nodded. He flashed his gaze to where Avie would have been seated for a fraction of a second, desperately wanting her to be there to witness his testimony, before looking up.

"It was her birthday. We previously made plans together, but after the falling out, Avie wouldn't speak to me. I went to her apartment to give her a gift and at least say happy birthday in person before the night was up. When she answered the door, she was very short and impatient. She expressed that she didn't want me there, even as I gave her the present. I noticed a mark on her chest area, right here," he gestured to the clavicle on himself.

"What did the mark look like?"

"It looked like some sort of puncture mark with light bruising on the bottom of the area. I thought she had gotten hurt from traversing the woods again, so I brought it up. She then loudly exclaimed that she was seeing someone, and to leave her alone."

"That must have been another blow to you, did you end up leaving after the exchange?"

"No, I knocked endlessly at her door, I was terrified she was now being promiscuous, adding to her out of character act. I was terrified she wasn't being safe in that regard as well, I just wanted to talk about it further, but she didn't answer."

"And in this worried state, you decided to wait at her door all night?"

"No… Her neighbour caught me and told me to quiet down. I had a spare key that I ran home to get. And I entered her apartment to find that she left, presuming in the time that I had moved."

Mr. Gabriele was pacing back and forth, his hands clasped behind his back.

"Mr. Zagorski … Did you see what happened when the victim returned to her apartment?"

"I did."

"As clear and with as much detail as you can, please explain what happened in those moments."

Leaning back, Owen huffed, "She returned to her apartment about eleven-forty in the evening, coming through her bedroom window. I was waiting for her inside in the living room, the door between both areas was closed so I could only hear her return through her voice. Avie came out of her room, seeing me immediately. She smelled so heavily of alcohol while she screamed and grew hysterical, calling me a slew of curse words and shrieking how she hated me. Avie ran up to me hitting at my chest and kicking at my legs, trying to attack me. It was completely unprovoked as I didn't retaliate, I only tried to hold her back. I feared for my life, she was absolutely feral in that moment. I managed to kick her back, but I tripped and fell. She got back up, lunged towards me again with a blunt statue that she grasped from her bookcase, I reached for the gun tucked into my belt and I shot at her, only once. I don't remember anything else after that, I blacked out until I was being interviewed."

"You felt no choice but to fire a gun to try and stop her?"

"There was none, she would have killed me in that state, there's no doubt about it. Her sanity was gone, I panicked."

"You are quite tall in comparison, six foot two on record. You could not keep a small five foot three woman from attacking you, the only way you saw fit was to shoot them?"

"Like I said, she persisted with animal-like strength in her drunken haze, I didn't think she would be able to stop, it took all the strength I had just to push her away from me. I only shot in self-defence."

"You said that she attacked you, where exactly did she manage to land her blows?"

"Mostly on the chest and stomach, she tried to aim for my face, but I kept her far enough away. She managed to get a few kicks onto both of my shins."

"Thank you, Owen, that's all the questions I have for you."

The opposing woman stepped up for her interrogation on matters. The tip of her tongue pressed into her cheek, eyeing him before she spoke.

"Mr. Zagorski, the victim had stated that when she arrived, you shot at her without a struggle happening. And here you explain that the events differed dramatically. Even in the event that she attacked you, why not just flee or run out of the building?"

Owen bit the bottom of his lip in hesitation. "I was terrified, frozen in fear. There was no way I could stand properly, let alone move fast enough in that moment. All I thought about was how she could be stopped."

"But you stated that you loved this woman."

Fuck.

"Well, I-I mean I, yes I did," he sputtered.

"You thought the best scenario was to shoot her? How is that, in any way, an act out of love?"

"I couldn't think clearly, the situation was out of control," his voice came out quiet.

"I don't know about you, but shooting usually isn't on someone's mind unless there were other underlying motives." Owen frowned, painted into a corner, unsure where to go from that statement. Luckily, she continued, "And after firing the weapon, did you call emergency services?"

He cursed internally. "I don't know, it's all blank after that. My last memory was the sound of the revolver, and then talking to Det. Arcand a few hours later."

"Thank you for your time, that's all I needed."

The side of his face pulled into frustration as he stepped down, returning to his table, observing the tart lawyer in front of him as they continued on. Frustrated features held in a moment while he sat, before his face held neutral once more.

It was all a blur of hours, stretching into days.

The Crown prosecutor and defence lawyer argued their points, bringing out ever-increasing forensic evidence and passionate speeches to further prove their side. It was exhausting to keep up with, having to relive the night over and over as they went through every little detail. Avie was able to sit at the bar finally, allowing her to watch the rest of the court proceedings as witnesses to the initial crime had done their piece.

For three days, the court proceedings dragged on.

The woman was nervous. The defence attorney really painted a picture that she had been slipping in reasonable behaviour, drinking away troubles and taking out frustrations onto Owen. Of course, she knew the truth, even Owen did, yet how the information appeared to the jury was very compelling to his side of the case.

The Crown counsel argued fantastically with points about what really had gone on. The redhead figured it was the only reason that the trial had taken so long—there was always some argumentative point to be made by the other party.

Each night, Avie would return to Rhulle, sick to her stomach with worry. Not knowing how the court favour would work, she feared that he would be released, or that she would be the one in trouble instead. And each night, he held her while comforting her mind.

"No matter what happens, no matter where you go, I will always be with you. I will wait forever if I have to."

Both parties gave out compelling arguments for their side, but the counsel woman stated something that was odd on the fourth day, bringing up the initial statement of Owen's mention of a creature in the woods.

"Does that sound like a man who one hundred percent can be trusted with recounting events? Exhaustion mingled with stress could verify a hallucination of the creature the defendant had claims to see, however—"

"Ask the victim about it, she's the one fucking him!"

Her head never turned so fast, pivoting to her left to see the blond standing, palms on the table with an ugly sneer plastering his face. She couldn't believe it. Avie truly thought Rhulle wouldn't be brought up in that sense at all, he remained quiet about it in her mention of a relationship, but now as soon as he was detailed as a creature, Owen spoke up.

People murmured all around them.

She fought to keep herself ignorant, knowing he wanted a reaction from her.

"Order in the court! Mr. Gabriele, please control your client," the judge's gavel boomed, final as his words.

With a quick apology, he got Owen to sit down with him after a second of resistance. Clearly wanting to say more, a conflict fought itself out over his face, turning to look back at her. Avie met his eyes in return with only a questioning brow to his pouting grimace. This certainly did not look good for him.

The case continued, finally finishing through all evidence, pictures, forensics, character studies, testimonies and statements. All that was left was for the jurors to discuss over the verdict. One by one, they left in a single file to deliberate in the back.

Avie's heart was in her throat with her stomach in knots.

She thought over every word she said, and every word retaliated by Owen's attorney. The woman prayed, desperate that she could remain safe and that Owen could receive the help he needed to become a better person, the one he used to be. Hands clasped in her lap, she bowed her head with eyes fluttering closed, praying silently to a Guardian Angel she was so often told she had.

An hour passed.

Two hours.

Three hours.

Without announcement, the loud metal door clicked open, snapping her attention to the juror's bench as they filed back into their stand. It felt as if they were walking extra slow, wading through molasses as time progressed slowly, awaiting news of the verdict.

She felt dizzy, watching with such focused intent—briefly wondering how Owen was affected by all of this as well.

Calmly, Judge Neish questioned, "Has the jury reached a verdict?"

The representative rose, handing the piece of paper to the bailiff, "We have, Your Honour."

He took the verdict from the legal officer, reading it over, before nodding approvingly and sending it back to the juror dressed in a regal blue.

On the edge of her seat, she could almost feel the collective room take a deep breath and await the final verdict.

Nobody made a sound, only the hum of the lighting above could be heard as it buzzed in the silent room.

CHAPTER 25

"**W**e, the jury, find the defendant, Owen J. Zagorski, guilty of attempted murder of the second-degree."

"Granted. Owen Zagorski, I sentence you to seven years in federal prison with a professional evaluation done by the province's mental institution due before rehabilitation."

The redhead started crying, feeling relief flushing through her. Justice was served today, not only that, but they too saw what she tried to convey, that Owen was a man that needed help, and now, he could receive it. If anything, she was hoping this gift would be extended to him, knowing what it was like to be lost as a person. That's all he was, lost to someone else that had taken over.

The silent sobs wracked behind her clasped hands, covering her mouth. Todd turned to console her, hugging her shaking form.

"He can get better. Oh my stars, he can get better now!" she sobbed into his shoulder, returning the embrace.

"No! No, you go out and you search the woods, that demon is out there! He has taken hundreds of lives and he will continue to take more! Just ask the *monster fucker* where he is! Her and her disgusting relationship has to end!" Owen stood and shouted, having the officers restraining him while he fought to have his voice heard, kicking and screaming to all that would listen.

Crap…

No doubt about it, the outburst would inevitably draw people to the woods now. Avie watched as he was escorted out of the room and out to who knows where. She only knew that it would be a number of years before she may ever see him again.

History has a funny way of repeating itself. The woman now saw two close people in her life fall through the grasp of reality and take out what they were feeling, all the frustrations, stressors and emotions out on someone close to her; someone that was close to *them*.

She walked out of that courtroom with a weight lifted off of her shoulders. Owen would get better, she knew he would, and he would be able to think over all the situations he put her through with a clear mind. Avie would still be the person that held him accountable, but he himself was the one to place his being behind the bars of a prison.

The redhead walked up to a pay phone, dialing out after placing a few coins in the slot.

"Hey sugar, you done already?"

"Sandy… Owen was found guilty."

A pause, "No way! What'd they say would happen?"

"He's going to be evaluated, Owen will finally receive counselling. Sandy I-I think it's finally gonna be okay."

"I'm coming to get you, hang tight."

Waiting in the atrium, she finally spotted the familiar blue truck pull into the stall down the lane. She hustled, trying to keep what warmth was in the building with her as she made her way to Sandra through the snow and ice.

"As soon as I'm paid, I'm giving you gas money." Huffing from exertion, she settled down on the fabric seats.

"Listen, sugar… I've been wanting to say somethin' about the whole situation…"

Avie watched and waited for her to continue. Sandy took a breath, trying to force the words she held onto out, "Owen might get the help he needs, but that doesn't mean he will be the same person as before. He will still blame you for a lot of things, he may see the error of his ways, sure, but to him, you will always be the villain for not takin' his side."

She looked down, away from the brunette. She knew that it was the most probable outcome of all things, but Avie wanted to remain optimistic. Hoping that Owen and herself could one day, in the future, at the very least communicate. With her future goals, it was a bit of a far-fetched idea, and the blond would come out jaded, no doubt, in some way from the experience.

However, she didn't make him pull the trigger on her. He made that decision.

No, she knew deep down that he would no longer be a part of her life, it just hurt to accept it, that things couldn't go back to the way they were. Avie changed him, and not for the better.

"But you can't help everyone, some people are beyond that," Owen's voice echoed through her mind.

"I think I always knew that. I was still holding out hope that the future may have a surprise down the line," she laughed weakly, "I can take that he will hate me, I can take that I will probably never see him again. But I couldn't take that I was the one that broke him and left him in that state. I just want him to return to his senses, and now I think that's possible."

"Aww, sugar bear, come here," Sandra reached over to pull her into an awkward hug, "I think you're right; he will come back to himself eventually. And in the end, that's the most important thing, right?"

"Yeah, thank you for talking to me, I needed to hear it. And thank you for understanding."

"Always," they broke apart, "listen sugar, my house is hectic, especially in the mornin', but if you need to spend the night, my home is open if you don't want to be alone."

"Oh, that's so amazing for you to offer! I was actually going to go out of town for maybe a few days."

"Shit, what's his name already? You said after the trial you'd tell me all about him!"

She smiled, "I said I could tell you about him, but his name is a secret."

"What? Aww, c'mon, sugar. Why? He some kinda celebrity?"

"I don't know if you would believe me…"

Avie giggled, before recounting how they met—the first meeting interesting in its own way, and how it seemed like he wanted nothing to do with her. But he kept coming to her, finding out he had an odd curiosity, wanting to know more about her as much as she did with him. The two of them bonding over movies, books, dancing, and family matters over time.

"He was so difficult to read; I could never know what he was thinking. One night, he asked me to dance just out of the blue, and all I could do was stare at his face, his eyes, his *lips*. That night I kissed him, and I thought I had made a mistake until he was kissing back."

"That's so romantic, y'all are out of a storybook or somethin'. You absolutely light up when you talk about him, you know that, right?"

She blushed, looking out the side window, "I always figured, he told me recently that he doesn't believe in fate, but he believes something greater must have brought us together. I couldn't agree more. I love that man with all of my heart."

The two of them pulled into the parking lot of the apartment complex. Exhaling through her nose, she had to think about what to do with the information let out in the courtroom and how people will search for something in the woods. They may dismiss it as a wild rambling tale, but she knew there would be at least a few curious patrons as word spread that would make their way through and find Rhulle's manor.

"He better know how good he's got it with you, never seen someone with a heart as big as yours, sugar bear."

"Thanks, Sandy. And thank you for the lift, I'll come to bug you at *J&K's* soon!"

Avie entered her small residence, flicking on the light and looked over her home. It was cozy, and it was hers, but it missed the warmth that Rhulle possessed with him. She would have to return to him and talk over what to do with individuals coming to look for him now that the proverbial cat was out of the bag.

She collapsed onto the sofa, staring up at the ceiling. The redhead thought of the future, in a few months' time, the snow would melt, and make way for lush greenery and fauna nurturing in their natural habitats.

Avie loved the winter, but it halted her plans, and all she could think about was the need to start and to start now.

Would people be able to stumble upon the manor so easily, or was she over thinking things? It wasn't a well-known place in Blacken, some only finding it in the past as shelter or for more unfortunate circumstances. The police department located it with no qualms because they knew all of Blacken and its surroundings. The general public didn't care enough to figure out why people were drawn into town to begin with.

She felt the itch of Rhulle's need to feed wash over her; the feeling she lacked since the first time he tasted her blood. It was agreed upon that she would go to him when the need arose, but in this moment, Avie wanted to keep a low profile, she didn't want to be seen sneaking into the forest. Was she being too paranoid too soon?

With a quick change of wardrobe and layering the winter wear, she left to seek him out as the vibrating rattled more intensely as the minutes ticked by.

The woman was able to pick her speed back up to almost normal as she trudged through the snow-laden woods, having her wounds heal to a purple scar that faded every day. Avie was thankful that she had mobility in the first place, some were not so lucky in less severe circumstances. Her stride was slower in comparison and had a slight limp with her unable to take bigger steps, not to mention the lack of ability to run or walk for long distances; it still was nothing short of a miracle in her opinion.

Rhulle came out of the manor, seemingly watching for her arrival as he glided over, scooping her up in his arms.

"Darling! I have missed you; do you feel it again?"

"I've missed you too, my love! You need to feed, I felt it just a moment ago."

He leaned down, pressing his forehead to hers while he carried her back to the warmth of the manor, "I had it start this morning, it was only a matter of time. I did not want it to interfere with your business. How did it go today, dear Avie?"

They entered the living room, temperature warming the pink frost touched skin as she was set down on the couch, Rhulle joining beside as he awaited her report.

"It happened, what I hoped for... Owen will be going away to get proper help from professionals, also serving time for what he did afterwards. They made the verdict today."

"That is wonderful news, he may not recognize it now, but you have taken the steps to give himself back!"

"That's my wish for the future, but it may be that he won't forgive me entirely instead. I don't really know what could happen, but I don't think I will ever see Owen again."

Avie held out her hand, palm facing up for Rhulle to take, "Darling, I have seen stranger things happen, he seems to be one of the few that fall into the category of his own shortcomings are projected onto others. No matter how he is, he will want to shape a false story to weave you as the one in the wrong, even in knowing the truth. And once he is much, much older, he may finally admit it."

Using the sharp end of his talon, Rhulle punctured the pad resting under her thumb where a vein could be visible as he spoke.

She winced, watching a few droplets float away from the puncture as Rhulle brought her palm to his face, mouth latching onto the cavity he had just created. The small burn of pain eased away, the intimacy of the action causing a stirring sensation instead.

"*Ah!*"

Avie couldn't help it, a small moan slipping from her lips causing Rhulle's eyes to peak open, catching hers. He smirked on her palm, still connected there.

He broke away, getting his fill, lapping at the few remaining strands that fell from the vein, "You have talked so much about the trial, now that it is over, should we discuss *other matters?*"

The redhead's mind cleared, his need for blood fading from her body. All the stress and anxieties she had over the past few days would no longer have to take their hold on her, Avie could finally put that chapter to rest. And as much as she wanted to continue chasing the feeling Rhulle gave her, she still wanted to express her worries over townsfolk attempting to locate him.

"Rhulle, I—actually I'm worried about people trying to find you here, Owen had mentioned—"

With the hand he still held in his, the feathered truxen pulled her forward to him, locking his lips with her own before she could finish, tasting the copper of her blood still lingering on his mouth.

"I have told you," he said as he broke away, placing a single finger over her lips, "I am not concerned, if the worst came to worst, I can still manage inside of the forest and not just in this dwelling."

Grabbing the offending hand, she laced it with her own, "I just want you to be safe, how am I supposed to sneak off to see you when others are looking for you?"

He laughed at her facetious question, moving to allow her to stop the blood beading at the surface of her skin, "Have you ever hosted a creature of the night?"

Cherry eyebrows raised, "My love… I don't want to make you uncomfortable. It's still in town and surrounded by others."

"A perfect hideaway. They would never expect it. And I would feel better about being able to see you, if those do decide to drive me into hiding for a while."

"If you're sure, I can accommodate as best as I can," she spoke, running digits through coiffed plumage at the back of his head, excited to hear that he could be beside her. Somewhere that could be, for all intents and purposes, safe. Where she didn't have to worry for him.

"It would be a new experience," he chuckled, "and I could use some more knowledge on human culture through immersion."

"Thank you," she expressed genuine gratitude, Avie knew it was something he struggled with, yet he would do it to place her at ease.

"The weather will turn and I will build you your very own house soon," Rhulle leaned in, kissing while pushing her back into a lying position, smiling as he spoke close to her lips, "far away from everyone, no one could bother you, bother me, bother us. We could live without worry, yes, very soon, dear Avie."

He hovered over top of her, a tongue tracing over her lips before playing with her own. Rhulle's words dripped out like honey, seducing her with only his tone of voice, it caused a shiver to course through her body. It had been far too long since they had been intimate.

A dark hand snaked up, skilfully unclasping buttons and peeling away layers while a gentle purr radiated from the body above her. She panted as they separated, only for a moment, to completely strip the fabric from her upper body. His mouth moved down, licking and nipping the flesh of her neck with hot breath ghosting over the motions.

"*Going to have you every day. Just like this, all to myself. My vovii, all mine.*" Rhulle's words rolled out in Truxen, the woman finally able to translate his language after weeks of learning it alongside him.

He kissed down her scars, shifting back on the couch until the lips met her pants. Rhulle's eyes flicked up to hers, the red outlines of them giving off a predatory look, matching perfectly with the desire igniting within them.

"*All yours. I am all yours, Rhulle.*"

His bottom lip was caught in his teeth briefly before it was released with a shaky breath and coy grin. She had given him permission, her desire matching his to be together as he grasped at her jeans, slipping them off along with the panties underneath.

Rhulle stared down at her as she lay exposed, looking to be considering all types of thoughts racing behind those eyes. They locked once again with hers, keeping direct contact as his face lowered, and lowered. Avie's heart rate picked up.

He's not going to…?!

The dark tongue poked out, lapping at her most sensitive spot, drawing out an audible gasp as her head arched back. The muscle swirled, mapping out the new area, tracing delicate patters as it danced across aching arousal.

"*Oh! Keep doing that, oh please do not stop!*"

Rhulle's pace picked up with vigor, applying more pressure, the appendage dipping into her and earning a choked gasp, her hands weaving into the feathers at the back of his head while letting out embarrassing noises she couldn't hold back.

"Yes, ohh, Rhulle," she moaned, words drawing out, he was getting her close, the rush of such an intimate act carried out for the first time pushing her forward.

Green eyes locked with rust ones, watching him observe her face while he carried out the performance with a blush heavy on his skin. She panted, huffing out short groans as the coil grew tighter inside of her, pulling her core deeper in heat until the control snapped. Fingers gripped tight as she came, squeaking out high pitched with eyes clenching at the sheer pleasure while legs shook around him. It lasted seconds, as her hands detangled themselves, allowing Rhulle to come up, plunging his tongue into her mouth once more in desperation.

She felt his erection warm against her as they kissed, hot and heavy and damp, the connection full of needy wandering hands and desperate hot grinding. Avie felt flush, the naughtiness of tasting herself on his mouth made her lust for more.

"I need you, let me remind you of my love. Let me take you, mark you, let me have all of you," he sounded frantic, almost as if he wouldn't get another chance. This whole time, Rhulle must have been keeping the urges suppressed, having all of the blocked feelings come loose in this moment.

"I need you too, I need to be yours, I need you to be mine."

He crooned, turning into a groan halfway as his teeth caught his bottom lip once more in a quick action. Hands on her hips, Rhulle repositioned Avie as he guided himself in, adjusting inch by inch as both puffed in heavy anticipation. Delicate hands wrapped around his back, finding perch under the muscle where wings attached, meeting his thrusts as Rhulle started a rhythm. She turned her face into him, kissing every inch she could reach on the side of his and down his neck.

*"I have wanted you again for so long. I have been thinking about this, about you. The feeling of you around me, your little sounds—drives me **wild**, Avie. Too long... I waited too long, I—"*

Rhulle rose up, his gaze fixated while he lifted her hips, helping them to meet his as he filled her completely, the new angle causing stars to explode within her, glimmering behind her vision.

"I cannot help myself."

She could have sworn he growled in that sentence, too lost in the throes of pleasure to be completely sure. The words he spoke were enough to be lost in him, the woman clinging on desperately to the couch below her as he had his way, not wanting him to stop. The day turned into a whirlwind of pleasure, overloaded with Rhulle and all of his pent-up need for affection.

He admitted their first date how he never had that experience before, and now he couldn't get enough of the intimacy since they first joined. Rhulle had been young when he first came to Earth, hardly out of adolescence and early into adulthood, never having the compatibility with anyone he lived with to become vovii. Almost embarrassed, he confessed that he only ever kissed before.

Now being so closely woven with Avie, having that involvement, it awoke his need to explore and make up for lost time with her. They lay there, sweating and panting from the excursion while lightly caressing the other with gentle touches.

"I want to fill you with my love. I want you all of the time, I cannot stop thinking about you. I cannot get enough. I want this everyday, Avie," Rhulle propped himself up onto his elbows, staring down into her face with poignant eyes.

Even though he expressed how he was in control of himself in the past with his hunger, he now stated he couldn't control the addiction to Avie, her love, her person, everything she offered to him.

"It's a good thing we have forever. I'm absolutely crazy about you, you make me feel so good, Rhulle. I already drown in your love, it surrounds me every minute. I love you with everything I am," she rose up, bringing her forehead to his, "I only hope I can show you how much you mean to me in return."

"You have, the moment you broke down the barrier of our differences and initiated romantic interest. I love all that you are, dear Avie. You mean everything to me."

CHAPTER 26

Avie heard whispers around the town, listening through the grapevine that Owen had left. He was finally gone, out to a completely different territory to receive treatments and counselling, and to serve time for his actions. Avie always imagined she would be there before he left, saying one last goodbye, but it couldn't always be as perfect as the mind makes it out to be.

Her previous best friend was gone, with no proper goodbye; perhaps for the better.

She would never see him again, but her thoughts would more than likely drift over to him, filling out her mind with memories of the time they spent, both the good and bad. And he would always think about her, no doubt about it.

The woman wondered if he would honestly get better, or if this was all a metamorphosis for who he really was, the events they shared together kick-starting a new chapter in his development. Actions of the past bringing out his nature buried underneath—akin to that of her father. Still, she hoped to everything beyond her that Owen could come back to himself in the future.

She would have to live with the fact that she probably would never know, it was unfortunate and painful to think about, but it was part of life. There was no way to have all the answers, the only way was to move forward. It's what she had to remind herself about constantly, caught up too many times in 'what ifs' of the past.

Avie looked to Rhulle, the chestnut-plumed truxen perched in her chesterfield as he read through a novel. Pondering, she ran through the striking thought of what could have happened should the initial roles between the two males she grew close with never changed. Rhulle had been cold and intimidating at first meeting, while Owen had been uplifting and warm in contrast.

What could have happened if the roles never switched?

Rhulle was an unstoppable force long before she entered Blacken. He would continue to draw in those from outside town lines in order to feed for perhaps decades longer into the future. Would he lose himself completely in his isolation? Could Avie have even survived such an encounter if she was the only one to wander into those woods?

And Owen… If Rhulle remained as an evil entity in his eyes, would the truxen eventually have been vanquished? Were the strands of fate weaving a future where Owen was supposed to have been the hero, saving Avie from the beast in the woods and subsequently causing her to never know Rhulle as she did now?

It was weird to think about. She couldn't imagine her future without Rhulle even before they were unofficial vovii.

Fate always intended them to be together, there was no other way their lives were supposed to go. Owen made up his own outcome, making choices that lead him to pilot the ship he sailed in, his relation to her was a mystery, a lesson, rogue in its intentions. Another question the woman would never receive an answer for.

Rhulle raised his brow, reading over something intriguing as he looked off to the side, catching her staring at him.

"I see you are thinking too much again," he stated, a smirk gracing his features with a warm tone.

"I am, too many silly things are taking over my mind. I guess I have too much free time now."

The trial was done, legal proceedings were completed, the mystery of Blacken was solved, even the murmured rumours of the thing in the woods were dying down. She was back to her routine regular life.

Rhulle stood, closing the book and outstretching his hand for her to take, pulling her to stand with him, "Let us find something new then."

She mirrored his smile, his mood always so infectious.

The truxen had been staying with her for a week, the apartment altered to constantly have the blackout shades drawn, keeping the windows blocked off and a barricade added for the wooden door. Since he did not need to come to her any longer, Avie found a way to keep her bedroom window locked properly in the meantime.

The pair made their way into the bedroom. Avie received a computer as an early Christmas gift from Sandra, with her stating how she couldn't wait any longer and needed to give the present early. Ecstatic at the surprise, Avie almost rejected the expensive gift at first sight, but Sandra insisted it was fine. It was a bit of an older model; however, the woman deserved the system nonetheless—Sandy expressing how much her own kids enjoyed playing on theirs.

She set the unit up, purchasing a few accessories such as speakers, webcam and games to test out, showing off the finished product to a questioning truxen and explaining how it all worked.

Rhulle sat her down at the desk, "You told me that this can help you find whatever you wanted, why not ask it to find a new interest?"

Avie hadn't even touched the world wide web yet, not knowing where to start into the deep dive of information. Still, she was excited to test it out.

"Good idea! Sandy gave me some tips that her boys discovered, let me grab them," she went over to her closet, patting at the top shelf for the folded piece of paper she had received that was placed inside the manual. Finding the items, she pulled in a sweeping motion, causing something else to come loose and fall from the shelf.

It was the birthday gift Owen gave her; she completely forgot about it.

He noticed her shift in demeanour as she bent to pick the purple box up off of the floor, "What is it? What is wrong?"

"Owen gave me this on my birthday, the same night everything changed. I don't know if—should I even open it?" She thumbed over the packaging, watching as the small layer of dust collected on her digit as it streaked through.

"I believe you should, it would not do you well to throw it away without knowing."

She nodded, just another reminder that the blond would never really be forgotten by her, constantly leaving little reminders in everything.

Tugging at the ribbon, Avie ripped at the shiny magenta wrapping paper, opening the cardboard lid underneath. Inside was a small silver key, and a folded note. Confused, she set the key and wrappings off to the side and expanded the note to read.

> *Hey Aves,*
>
> *I know things have been weird, and I know everything's been falling onto you, but I thought we could try to get the Dewey Decimal team back for another mystery to solve, something different. We've had our disagreements on 'certain aspects' but I think maybe the mystery was the only thing we could see eye to eye on and I want to continue that with you. I'm not supposed to do this, but I got an extra key made for the library archives for you to use, that way you can look at them if I'm not around. It's not like anyone is there much to begin with.*
>
> *I guess what I also wanted to say was I'm sorry. You've been stressed from Garret and your condition and I've been too busy stringing you into all of this to stop and really listen to your side. So, I'm sorry, Aves.*
>
> *Your birthday is coming up so I'm probably just going to give this to you then, I hope you're not sick of the library by that time.*
>
> *Happy Birthday Avie!*
>
> *From your friend,*
> *Owen.*

The woman read through the handwritten note again, she couldn't be sure, but it almost felt like it was written after he met Rhulle, before shit all hit the fan and he started to rapidly change. The question also came across if he even remembered all that he wrote when he decided to present the gift to her, his mind certainly changing on topics written inside from his behaviour.

It caused her to hiccup, gasping in stilted breath with a sad heart but an optimistic outlook. She finally got an apology, a possible glimpse that while Owen changed into the person he now was, he was still in there—this letter proved just so.

"Are you alright? What does it say?" Rhulle asked, hints of worry filtering through.

She wiped at watery eyes, "He gave me a key to the library, telling me happy birthday and that he was sorry for his behaviour. He will come back to himself; I know he will. This is the last bit of the real Owen I'll get to see and it's an uplifting one."

He enveloped her, "You have some peace of mind."

She returned the hold, nodding into the softness of his chest, "Yes, I think I finally do."

He flipped through the notebook, finding the phone number he was looking for.

Avie was out at work, and he hoped this plan would all go off perfectly. Rhulle hesitated over the counter for a beat, clenching and releasing his fists as he thought over the conversation with his vovii just a day prior.

"Would you tell me more about Christmas, and why you all have to celebrate so much of it?"

The holiday was in full swing, Avie had been placing a few things under the tree addressed to friends and herself, the small space of the apartment chalk full of decorative set pieces and multicoloured lights. She explained Santa and Saint Nicholas to him and even the tale of Mary and her virgin birth to Jesus Christ, yet it all did not seem to warrant this level of obsession.

"The spirit of Christmas is to give, spread joy and be with loved ones. I think it starts earlier and earlier every year just because people want the magic to start as soon as it can. That, or people are corrupted by consumerism and the need to buy and spend as commercials for Christmas come on as early as November sometimes. But I like to believe it's the holiday magic."

"You have perked up in these last few days, it must be the magic. What do you like best about Christmas time?"

It was his first celebration, noticing the change in environment and only reading through various novels in passing enough to recognize the holiday, but still unaware of the intricacies that entailed with it.

His vovii smiled, opting to sit beside him instead, "Decorating, the music may be tied with that though. Christmas movies are often cliché but always make me feel good."

"And what of gift giving? How do I get something for you for the spirit?"

She paused, "You don't have to, I'm not expecting you to have to worry about that."

"Are you giving me anything?" He wanted to celebrate things right by her, she deserved a proper festivity.

Avie looked off to the side, speaking embarrassed, "I am, but that doesn't mean you need to as well."

He placed his hand on hers on the couch, "I want to, darling. Is there any way?"

Turning to face him, she let out a long exhale, "I can show you a few things, and you can pick out which one you would like to get me, how does that sound?"

"I thought the point was the surprise of opening it up on December twenty-fifth," Rhulle chuckled.

"That's part of it," she smiled in return, "but I don't know what else we could do."

Shrugging, "If it is what I can do, then I will, gladly."

He caught the recognition in her eyes, he did not fully believe his own words either.

Cocking his head, Rhulle tried to work the phone, seeing it only demonstrated a few times.

"Hello?" a female answered, there was no backing out now.

"Hello, is this Sandra?"

"Yes, it is, who's this?"

He paused, "My name is Rhulle, I am Avie's... *boyfriend*. Do you have a minute?"

"YOU'RE THE ONE WHO'S WITH SUGAR BEAR?"

The truxen cringed, moving the receiver away from his face as the loud shrilling continued through, picking up bits of speech as the slew of words cascaded out.

"Of course I got a minute! I got about a million questions 'bout you that Avie's avoidin' specifically, what was it ya said your name was again?"

"It is Rhulle, I um, I wanted to get her something for Christmas. She implores that she does not want anything, and I am desperate, Sandra. I do not have much cash, and I cannot go out into town anytime soon. Is there any way you could help me out in this situation?"

"It'll cost ya. How about you answer some questions and I can run out and get somethin' to help?"

This woman thought he was a human. That was fine, he could act... *human*.

"What do you want to know?"

"Let's have a sit down with coffee. I can come by in, say... 'bout an hour enough time?"

"No!" He cleared his throat, "I mean—ahh, I cannot presently... otherwise I would. Could this happen over the phone?"

"Well sure, that works. Tell me, Rhulle, do ya love her?"

"More than anything," he didn't even hesitate in his response.

"You ain't playin' around with her, right?"

"Playing? We have fun together, but my intentions *are* serious."

She hummed, "Good, just what I wanna hear. Because she sure does love you."

He blushed; just how much was she speaking of him? Not that he minded, but to hear someone else know of their relationship, and that Avie spoke so fondly about him...? Rhulle's heart fluttered, echoing in his chest.

The phone interview continued, this woman leaving him with an over-bearing mothering feeling towards Avie, asking questions that caught him off guard and leaving him feeling a bit odd about answering them so freely when just months ago he was reserved.

It was for Avie, he wagered.

No. That wasn't right. It was *because* of Avie.

"Did you go into debt from buying that engagement ring? Should've done that payment plan," she laughed, tone not completely serious.

Engagement...?

"I will have to remember that for the next big purchase."

"Right, well, ya sound good for her. She thinks the world of you, you know? Wouldn't have to get her nothin' but a Christmas card and she'd love it all the same."

"She has not had a proper Christmas in her life, and her birthday was ruined so I wanted to at least do something. And I know my predicament may sound odd, but Avie trusts you so I know I can too. I can explain more soon."

"No need to worry 'bout it now. When it's right you two will fess up to the secrets, until then I'll stop by with somethin' for you to give. What's the budget?"

"Budget for money? I—ahh... two twenties and a fifty?" He worried if that sounded right.

Rhulle collected a few bills over the years on Earth, keeping them with the stash of odd items catching his interests, such as the ring he presented to her. Gathering the coloured papers in the dead of night just this last evening and keeping them hidden from Avie. He hoped that was enough to buy something, *anything*.

"Gotcha, sugar's been eyeing a painting at *Street-Neats* and I think it was going for about that price."

Painting?

"Oh, actually, Sandra, that gives me an idea. Could you pick up painting supplies instead?"

"Sure hun, just an array of colours for paint? Are you available if I go
and fetch that now?"

Avie did take a shining to the portrait he gave to her, having hung the
artwork up in her bedroom to look at constantly. It sounded like the perfect
idea, but would this Sandra want to see him? Would she come into the apartment and see who really was conversing with her? Did he have a choice?

"Yes... that would be great."

"See you soon then, hun."

The other end clicked, and a low monotone noise greeted him—the
same as when he picked it up for the first time. Rhulle figured he could be
done with the conversation and placed the phone back in its cradle. The
stars above, how would he pull this off?

Sandra picked up a rainbow of coloured acrylic paint, a large canvas,
and soft paint brushes, the nice stuff from the corner hobby and art
supply store. Handing over cash with a smile and an exchange of holiday
expressions to Bobby at the front, she was out the door towards the little
apartments Avie called home.

The brunette thought over her conversation with the man on the
phone, he had spoken in a very stilted manor, like he's never been around
people let alone talked with them. An accent was attached to the warm
voice that she just couldn't place, running it all over as she walked.

This Rhulle guy didn't seem too bad, just socially awkward if she had
to wager anything. Maybe that's why she couldn't meet him, or why her
sugar couldn't have him out and about with her. She thought about the
poor guy working himself up for days trying to get something together for
Christmas.

Still, Sandra was honoured that he managed to call her out of anyone
and ask for her help. She knew that sometime soon, she would be able to

meet the mystery man. If anyone could help him come out of his shell, Avie could. That woman had the patience of a saint.

Lugging the awkward frame around, she finally managed to reach the top floor, apartment 516 and knocked heavily at the door.

"It is open!"

His voice barely registered through the wood, regardless, Sandra heard it and entered the small flat, flicking on the light and taking in all the tacky decor. Man, she loved the gal, but it looked like the north pole threw up in the space.

"Hello, Rhulle?" The door behind her closed, walking up to the dining table and leaning the frame against it, she saw the bills laid out on top.

"Hello, yes, forgive me but I am not feeling well, just in the washroom. I left the money on the table; I hope it is enough?"

She took the bills, snorting out an affectionate giggle, "You ain't gotta be so shy, hun. Avie loves ya, so I will too. This is plenty, I've got some change to give back, I'll leave it here."

The few dollars were placed there instead as she walked towards the bathroom, knocking lightly at the door, "Listen, hun, you went outta your way today to do something for her. I respect that. Thanks for coming to me for a hand, you call me anytime for anything, ya hear?"

"… I understand. Thank you for everything, Sandra."

"I'll skedaddle, I want to properly meet you soon too, Rhulle. Alright?"

"Yes, I would like that as well."

She smiled, picking up her purse on her way out, making the noise of the door loud enough for him to hear. Sandra laughed once, shaking her head and turning to go back home.

What an odd fella.

CHAPTER 27

People were all wrapped up in the spirit of the holidays, their minds on the hustle and bustle of family, decorating and last-minute shopping. Avie was able to have Christmas Eve and Christmas Day off, happy to have the time to spend with Rhulle on his first celebration. Even the odd questions from townsfolk about Owen and the trial tapered off, the inquiry of something out in the woods making its way back into obscurity as no curious explorer managed to find anything.

The redhead woke up first, eyes flashing open of their own will before her mind could process that it wanted to be awake. She blinked away sleep, registering her surroundings as consciousness fought for dominance, finding an asleep Rhulle holding her into his chest. She smiled, seeing the serene look on his features, amazed that she was able to once again wake up to this; to him.

A hand was raised to further wipe away sleep from her eyes as she rolled, delicately trying to move the arm acting as deadweight from around her waist. It grasped at her instead, pulling her flush against the body behind her.

Her vovii nuzzled his nose into her ginger locks, sighing, "Good morning."

"Good morning! How did you sleep?" she asked with a laugh, Rhulle was always extra affectionate in the mornings.

"Amazingly, and you?"

Turning her head, she was able to face him while keeping the position, "It's always much better when you're here beside me."

He smiled, cupping the side of her face, "I have got a taste of being with you for days now, admittedly, it will be difficult for me to return just to sleep alone."

"It would make the reunion that much better," she turned fully, kissing him a few times while she idly played with the silken chestnut feathers at his chest.

"Merry Christmas, Avie," his voice was soft and smooth, whispering over her skin in a tender affection as they broke away.

She let the words course over her, offering her own smile with bright eyes, "Merry Christmas, my love."

Without warning, Rhulle sat, scooping her up bridal style in a lithe fashion—standing and carrying her out towards the living room where the glistening Christmas tree beckoned with its cheer. The action never ceased to make her burst out in a fit of giggles, graceful arms wrapping around his neck just to stare into the face she adored so much. He placed her down onto the sofa, holding up a singular finger in an action for her to wait. He knelt down, reaching into the pile of gifts that littered underneath the tree and pulled back the wide box marked with his name, as well as a long and thin one that camouflaged in the back.

Rhulle handed the one addressed to him to Avie, smiling in a giddy apprehension while returning to her side. She looked down at the gift she held, then to the foreign one he held in his hands with a cocked eyebrow. What did he get up to?

"Ready to exchange gifts?"

The woman went with the flow, shaking her head with a soft laugh, "Yes, of course."

He proudly thrusted the gift into her lap, the rumpled edges and over-taped wrapping paper endearing to see. She took the object, handing over her gift-wrapped present in return. Rhulle grasped the item, fingers tracing over hers in the exchange before tapping his talons, hearing the hollow echo call back to them.

"You open yours first," he claimed, excitement hardly able to contain itself in his voice.

She clenched her lips in her teeth, the thrill of opening a gift from her vovii was not something she expected fully, overjoyed with just the idea of spending the holiday with him. He had gone out of his way to try and do something for her, and she couldn't wait to see.

Tearing off the decorative paper, she was greeted with a painted landscape. In a lush green forest, the two of them stood facing each other in an embrace—standing happily in front of a cottage with vibrant flora adorning the canvas in such a picturesque scene it caused Avie's heart to tighten.

"My love, this is beautiful... I'm speechless... Is this—could this really be our future?"

"It will be ours in no time, I had hopes for you to look upon this if the present gets hard to handle. You could remember that better times are coming, and the worst is behind you now. Our future is ours to make."

Her chest tightened, constricted with the love he shared for her, it took her, overloaded her, yet she couldn't get enough of it. Rhulle was the driving force to give her life new meaning, to change as a person and learn new skills with a new simple life, one she dreamed about for decades. And he offered it to her.

"I love it, it means so much that you made something... You'd better open yours before I get too emotional," she said, wiping at brimming tears with a shaky laugh.

Leaning across, Rhulle kissed the damp cheeks, "I am so delighted you enjoy it, I wanted to surprise you so desperately."

"You did! You really did," she kissed him back in the same fashion, "how were you able to paint this anyway?"

"I called your friend Sandra, she helped me with purchasing materials," he stated, a little sheepish.

"She what? You what? How did that happen?" Bewildered, Avie's eyebrows went into her hairline, trying to envision a scenario of Sandy meeting Rhulle where it wouldn't be made into a big deal. She wasn't trying to sound accusatory in her questions, more rather confusion slipping through her statements.

"Do not worry, she did not see me, I only conversed over the phone. She seemed happy to know a little bit about me, and when Sandra dropped the items off here, I was in the bathroom. I think she figures that I am just shy."

Avie laughed, "Now she really won't stop hounding me to meet you. I don't know how I'm going to get around this one… That was a huge risk to go through, but I'm glad you did; this is even more beautiful than your last work. Will you open yours?"

Rhulle returned to his proper spot, playing with the ribbon, admiring the wrappings before clawing at the striped paper in anticipated excitement, lifting open the lid and discovering folded material within. He pulled the garments out, turning them around in his hands, blinking at them in a stunned silence before meeting her eyes in the twinkling light.

"Avie… How did you… do this?"

In the past, Rhulle expressed to her, only twice, the importance of insignias to his race—to bear symbolism of who they were, their family, and their values in lettering and crests with their tunic-esque clothing.

In drawing out various items from Celisc, he sketched a rough outline of an outfit; the block pattern on the chest detailed from his pen more than the feathers on his fictional truxen—adding in a quip that it stood for family. Avie saved all his drawings, admiring them, learning everything about him, his culture and even history. She worked off of the details he drew day and night, trying to get everything perfect.

"Mrs. Harris let me borrow her sewing machine. I made it a little bigger just in case my measurements were off, I had to guess a lot, but I can make it fit nicer now that you can actually put it on. I know it isn't the same as the ones on Celisc, I made some adjustments for your new life here on Earth instead."

"I renounced them. All of them. My whole race the night I crashed into the forest here. The old clothing that fastened my ties with them, I stripped and buried somewhere out there to be forgotten. For years I lost who I was, not knowing my identity outside of the colony I grew up in. But *this*? It only shows that you are supposed to be my family, that I truly can start over with a new life. Darling, this is the most amazing gift, would you be willing to dress in one as well?"

Her fingers steepled over her mouth, reveling in his appreciation, for weeks she fought over the conflict of it being a terrible idea or a fantastic one.

"Look again," she whispered.
Rhulle looked down, back into the box, finding another feminine matching garb in a smaller size. He hiccupped, "*Family. My family. My vovii.*"

He pulled her into him, kissing with passion, leaving delicate pecks over her face and crown.

"Would you try it on? See how it fits?"

He was up in a flourish, threading his wings through the gap and lowering the cotton material onto his body as he stepped into the matching shorts with their hem reaching just over the knee. The tunic was a bit loose, but she was glad to see it could be easily adjusted to fit properly.

"How do you like it?"

He spun once, trying to see all the detail in the yellow lighting. Rhulle moved to the full-length mirror in the bedroom, seeing most of himself and the outfit as Avie trailed after him. "It is stupendous, it is the best gift I have ever received! I love you, dear Avie. This is so exciting; we need to celebrate every year."

"I love you too, Rhulle. We will then, every year together, forever. You have made Christmas truly feel like Christmas, thank you."

"Y'all are eloping away, aren't ya?"

Sandra's question hit Avie from left field. She was over at her house for coffee, the first signs of sunshine and warmth showcasing in the late February month and the young woman was conversing pleasantly with her friend until the out of the blue statement.

"Excuse me?"

"You and Rhulle. The both of you are moving away, aren't you? A few of the townsfolk were startin' to. And you kids are all but married on paper, it makes sense you'd be leaving to go somewhere better than Blacken."

Well... she was right, in a way. "I haven't even mentioned anything about it, how did you know?"

Sandra had a knowing grin on her features.

The residents of Blacken slowly came to the realization that those who travelled here, were no longer bound to stay. They could leave without the overwhelming affliction plaguing their blood and body, and a fraction of those with the affected blood type decided to return to the cities they left—or move on to bigger and better things. A majority still stay in town, becoming accustomed to the lifestyle over the bulk of years.

"Sugar, I can see it all over your face. You're movin' on from this small town, starting a life with Rhulle probably somewhere that I won't be able to see ya. That's why you look guilty, you don't want me to know."

"It's not like I didn't want you to, Sandy. You have been amazing to Rhulle and I, but you know he can't stay out there forever."

Sandra took a sip, agreeance in her nod and twinkling eyes.

It had been a full month since Sandy officially met Rhulle. The couple had lengthy discussions about the event and if another person learning of his existence would have any benefit. Her vovii finally gave his answer; agreeing to meet the Sandra he had only verbally communicated with and finding that there was indeed value in their meeting.

Avie asked if he had been absolutely certain in the decision, he nodded.

"She will meet me with a proper introduction and plenty of precaution. Sandra is a kind and understanding woman, having the preconceived notion of me from your actions and words. She knows of my character before meeting me properly, I think that will help a majority of the shock."

And the brunette was incredulous when they wandered the woods at sunset, coming up to the abandoned manor, thoughts and cognitive connections written over her features as Avie once again made sure she was alright, and to subvert her expectations.

"Sugar, it's fine, I'm fine. If I was worried, I would have turned back before you led me into the woods and to this place. I'm excited to meet this mystery man, honestly. Y'all are lettin' me in on whatever it is you gotta keep hush hush. I trust you."

They entered, seeing the fire lit and casting warmth into the room.

"Rhulle? It's us. Sandra's here to meet you."

He rounded the corner from the dining room, walking into the light for Sandy to properly observe. She gasped, grasping the forearm beside her, but she wasn't frightened, she didn't scream, she didn't run, she didn't try to hide; she simply observed.

"It is nice to finally make your acquaintance, Sandra."

Sandy breathed out, heavily. Turning to stare wide-eyed at Avie, and then back at him. She shook her head, steadying her breath and closing her eyes for a beat, releasing her grip.

"I can see why ya took so long, I had my suspicions, but I really was not expecting anythin' like this. However, it is nice to meet you all official-like, Rhulle," she raised her hand out in front of her, ready to greet properly.

He only pressed his palm to hers in the greeting.

"Are you, alright? I understand this is a lot, would you like to sit?" He conveyed calm much better than Avie could attempt, beckoning them towards the chesterfield.

They sat and talked hours into the evening, Sandra warming up to the truxen more and more as the minutes ticked by. The redhead felt reassured, having the pair's meeting go infinitely better than how Rhulle and Owen started off. Hell, Even Rhulle and Avie in their first meeting.

She snapped out of her reverie as she realized Sandra was talking once again.

"—And even if he stayed out in that glorified shack, that's no life for either of you. So, I do understand, and I support your decision. Are you guys plannin' to live off grid, livin' off of the fat of the land?"

She coughed once, trying to disguise that she only heard part of the speech, "Right, he knows everything about what we would need to do. We were going to start building soon now that the snow is melting. It would be somewhere in these woods, though I don't know exactly where, or how well I could maybe even come back to find the town."

"I want to help, any way I can, sugar. You need tools? I got 'em! You need food or blankets or anythin', I can be there. I want to still see you grow, you and Rhulle. If you'd let me, I can take time off and assist with some of the building, that way I can know where y'all are and visit every month... Discreetly, of course. I used to be quite the outdoors woman in my prime!"

Avie could have dropped her cup. She so desperately wanted that connection to Sandra, wanted so badly to keep her friendship after everything. The woman was tempted to ask if she wanted to live out there too, to have her own cabin in a sanctuary of woodland. To hear her avidly wanting to help the couple in building and even visiting, she couldn't pass it up!

"Sandy... Would you, really? That sounds amazing, it's not too much?"

She laughed, "Of course not! I'll be sticking 'round here in Blacken, and y'all deserve someone on the inside that can lend a helpin' hand. You two have been survivin' on your own for so long, it's all right ta ask for a lil' help."

"I forget that's an option sometimes. Sandy, thank you, from the bottom of my heart."

They exchanged a hug, "Do ya ever think about how people will never know?"

"Never know what?" The redhead returned to her seat.

Sandra hummed, "Every person who has lived in Blacken knows 'bout the odd phenomenon that brought people in ta stay. But no one will ever know that it was you who put a stop to it, that you found out what was really causin' all of it to happen and found a way to fix it all. Do you ever want people to know?"

Avie smiled.

Yesterday, with the sun low in the sky, the rays glittered through windows of the library, guiding her to the back. Descending the steps into the restricted area, she used a small key to open the metal door, the hinges protesting loudly at her entrance. Striding in, it became very evident that not a soul tread here since Owen, her footprints leaving tracks in the settled dust.

His notes scattered about, still unbothered, locked within their own time capsule. The woman picked up a random hardcover, flipping pages to see his handwriting lingering in the margins there too. The room filled with a mystery unsolved.

She sighed, bittersweet. The silver key used to gain entrance was placed down on a desk beside his notes.

The mystery of Blacken was never really of anyone's interest. As long as it had been going on, it suddenly stopped, leaving people to wonder and speculate from the abrupt shift; it had been normal for them after all. There were a few others in the past who also took an interest, who knew how far they got before giving up or being compelled to stop. There were only two that had seemed to find the answer. One embraced it, the other wanted to eradicate it. Would anyone else in the future take an interest in the odd tale about the small town surrounded by forestry, and why so many people came and went?

It was all just a part of history now, another chapter to be locked away in the archives.

"No, I don't. Let it be a mystery, let people be entertained with it if they choose. It's more fun that way."

EPILOGUE

Taking the well-versed dirt path that guided her home, Avie reached out to her side, allowing the leaves and tall grass to tickle her palm as she walked, her other arm cradling a basket filled with a mix of flowers and berries.

A babbling brook sang to her in the near distance, sunlight gently touching her skin. The woman paused for a beat, allowing the golden rays to wash over her face, soaking in their warmth as they peeked through the trees. Playing with her hair, she flicked the strands to one side as they kept tucking into the woven basket's handle as she walked.

The small cottage came into view, smoke billowing out of the pebble chimney as her vovii dug up potatoes from the garden. He stopped as soon as he saw her, smiling as Avie approached with the happy giggles of their small child being lifted into his arms.

"Welcome back."

"Mama!"

She kissed both of them while a hand encircled the small bump of her stomach, *"There are my two favourite boys. I am thinking about making some jam, can anyone help?"*

"Me, mama, me!" Erik raised his hand, squirming in his father's grip as he waved the appendage in his volunteering. It caused him to be set down, immediately running back into their home, awaiting to start.

The couple shared a laugh, before Rhulle turned her towards him, catching her chin to bring her in for a kiss, the other palm meeting hers on her growing abdomen. *"Have you thought of any names for this one yet?"*

"I was thinking of Hans if they were a boy, but if they are a girl, I wanted to name her Aubree."

Rhulle named young Erik after the pivotal character that helped change his outlook over Avie, ecstatic in the news that they conceived a child together. Even through the uncertainty and concerns, she too was excited to welcome the little one into the world. After all, if they had been able to create life together, there was no doubt that their child would be born perfectly well.

Sandra, true to her word, came to visit every month to check on the pair, giving all support she could, especially with a child on the way. She brought all the books, passing down all knowledge and gifts that she could carry with her, even staying after the three months term to help with care.

Then in just a few short years it happened again.

"My dear Avie, that sounds perfect."

She looked back up into his eyes, and then over the house they built and resided in; little Erik, who so closely looked like his father, jumping in the window with jade eyes delighted.

It was perfect.

All of it was.

Manufactured by Amazon.ca
Bolton, ON